THE INSPECTOR'S DAUGHTER

THE INSPECTOR'S DAUGHTER

Alanna Knight

CHIVERS

THORNDIKE

This Large Print book is published by BBC Audiobooks Ltd, Bath, England and by Thorndike Press®, Waterville, Maine, USA.

Published in 2006 in the U.K. by arrangement with Allison & Busby Limited

Published in 2006 in the U.S. by arrangement with Allison & Busby Limited

U.K. Hardcover ISBN 10: 1–4056–3888–5 (Chivers Large Print)
                ISBN 13: 978 1 405 63888 3
U.K. Softcover ISBN 10: 1–4056–3889–3 (Camden Large Print)
                ISBN 13: 978 1 405 63889 0
U.S. Softcover ISBN 0–7862–8963–5 (British Favorites)

The text of this Large Print edition is unabridged.
Other aspects of the book may vary from the original edition.

Set in 16 pt. New Times Roman.

Printed in Great Britain on acid-free paper.

British Library Cataloguing in Publication Data available

Library of Congress Cataloging-in-Publication Data

Knight, Alanna.
      The inspector's daughter / by Alanna Knight.
        p.   cm.
      "Thorndike Press large print British Favorites."
      ISBN 0–7862–8963–5 (lg. print : sc : alk. paper)
      1. Women private investigators—Scotland—Edinburgh—
Fiction. 2. Daughters—Ficiton. 3. Husbands—Fiction.
4. Women domestics—Crimes against—Fiction. 5. Scottish
deerhounds—Fiction. 6. Edinburgh (Scotland)–Social life and
customs—19th century—Fiction. 7. Large type books. I. Title.
PR6061.N45I57 2006
823'.914—dc22   2006024957

For Eileen and Ian Ramsay with love and thanks for Thane.

Chapter One

Soon I would be safe.

The journey from nightmare was almost ended. Every turn of the train's wheels, every drifting smoke wreath closed the door more firmly on the past.

Beyond the hills, the blue glimpse of sea, Edinburgh was fast approaching, epilogue to ten years in America, so-called land of opportunity but for me a land of tragedy and loss.

Home! The train gathered speed, echoing the magic word as it plunged into a familiar landscape welcoming the exile returned with a perfect summer's day. Under azure skies, fields spread with the delicate fuzz of green, trees radiant in blossom, were heralds of hope.

May 1895—a time to be remembered always, the day I began life anew and severed the past for ever.

Or so I thought. For as I was to discover, there is no escape from the painful experience of adversity. Loss invades each corner of the mind, scars body and soul. A ruthless part of every day, of living and breathing, it waits to erupt like a malignant disease when, cocooned by new happiness and security, we least expect it.

But mercifully unaware of what the future held, I smiled delightedly, radiant with excitement as the train steamed into Dunbar Station.

In less than an hour, I told myself, Vince, beloved stepbrother, would be waiting on the station platform in Edinburgh. Did he feel the same emotions at the returning prodigal, I wondered? Closing my eyes, I pictured him leaving the house in Sheridan Place with his dear Olivia, the practical wife, urging him to make haste: 'Hurry, dearest—we must not keep Rose waiting.'

Imagination painted no further pictures beyond that blissful moment of being reunited with them both. If only Pappa could be there waiting with them, happiness would have been complete.

But I had learned long ago the bitter lessons of one who expects perfection. All I needed of a future was waiting for me in the house in Sheridan Place. Reassurance, comfort, the safe warmth of a loving family circle would heal wounds, allow me to forget . . .

'Dunbar!' called the guard and the family who had taken the five remaining seats in my compartment at York—father, mother and three disagreeable children of assorted ages— noisily took their leave, scrambling across my feet, screaming angrily at one another.

Peace at last. I gave a sigh of relief. But

their presence, although obnoxious, had not been without its reward for concealed by my shawl I had made several interesting sketches. Something of an amateur artist, this was my refuge for keeping sane and calm during many long and wearisome journeys across a continent, from Dakota to New York.

Beyond the carriage window the weather was kinder than the rain that had poured down when I took leave of Scotland on the outset of my long voyage to join Danny McQuinn in America a decade ago, regardless of omens, brimful of confidence and quite delirious with passionate hopes for the future.

How I had laughed at my family's misgivings, their solemn faces, dear Olivia trying not to cry, horrified at a young girl travelling unescorted, without even a maid to accompany her, halfway across the world.

But I was determined. Danny was waiting for me. He will be there, I told them firmly.

'A savage country, wild, untamed and dangerous. Let me get settled first, find a place for us to live. Then you can come.'

Danny had exhausted every reason for persuading me to stay at home. And as he ran out of arguments, so I ran out of patience, believing I would thrive on danger and hardships faced together would make our love stronger.

I would prove right Pappa's boast that his Rose was utterly fearless, no milksop ready to take the vapours at the sight of blood.

And there was plenty of that. I thrust the thought into the black depths of my mind. I was older, wiser now. Thirty years old, bereaved of husband and child, I had seen more blood spilt in the last eight years than most genteel Edinburgh women ever saw in a lifetime—

But what was happening on the station platform? A middle-aged couple had walked three times past the window of the compartment. Were they searching for someone on the train? Worried expressions, furtive rather than welcoming, hinted at some less pleasant motive and as the guard blew his whistle they came to a sudden decision.

The man opened the carriage door and thrust the woman before him into the seat opposite me. He sat close to her, both ignored my polite greeting, their manner preoccupied, apprehensive, watchful.

I didn't need Pappa's expertise to tell me that the newcomers were most likely absconding lovers, frustrated by their attempts to find an empty compartment; observations confirmed by the fact that the Edinburgh train had only a short distance to travel.

What was so urgent? What matters needed to be discussed? Why that desperate need for secrecy? Then I noticed the man grope stealthily for his companion's hand inside her muff.

Their behaviour suggested that they were facing some imminent crisis. Huddled close together, an occasional whisper, a nervous, darting glance out of the window.

As they seemed completely unaware of me, here was an excellent opportunity to make further use of the journal-sketchbook. A challenge indeed to capture those fleeting expressions, their scared, furtive looks. Their true personalities, the passion latent in them that was so much at variance with their apparel.

An unlikely pair of tragic lovers, were they a middle-aged Tristan and Isolde in modern dress?

The man was sweating. He took out a pocket handkerchief and removed his tall hat to wipe his brow. His hair was thin, sideburns and moustache slicked down with macassar-oil.

The indications were that they had bolted, but had not travelled far. Neither had hand luggage, cloak nor umbrella. The last a curious omission since Scottish weather in early summer is not infallible and cloudless skies are not entirely trustworthy.

The man's rather loud checked trousers and jacket would have been more at home on the golf course and a faux diamond tiepin, rather too large and showy in his crumpled cravat, were at odds with the down-at-heel scuffed patent boots. Hands, beringed with

5

flashy stones, were less than gentlemanly and proclaimed the dandy.

But it was the woman who drew my attention. Nearer to me than her companion, in purple and grey half-mourning, the veiled hat did not become her and looked as if it had been borrowed by necessity in some haste.

In the game Pappa and I played on train journeys he encouraged me to speculate from appearances the background and condition of our fellow travellers. While providing a pleasant way of passing the time it was an early and valuable lesson on observation, which I was never to lose.

As for the woman leaning so close to her companion, Pappa would have speculated an upper-class servant hoping to be taken for a lady. Unlike her companion, her only jewellery was a beautiful pendant, a gold dragon with jewelled eyes and wings—no doubt as false as the man's tiepin but nevertheless an impressive ornament.

Unobserved, my pencil flew across the page. A few deft strokes to capture the hard face, the thin lips, the flamboyant necklace. Instinct, observation said it was newly acquired, for she touched it constantly, nervously as if to reassure herself of its safety. Had it been borrowed too? If so, why?

At last the train slowed down and slid along the track past Salisbury Crags and the ancient Abbey ruins at the Palace of Holyroodhouse.

'Waverley Station,' shouted the guard.

Ignoring my efforts to lift down heavy luggage from the rack, the couple were in such a great hurry to leave they almost fell across my feet as they scrambled out of the carriage.

No apology and no gentleman, either. I had been right. Even the humblest working man would have offered assistance. Curious to see what happened next, I watched them separate like strangers, with never a look or a word of farewell exchanged.

As they disappeared I felt quite disappointed that my supposition of their illicit dalliance would never be confirmed.

But in this, as in so much else that was to happen, I was quite wrong. Destiny had not yet finished with the ill-assorted couple and myself. We were to meet again in less agreeable circumstances.

*　　*　　*

With my luggage piled alongside, how eagerly I scanned the platform for Vince and Olivia. As the clouds of smoke dispersed from the train I expected to see their familiar carriage.

There was none.

Passengers were being greeted, hurrying away on foot or seizing the waiting hansom cabs. I looked around. The platform had emptied and I was alone.

Vince—where was Vince?

What had happened to him? Why wasn't he here to greet me? I had sent him a telegram before boarding the train.

I told myself to be calm, but still that rising panic. There could be many reasons. Telegrams could fail to arrive on time, be interpreted wrongly, be delivered to the wrong house.

I had been in much worse situations than this and recently, too. There was only one sensible way to find out what had happened: go immediately to Sheridan Place.

I closed my eyes, thought ahead to their surprised greeting. Their delight in this unexpected arrival. Some simple explanation such as: 'Rose! But we thought it was tomorrow you were arriving!'

A porter sauntered along, noticed this forlorn, uncollected passenger. 'Carriage, miss? Follow me.'

The rank of hiring carriages was empty.

'Shouldn't be long, miss,' he said consolingly. 'Most of the folks are short-distance fares. It's always like this when the London trains arrive. You have to look sharp, make a dash for it. Not quite the thing for a young lady though,' he added apologetically.

'I was expecting to be met.'

A hansom appeared, the porter put my bags aboard, received my tip and said: 'Where to, miss?'

'Sheridan Place.'

He repeated this information to the cabman who had already assessed the shabby luggage. Although I appeared to be respectable enough, it was unusual for a lady with an address in that elegant area of the town to be travelling without a maid. Unless she was a certain class of woman, of course, and he got plenty of them, after dark. Curiosity overcame him: 'Been away long, miss?'

'A while.' I looked around. From what I could see, Edinburgh seemed much as I had left it. 'Nothing changes, though.'

In reply he pointed with his whip to the newsboy and the billboard at the station entrance: 'Horrible Murder. Killer at large. Aye, people still get themselves murdered. And in that respectable neighbourhood you're heading for,' he added, his laugh betraying a certain satisfaction. 'Make sure you're safe home before dark, miss.'

What a homecoming, I thought. One Pappa might have relished.

As the hansom rattled along the cobble-stones down to the Pleasance towards the Dalkeith road, I saw beyond the city centre that Edinburgh had indeed changed.

Posters advertised a Wild West Circus in Queen's Park.

A circus! They saw the Wild West as an amusement, an exciting entertainment, not a brutal reality. But then, in ignorance, so had circuses seemed in my childhood.

9

Edinburgh had more permanent changes: tall houses on the skyline hiding the view of the Firth of Forth to the north, and the once unbroken view across to Craigmillar Castle and the Pentland Hills to the south.

Progress was with us, new buildings everywhere, the clang of hammers from labouring men perched precariously on tall scaffolding.

What I remembered of the approach to my old home in Sheridan Place had changed most of all. The fields that had bordered Arthur's Seat with Nelson's Printing Works, flanked by St Leonard's Hall and Salisbury Green, and a few Georgian houses discreetly concealed behind high walls, belonged to a pleasant rural area no longer. They had been overtaken and sadly overlooked by streets of tenements five storeys high. For the more affluent newcomers, terraces of modest villas offered gardens, with iron railings and gates for extra privacy. And where travel to this remote part had been only by carriage or gig, there were omnibuses running on rails in the roads. A novel innovation by which a greater number of passengers, and those lacking carriages, could travel in comfort and less cost from the outer reaches of the city.

*   *   *

At last, the gates of Sheridan Place. We turned

the corner and there was the familiar house.

Only it wasn't familiar any more. The garden was overgrown, the windows shuttered. It was empty, deserted.

At my cry of astonishment the cabman said: 'Looks like someone gave you the wrong information, miss. Are you sure this was the right address?'

I was speechless, almost in tears. I couldn't start arguing with him that I had lived in that house, that it had once been my home.

Almost hidden by shrubbery, a 'For Sale' notice: 'Apply to Blackadder and Co., George Street, Edinburgh.' I remembered Mr Blackadder. He was the family solicitor.

But what had happened to Vince? Had some ill befallen him and Olivia, and little Jamie?

Bewildered, scared, I had thought that reaching Edinburgh all my troubles would be over. And as we made our way back through the city, I tried to suppress feelings of panic by observing the passing scene in Princes Street. More carriages than I remembered, new buildings. Ladies' fashions had undergone a transformation too. Tiny waists and enormous hats, beset by plumed birds and vast quantities of fruit.

The modern craze for bicycles was evident too.

But as the hansom turned into Hanover Street and down towards Mr Blackadder's office my heart banged against my ribs, thumping with dread for what awaited me there: the terror that this was a continuation of the nightmare I had lived through and believed to be past; and with it the certainty that my strength to face any further personal disasters was rapidly fading.

Chapter Two

I walked up the steps and rang the doorbell of the solicitor's office in George Street, realising that I had never set eyes on Mr Blackadder in all the years he had served my family.

Invited to enter and state my business, there was some little delay in which I was certain of being watched surreptitiously through the window which separated Mr Blackadder's sanctuary from the main office. My arrival had created a small stir and I was the object of some curiosity among the three clerks, busily writing at their high desks.

At last the door opened and Mr Blackadder introduced himself. A gentleman of ancient vintage whose somewhat grey and dusty appearance suggested a lifetime spent in the company of dry legal documents.

Invited to be seated, my first question concerned my stepbrother: 'Dr Laurie? Is he well? And Mrs Laurie?'

Assured that they were in excellent health, I gave a sigh of relief and told him about the telegram I had sent to Sheridan Place, my dismay at not being met and the further anxiety at finding the house for sale.

He held up his hand. 'Allow me to explain, Mrs McQuinn. First of all your telegram must be lying in the empty house. Doubtless the delivery boy made the mistake of thinking it was occupied by a new tenant. Here is your further explanation—'

He pushed several envelopes across the table. I recognised Vince's handwriting and my sister Emily's.

'These were returned to us from the American bank some time ago since they had lain there unclaimed and they had received no forwarding address from you.'

He paused and looked at me. 'Mr McQuinn?' he asked.

'I am a widow.' How I hated that final word, closing the page with the formal acknowledgement that Danny was dead.

Mr Blackadder sighed and placed his fingertips together. 'My most sincere condolences, Mrs McQuinn. Most sad, most sad.'

'Dr Laurie—where is he?' I asked, trying not to sound impatient at his leisurely explanations.

'They have recently moved down to

England.'

'Why on earth—'

'When Dr Laurie heard from New York that you were returning home, he instructed me to deliver this letter to you. It will explain everything.'

Handing it to me, he leaned forward confidentially. 'Dr Laurie has been looked upon favourably by Royalty.'

A bell sounded in the outside office. 'That is a client I am expecting. No, no. I shall only be gone a few moments—'

I stood up, clutching the packet of letters he handed me.

'Thank you, sir, I am most grateful to you for seeing me without an appointment. I apologise for this rather unconventional behaviour but I was quite distraught—'

'My dear young lady,' he said and compassion showed on his face for the first time. 'Please remain seated. I shall return shortly and we have many other matters to discuss regarding your future.'

'My father—is he well?'

He shook his head. 'I have no recent news regarding your father but the last indications were that all was well with him.'

He paused for a moment to let this sink in before continuing: 'But there are certain important financial matters—if I may crave your indulgence for a little longer—'

As the door closed on him, I opened

Vince's letter. It was two weeks old and written on elegant notepaper with the Royal crest.

Dearest Rose

Welcome home again! I trust you are well and that the sea voyage was pleasant and agreeable at this time of year for yourselves and the little one. I apologise for not being at hand to greet you and trust you will understand and forgive when I tell you of my amazing change of fortune.

Destiny has smiled on my endeavours as an Edinburgh doctor at last and by Her Majesty's command I have been appointed as a junior physician to the Royal household (at Osborne, Windsor—or wherever!). Balmoral is quite high on the list, which means I may expect to visit my native land en route at Holyrood on brief occasions.

Dearest Rose, I am quite overwhelmed by it all. Such a privilege, such an honour, although we were sad to leave Sheridan Place, our happy home of many years, with all its memories of dear Stepfather, of you and our dear Emily. I do not doubt that Olivia will settle very happily in our new life, especially when it will afford such excellent opportunities and prospects for the children.

Jamie is almost eleven, a popular playmate with the young Princes, while the older Princesses make a great fuss over little Amelia and Eliza (who as you know are now six and four). I am delighted to tell you that we are expecting a further addition to our little family in the autumn!

As I had not received any communications from Vince in recent times mentioning the little girls, I had no knowledge of any babies after Jamie. This was indeed a surprise.

You will need a place to live. And I am happy to inform you that I have transferred the title deeds of Solomon's Tower, which I inherited three years ago, to you. It is now yours to live in or dispose of as you wish. Mr B. will give you all the details. Enjoy it with Danny and your own small brood—it pleases me to think of that ancient house being full of the happy laughter of small children—

I shivered at that. Ghosts of the children we had dreamed of and would never have. Poor Vince. So he didn't know. None of my tragic news had ever reached him. As for this information regarding Vince's inheritance, that was strange and quite fortuitous, something of a miracle in my present low financial state. To find that I had a home of my own, although recalling the ruinous condition in which I last saw it, this might not be such a boon after all. I continued reading:

When my duties with the Royal household allow me to travel north doubtless we will have an opportunity to meet. Perhaps on Her Majesty's visit to Balmoral? Rest assured I will make the utmost endeavour to look in and see how you are faring in your new home. Olivia has done a great deal to make it comfortable for you. She joins me in sending fondest love.
   I remain, Your obedient servant and devoted brother
   Vince Laurie MB, ChB

It was so typical of Vince. I couldn't see myself rushing down to the Isle of Wight or Windsor, or even London. What if Danny was alive? The forlorn hope persisted that the dead might rise again, and one day a door might open and I would find him waiting, as he did so often in my dreams. What if he came to Edinburgh (to return home together had been our ultimate plan)? What if he came, maimed or ill, and couldn't find me again?

17

Such thoughts tormented the sleepless hours of the night . . .

*   *   *

Mr Blackadder hadn't returned. There were three letters with Orkney postmarks from my sister Emily and, being Emily, they were written in haste with no dates.

Yesnaby House

Dearest Rose

Vince has written to me with the glad news that you are returning home to Edinburgh at last! Welcome to you and Danny and my little niece or nephew.

I long to hear all about the baby, a photograph would be lovely. Family groups are so popular these days. I am so looking forward to hearing from you, dearest Rose, and all about your exciting adventures in the New World.

Gran is well and sends her love as does

Your loving sister
Emily

There were two more written in similar vein, earlier and more distraught in tone. Why had I not replied to her letters? Had I not received them, etc., etc.

The remaining contents of the packet were

wedding invitations from two fellow teachers I had worked with in Glasgow. So long ago, like something from another world.

A note from a childhood friend, Alice, giving notification of a new address in Edinburgh. Once a dear neighbour, we had been very close and I had been at her wedding.

But there was nothing from Pappa.

*   *   *

Mr Blackadder returned, full of apologies for the delay. I said I had read Vince's letter.

'What is this about Solomon's Tower?'

'Ah yes. Dr Laurie inherited the property with a substantial legacy on Sir Hedley Marsh's death some years ago. He decided not to sell it since it is of local historical interest—'

I suspected that he might have difficulty in obtaining a buyer. Ancient and forbidding in appearance, it had acquired a bad reputation as a haunted house. It had been home to a murder just before I left Edinburgh—

'Dr Laurie decided it should be kept in the family, that is what Sir Hedley would have wished—'

(Obviously he was unaware that all the family knew of Vince's quite unreasonable dislike for the man who had always shown such a great fondness for him.)

Ignoring my look of surprise, he continued: 'Dr Laurie gave instructions that the property was to be restored and modernised. The deeds are in your maiden name,' he added, 'A necessary precaution should you wish to remarry.'

As he explained the legalities, I understood his small hesitation, remembering again how Vince and Pappa had been in full agreement with Danny's own wish that I should remain in Scotland until such time as he returned for me. Had their fears been based on some instinct for the disaster that was to overwhelm us both?

'Dr Laurie's wishes have been carried out to the letter and you will find remarkable changes in the old Tower, including regular visits from a firm of cleaners to make certain that it was kept in readiness for your immediate occupation. Foley, the gardener and handyman from Sheridan Place, is very reliable. He will also look after the exterior fabric of the building, coal supplies and so forth.' Mr Blackadder regarded me solemnly. 'That is, if you so wish.'

A gardener-handyman indeed. What a luxury, remembering filthy hands and an aching back, tilling the dry earth to raise vegetables in the patch of earth outside our cabin in Dakota.

Memories, some of them tender, came flooding back—

'Considering your present circumstances,' Mr Blackadder continued, 'you may wish to give it some thought. Perhaps an Edinburgh lodging would be a happier choice for a lady on her own.'

Then, hesitantly: 'The house, as you know, is somewhat isolated,' he added, leaving me with an unhappy feeling that there was much more he could say on the subject. A warning, perhaps, but he was unable to find suitable words.

Not that I would have heeded a warning. My sojourn in America had proved beyond any possible doubt that I was totally oblivious to anyone's advice. Now I remembered only how I had regarded as special treats visits to Solomon's Tower with Pappa.

The tribe of cats, the smell, the ruinous happy state did not worry a child and I decided boldly to accept Mr Blackadder's assurances of agreeable changes. As I had no other place to live and no money beyond a few sovereigns, it was in my best interest to take up temporary residence there. Until I wrote to Emily and told her of my plight—

Mr Blackadder was watching me. 'Are there—is there any family, Mrs McQuinn?' He cleared his throat. 'I understood from Dr Laurie . . .'

'No,' I said sharply before he could utter more condolences, which would only succeed in opening the floodgate of tears, that bottomless well of grief . . . 'I have only my sister Emily. I may go and stay with her in Orkney eventually. Meanwhile the Tower will serve my purpose,' I added, certain that when Emily knew of my sad circumstances she and her husband would offer me a home. There is always a place for widowed sisters or those female relatives beyond hope of marriage in a family where there are children to attend or a large house to manage.

But even as I spoke confidently of Emily's response, a small voice questioned: did I want to return to my childhood years spent on an island remote from the rest of Scotland? Did I want to become a dependent relative, an unpaid but much loved servant, for the rest of my life?

The bell in the other office signalled another client.

I stood up this time to take my leave, thanking him once again.

'One moment, if you please.' Reaching for a key, he unlocked a drawer and withdrew a purse. 'This should tide you over for a little while, see you settled.'

He looked at me steadily. 'And I would urge you most strongly, Mrs McQuinn, to acquire the services of a maid without delay.'

I opened the purse. Guineas, banknotes—

At my gasp of surprise, Mr Blackadder smiled. 'Obviously Dr Laurie did not mention in his letter that he had a draft sent to the bank in Dakota giving them authority to pay you one hundred dollars. This was particularly to finance your return to Edinburgh. It has been returned to us—'

I was staring at the money, counting it in my head. In my present state this was a small fortune.

Mr Blackadder smiled. 'This is merely part of the legacy of one thousand guineas from Sir Hedley Marsh's estate which we hold in trust for you.'

I gasped, 'One thousand guineas!' I was rich! 'I don't know what to say.'

Mr Blackadder smiled. 'It is your stepbrother you should thank, Mrs McQuinn, and I am sure you will do so.'

The bell rang again.

'My senior clerk, Jeffries, will escort you to your hotel.'

I looked at him. 'I haven't one. I thought I might go straight to Solomon's Tower, since it is kept in readiness for me.'

Mr Blackadder bit his lip, frowned and opened his mouth, like one about to offer advice. Then, thinking better of it, he sighed and from a drawer he handed me two large keys. 'Jeffries will accompany you to make sure that all is in order. I have already instructed him to collect provisions for you from a reliable grocer in Broughton Street.'

'Thank you, sir. You are very kind, but if the farm in St Leonard's is still there, it is just a short distance from the Tower. Our housekeeper at Sheridan Place, Mrs Brook, relied on it for our supplies of milk, eggs and bacon—'

And I remembered delicious newly baked bread thickly buttered by Mrs Brook. Dear Mrs Brook, who was like a second mother to Emily and me. Had she gone with Vince?

'No,' said Mr Blackadder. 'She retired some years ago and went to live with a cousin in the Highlands. Dr Laurie keeps in touch, I believe. He will give you her address.'

Jeffries, summoned, was just a shade junior and a shade less dusty than his employer.

'Jeffries will call a carriage for you. You will find him most reliable,' I was told as he proceeded to gather up my luggage. As he had probably been with the firm since before I was born, I felt guiltily that I was fitter and stronger to carry my own array of packages.

At the door, Mr Blackadder took my hand. 'Let me know how you fare and, if there is anything you need, you have only to ask. This firm has always been happy to serve your family in any capacity.'

For a moment he frowned, staring across the street. 'Get a maid as soon as you can, Mrs McQuinn, see to that with all possible speed.' Again his tone was urgent.

'I have managed on my own for a long while in America—'

'I understand things are different there. But

Solomon's Tower is very isolated from other habitations and a fair walk into the city—'

'I have thought of that, sir. Since I have come into a great fortune, perhaps I can afford a bicycle.'

'A bicycle, Mrs McQuinn?' His eyes opened wide, an expression of horror.

'Yes, it would be very useful.' I didn't add that I had yearned to possess one ever since my first encounter with the new craze for bicycles on the streets of New York.

'But Mrs McQuinn, no lady would be seen riding such a machine in the city. It is considered, well, rather improper and most undignified.'

I smiled. 'Perhaps I don't consider myself too much of a lady to forgo the convenience of such an easy and pleasant way to travel.'

Mr Blackadder shook his head impatiently. 'Very well, Mrs McQuinn, you must do as you wish.'

As he led the way down the front steps, shaking his head sadly, I hoped he wasn't going to have a seizure. Handing me into the waiting carriage, he said once again: 'A maid, Mrs McQuinn, remember that is your first priority. Your stepbrother would not want you to live in Solomon's Tower alone. He would be most exercised about that.'

I thanked him for his concern and, sitting back in the carriage, I thought about my own change in fortune. No longer penniless, with a home, money to buy food and clothes—and a bicycle too.

Dear Mr Blackadder. I turned to wave to him through the window but he did not see me.

He was frowning, staring across the street and as we flashed past I again saw a newspaper placard: 'Horrible Murder. Savage killer still at large.'

Chapter Three

We drove down the Pleasance and I instructed the cabman to stop at Bess's farm. The smell of hot baking bread took me straight back to childhood and made my mouth water.

The old woman greeted me warmly and said she hadn't seen me for a long time, but I was as bonny as ever. I was flattered. She didn't look any different either. Perhaps she hadn't been as old as childhood's memory painted her.

As she sliced the bacon, weighed out the butter and counted out the eggs, she asked: 'Where's your basket, lass?'

'I haven't one with me. I'm sorry.'

Bess sighed and said: 'Then I'll loan ye one, but make sure you bring it back,' she added, lining it with newspaper and carefully wrapping each egg. 'Did you remember to bring back your milk can?'

I then realised that she really didn't know me at all, or that I wasn't a regular customer. 'Perhaps I could borrow one as well. And return it to you.'

She gave me a hard look over the top of her spectacles, decided I was honest and said: 'I'll get the laddie to deliver it to you every morning. Where is it you live?'

I told her and she wrote it down on a scrap of paper. 'Solomon's Tower, did you say?' Suddenly her head jerked up and she stared at me. 'Been empty for years, it has. That's no place for a young lady like yourself to stay.'

'I know it well. It's going to be my home.'

She shook her head and muttered darkly, 'I wouldn't want any of mine living there.'

And it seemed that nowhere was I to escape the sensational story of the murder not a mile away as, wrapping the bread, she added: 'Not after that poor lassie was strangled down by Grange. Respectable, clean-living she was too. I kenned her folk well. This was a decent safe place right out in the country before they built all these new houses.'

Jeffries appeared, hovering at the door ready to carry my provisions.

'The district is going to rack and ruin,' said Bess, including him in her observations, 'what with that circus down the road and all those queer-looking savages. A body's not safe in her bed any more.'

I handed over a shilling, got some change and she said to Jeffries: 'You take care of the young lassie there, sir. She's just a slip of a bairn,' was the parting shot.

I was thin and not very tall, with a small face and a head of yellow curls. But at thirty such flattery hinted that old Bess was in urgent need of new spectacles.

*   *   *

As we turned towards Queen's Park the massive expanse of Arthur's Seat stretched high above our heads. Pappa had described it as a lion couchant, this Edinburgh landmark that was millions of years old before humans took their part on the earth's stage.

The horses trotted through the gates of Queen's Park. Down the road to the left I glimpsed an untidy sprawl of caravans clustered around a high tent.

Woodsmoke, cooking and the gamey smell of animals drifted towards us.

'A circus!' I said to Jeffries. 'Have you been to a performance yet, Mr Jeffries?'

Jeffries shook his head. He looked mildly shocked at the suggestion, a disapproving sniff indicated his sentiments. I guessed that he felt it not only lowered the tone of the area, but was lèse-majesté too, situated in the park on the edge of the Royal residence of Holyrood.

'How long is it staying?' I said anxiously.

'It has been here for several weeks and there is no sign of it leaving.' His disapproving manner suggested that an immediate visit would be advisable. A return to magic childhood days of performing animals, acrobats and clowns. Another trip, like Bess's farm, down memory lane . . .

Pappa used to take Emily and me if he had time and wasn't involved in solving some crime or other. To this day I could recall the bitter disappointment when, as so often happened, an outing planned with Pappa had to be cancelled at short notice or delegated to the long-suffering Mrs Brook.

The carriage turned briskly on to the narrow road through Queen's Park, which led into Duddingston village. On our left, Samson's Ribs, the massive perpendicular rocks formed from basalt that had cooled into six-sided columns and pushed up from below the older, softer rocks surrounding the extinct volcano that had descended into recorded history as Arthur's Seat.

And there, at the base of Samson's Ribs, was Solomon's Tower.

At first glance invisible, a mere part of the foothills of that craggy mountainside, Pappa always said it didn't look like a 'house made by mortal hands'.

While the earth cooled and the summit of Arthur's Seat was twice its present height, the site the Tower occupied would have been within the volcano; I saw how accurate that whimsical description had been since stones and mortar blended so skilfully into the rocky backdrop, as if it had naturally evolved from the prehistoric eruptions that shaped the city of Edinburgh.

Sinister, dark, I could well believe that its early history, lost in the mists of time, might have revealed a refuge for the Knights Templar after their flight from Jerusalem during the Crusades. Its reputation as a convenient place for Royal conspirators had continued down the ages from Mary Queen of Scots to Prince Charles Edward Stuart marshalling the Jacobites on the ground above the city at Hunter's Bog.

Isolated, alone on its rocky perch, it did not need great flights of imagination to understand how readily such a place became the setting for superstitions, a place to be avoided, with tales of saints and devils. Certainly it had never been built originally with domesticity in mind, there was the hint of the monastic in tiny arched windows, and of defence and fortress in high unscaleable walls and arrow slits.

I sighed. Even the gentle golden light of early evening could not turn it into a home. But perhaps I could. I had dealt with log cabins in arid plains, far less attractive prospects than Solomon's Tower. In that moment I resolved to accept the challenge it offered.

As we drove alongside it looked much as I remembered. Closer acquaintance revealed a small, tidy garden with possibilities for a vegetable patch and a seat on sunny days sheltered by the rocky overhang.

I said the words out loud and Jeffries, who was regarding the building with evident dismay, stared at me as if I had taken leave of my senses. 'Rabbits and rats and deer will soon put an end to such schemes, Miss. To say nothing of the weather, which can be severe. Arthur's Seat gets the full blast of any storms sweeping straight across the Firth of Forth,' he added as if he had forgotten that I once lived in Edinburgh.

I didn't care about his gloomy predications. I'd transform this grim old building by investing some love and pride in its sad stone and mortar. Absurd as it is, I believe that houses have souls, a theory I would not care to admit to the incautious listener. And that houses said to be haunted have merely absorbed into their walls the hatred, agonies and cruelties inflicted on one another by human inhabitants.

The carriage stopped by the iron gate. I remembered that it creaked. Time had not changed that or produced oil for the hinges. I made a mental note to rectify the omission. Creaking doors set my nerves on edge. The ancient entrance was a heavy, studded oak door overlooked by a small turret, which had been built for defence against the invaders, with burning oil, arrows or gunshot in mind.

I declined to have Jeffries stay after he had opened the door and set down my travel bags. He fussed over me dreadfully. Would I be comfortable enough, warm enough—safe enough?

Gloomily, he emphasised the last, looking around with ill-concealed anxiety at the stone spiral staircase leading to the upper floors. I wasn't nervous, was I?

His attitude would have struck fear into even the bravest but I put a good face on it, reassuring him on all these issues. Thanking him for taking such good care of me, even more thankfully I closed the door and watched him drive away.

Alone at last with my new home, I sighed with pure contentment and wonder as I looked around me. This was the first house I had ever owned, an exciting thought. I went through a kitchen and scullery up a few stone steps into the sitting-room with a large arched window that earlier had been the entrance to the Tower, some ten feet above the ground, once approached by a ladder that could be speedily uplifted, a further indication of ancient defence.

In more recent times the unsavoury domain of Sir Hedley's tribe of cats, it had been transformed into a comfortable, attractive room. Furnished in Olivia's particular style and good taste, had I closed my eyes, I could have been back in Sheridan Place.

I carried the most immediate of my travelling bags through a door which led up a spiral stair to the master bedroom. The four-poster bed was there, no longer a sanctuary for the feline inhabitants; there were new brocade curtains, rugs on the floor, a massive wardrobe and a cheval mirror, the last thoughtfully provided by Olivia as every lady's necessity.

The sight it reflected was far from agreeable: an untidy image of windswept yellow curls, too much hair for the thin pale face and startled-looking eyes. As for the rest of the sad-looking woman, her clothes did little to inspire confidence.

Drab and travel-stained cloak, down-at-heel shoes, a gypsy who would have been turned away from respectable doors, I resolved to invest immediately some of those guineas Mr Blackadder had given me in the purchase of a decent wardrobe.

But Olivia had thought of everything. Had she foreseen my reactions, I wondered, as I opened a cabin trunk at the bedfoot? A note inside said these were clothes and shoes she would not have any use for in London. If they were unsuitable then perhaps I would be so kind as to donate them to some charitable institution.

My feet were shorter and broader than Olivia's but I guessed, as I took out petticoats, drawers, chemises and nightgowns, plus stockings, that this treasure trove of garments, all neatly darned, which dear Olivia had thought too shabby for Court circles, were, alas, far removed from the practical requirements of a lady bicyclist.

There were baby clothes, too, in several different sizes, all a little yellowed by constant wear. I felt my throat tighten as I fought back those tears again. In her usual caring fashion Olivia had guessed the impoverished circumstances of our life in America and had tactfully decided with sensitivity and insight that charity begins at home. I was much indebted to her.

A door led into a recently installed bathroom with water closet and a smaller bedroom, which I remembered had been Sir Hedley's study. The nursery, I thought sadly, complete with cradle, that forlorn reminder.

I followed the stone stair up to the next floor. Even as I opened the door I felt the atmosphere change. According to legend this part of the house with its stone vaulted roof had been the Knights Templar's chapel. All indications of its religious nature had long since vanished, but the aura of sanctity and dedication remained undisturbed by passing centuries. Below the tiny arched window, with its stained glass high in the wall, a raised dais in the floor hinted at the one-time presence of an altar. Painted murals of biblical scenes flaked off the walls, ghostly images of prophets and saints obliterated by the passing centuries.

Olivia and Vince had left this strange room untouched.

I would set an antique oak table on the dais under the arched window, with crucifix and candles I'd light for Danny. A devout Irish Catholic, he had been brought up by the nuns at the Convent of the Sisters of St Anthony in the Pleasance.

When I was at more ease with my surroundings, perhaps I'd get them to say a Mass for Danny. He'd have wanted that although I dreaded telling them the fate that had overtaken their beloved protégé, the clever orphaned lad they were all so proud of, whom they had educated well enough for a career in the Edinburgh City Police.

I did not want to remember the last church I had set foot in: a refuge for the women and children in a settlement attacked by renegade Sioux Indians. In a retribution raid for the massacre of their own women and children by white soldiers—The screams of the dying, the burning arrows—

*　　　*　　　*

Dear God—not even in nightmare, save me

35

from remembrance.

And feeling this was a holy place where prayers might be heard and supplications answered, I knelt down on that stone dais and prayed for the repose of Danny's soul.

And for all those who had died that terrible night.

If he is alive, I whispered, please send him back safe to me.

Down the stairs again and into the bedroom, I was suddenly overcome by weariness, too tired even to feel hungry. Wanting only oblivion I threw off my clothes, seized one of Olivia's nightgowns and, crawling under those pristine white sheets, I laid my head gratefully on the lace pillowcase faintly perfumed with lavender.

And there I slept dreamlessly until morning came.

Chapter Four

I awoke refreshed and for the first time with a sense of wellbeing and inner strength. No longer dreading the day ahead or haunted by past sorrow but with a feeling of delighted anticipation, I opened the window.

Beyond the garden, a thin haze over the summit of Arthur's Seat, the butter blaze of sun-gobbled gorse haunted by the buzz of excited insects promised another fine day.

Down the spiral stairs my hand lingered on the ancient rough stone wall. This was the first day, the dawn of a new life and in the parlour every piece of furniture held some memory of Sheridan Place and surrounded me with the comfortable feeling of having returned home at last.

No longer need I fear the future or wonder where my next crust of bread was coming from. All that was gone for ever. I could make plans, in time I might even obtain a situation as a teacher or governess. Although that idea did not greatly appeal at present, it could bring me a comfortable living when my vast fortune dwindled.

I took out the purse and shook out the coins. I still could not quite believe that all this—and much more—was mine to spend. Such wealth demanded outdoor wear suitable for riding a bicycle.

Out of the kitchen door and off to inspect the rest of my inheritance. A crumbling wall, the foundation of some earlier version of Solomon's Tower. Across a stretch of grass, a coachhouse-cum-stable with stall containing soft straw, fresh and dry, presumably the responsibility of someone who expected the new occupants to keep a carriage and horses.

Perhaps at some future date I might keep a few hens.

Returning to the kitchen, I saw that a fire

had been set ready for lighting. A peat fire that brought back memories of my Orkney days, remembering how, once Gran set it going, she said it need never go out.

This morning, however, with no means of boiling a kettle I poured a cup of milk. Delicious, with a slice of fresh bread thickly buttered and a piece of cheese. Bacon and eggs would come later, once I had mastered the kitchen range.

Carefully unpacking Bess's basket of eggs, I discovered they had been set upon a newspaper for safety: a copy of The Scotsman. That is was two weeks old didn't bother me, I was very curious to know what had been happening in Edinburgh of late.

The most important item—after news of unrest on the fringes of the Empire, places I had never heard of, and Mr Gladstone's latest pronouncement in Parliament—was the Edinburgh murder.

Molly Dunn, a servant girl in Saville Grange in Newington, a suburb to the south side of the city (and a quarter-mile from Solomon's Tower), had been found brutally murdered, her body on the kitchen floor. The back door was unlocked and she had been taken unaware for there were no signs of a struggle, although a candlestick lay beside her. The police were working on the theory that she had been awakened during the night and had disturbed an intruder who had assaulted and then strangled her.

The gardener, on his weekly visit, had discovered her when he knocked on the kitchen door for his customary dinner of bread and cheese. Access denied him, he found the door unlocked and her body on the floor. At first believing she was in a faint, he was horrified to find that she was cold and must have been dead for some time.

The newspaper report continued:

> Dunn was alone in the house at the time as her employers were in Stirling at a family wedding. Mr Elliott, a rich wine merchant in the city, stated that as far as he was aware the burglar had not got very far with his activities since no items were missing, although the house contains many valuable antiques and silverware. Mrs Elliott was in a state of shock when she spoke to the police who were carrying out extensive enquiries in the neighbourhood.

Saville Grange. I put down the newspaper. I couldn't place it but the name was familiar. I must have walked past the house many times in childhood days and afterwards, before Gran took Emily and me to live in Orkney when Mamma died with her stillborn baby who would have been our little brother.

Realising the murder had taken place so

near at hand must have brought a natural feeling of unease to any woman living alone and accounted for Mr Blackadder's anxiety. Her killer being yet at large some weeks later made me wonder if the police detectives were as skilled as Pappa had been at solving domestic murders.

I was still so engrossed with the news items in the weeks-old newspaper spread on the table that I got quite a shock when I looked up and saw a policeman's helmet framed in the window.

He tapped on the glass and, on my unlocking the kitchen door, revealed the rest of a tall, broad-shouldered man in his early thirties. A handsome 'chiel' in the Lowlands tradition of high cheekbones, thick, sandy hair, a well-shaped mouth and eyes so dark blue they seemed at first glance to be black.

'May I ask what you are doing here, miss?'

I was somewhat taken aback. 'You may indeed. I live here and may I ask why you are staring in at my window?'

'Your window, miss?'

'My window. Who are you?'

'Constable Jack Macmerry, miss,' he said, saluting me politely. Then danger over, his manner suddenly relaxed and he smiled apologetically. 'I do beg pardon, miss. I live down the road at Duddingston. I pass by this house every day and, although there was some activity a few months ago, I thought it was still unoccupied.'

He paused. 'We have instructions to keep an eye on it. Vandals and undesirables, if you get my meaning,' he added, with a heavy nod in the direction where the circus was sited. 'I take it that you are the new owner, miss.'

'I am and it's Mrs, not miss, Mrs Rose McQuinn. Would you like to see some proof? You may consult my solicitor, Mr Blackadder. The title deeds are with him—'

'No, no, I'll take your word for it,' he said hastily. Then, pausing to take stock of the surroundings, he asked, 'Aren't you scared, living here all alone—I mean, what with this murder nearby and all?'

I tried not to laugh since his textbook training obviously lacked a chapter on tactful and consoling speeches for ladies living on their own near a murder site.

Wondering how Pappa dealt with such exigencies in his police constable days, I pointed to the newspaper. 'I've just been reading about it. Fortunately I am not of a nervous disposition.'

Suddenly I interested him. 'Mrs McQuinn, did you say? Are you related to the Sergeant Danny McQuinn who was in the police here?'

'I am his widow. He died while were in America.'

'My condolences, ma'am. I'm right sorry to hear that; my father worked with him in the old days.' He smiled. 'It's in the blood.'

'I know.'

Rubbing his chin, he looked at me. 'I seem to remember that Sergeant McQuinn married Chief Inspector Faro's daughter. Am I correct?'

'You are.' He had a good memory too. 'Congratulations, Constable Macmerry.'

'Fancy you being his daughter. He is still a legend in the Central Office, you know. They all try their best, but there's never been a detective like him—never will be, I reckon.'

'Oh, I don't know, Constable, you sound as if you're doing very well,' I said, thinking this might be an opportune occasion to establish friendly terms with the police. 'Look, I can't offer you a cup of tea but would you like a glass of milk?'

'I would indeed, Mrs McQuinn. I left the house early this morning and I didn't have time for breakfast.'

He relaxed, took bread and cheese, and from across the table he looked around and said: 'This house has quite an atmosphere, I grant you that. But it's lonely for a woman on her own. Would you like me to look in each day—when I'm passing?' he added awkwardly.

'I would greatly appreciate that, Constable. But I am well able to look after myself, rest assured of that.'

I thought it better to avoid mention of the pistol I had learned to keep by me—and to use with deadly effect—in America, so pointing to the newspaper, I said: 'Have they got anyone for the girl's murder yet?'

'No. But there have been quite a few leads. We expect to make an arrest any day now.'

I thought that was a pretty well-rehearsed little speech that came quite glibly from the lips of policemen baffled by a killer's identity and singularly lacking in clues.

'The gardener who found her gave us some very useful information. He'd seen some savage-looking stranger near the house around the time of the murder. He's very concerned, having found the body. Earnest sort of chap, feels it's his duty to come straight into the station regularly to ask what progress we're making with our enquiries.'

He paused and gave a despairing sigh. 'Insists that the man looked like an Indian from the circus, whom he might recognise again.'

'The circus down the road? Is that why you're here?'

'Exactly, Mrs McQuinn. The police have their own ideas, but I've been elected to keep a sharp lookout.'

'The newspaper report said that nothing had been taken. So the motive wasn't likely to be robbery.'

I had already come to some conclusions of my own: the kitchen door unlocked—I knew what Pappa would have made of that. Poor Molly had most probably been killed by someone who knew her. Someone she trusted to let into the house. 'I'd be on the lookout for a jealous lover, rather than a circus performer who was taking some exercise,' I said.

He frowned. 'On the other hand, it could have been someone she was sorry for. A benighted traveller who needed help and she asked him into her kitchen. It does happen, you know. I suspect, Mrs McQuinn, that it's the sort of trusting thing you might do yourself,' he added with a note of triumph for his own shrewd appraisal of character. 'Now I must be on my way. Thank you for my late breakfast.' At the door he turned and saluted me gravely, looking rather anxious as if he felt I was taking his warnings all too lightly.

*   *   *

Hanging in the cupboard next to the kitchen range were a waterproof rain cape and a rather shabby straw shopping basket. The cape would come in handy for wet weather and the basket I'd press into immediate service for my visit to the shops on Princes Street.

I walked happily towards the Pleasance, enjoying the warm sunshine. Once, when there were only fields, this was a narrow track outside the city walls, part of rural Midlothian. Now, tall terraces of houses, close-packed, sprouted skywards.

Returning the basket to Bess, I walked on

past the Old Flodden Wall which once marked the city boundary. Built in 1513, it was intended to keep the English army at bay after the Battle of Flodden Field where the flower of Scottish nobility died at the side of their king, James the Fourth.

The changes in the city of Edinburgh since the sixteenth century were no less remarkable to my eyes than what had happened to the skyline in the past ten years and was doubtless fated to continue into the next century. Progress was with us in full fever as the clang of hammers and the mast rigging of scaffolding told of yet another building arching its outline against the sky.

Up St Mary's Street and skirting the railway station, across Princes Street to Jenners, an establishment dedicated to serving the needs of respectable middle-class Edinburgh ladies who might with propriety now shop there alone: a daring new innovation of which the older shop assistants disapproved, preferring their ladies to have a maid in attendance, a guarantee of special attention.

I felt quite courageous, and modern too, making my way to the ready-made sports department and, as I'm not one to fuss over what I wear as long as it is comfortable and reasonably attractive, I soon had all the garments necessary for a lady bicyclist. Wishing to avoid the look of horror on the more mature and less enlightened assistants rigid with convention, I chose my assistant with care, one of the younger girls who might understand and sympathise with my needs.

I found that my figure was well out of date and my uncorseted shape worried even the young woman who served me, especially my firm refusal to be laced up. The fashionable 'hourglass' was not for me. My sojourn on the unfashionable American prairie had brought some very decided ideas regarding comfort and the female form, as well as an unshakeable determination to retain the shape that nature had intended.

At last, happily carrying my purchases, I made my way back through the departments, with stationery in mind. I must write immediately to Vince and Emily.

I was also wondering where and how I might get information about purchasing a bicycle.

'Rose!'

I turned round. 'Rose—it is you!'

'Alice?'

What a piece of good fortune to have met my oldest friend on my first visit to Edinburgh.

As we hugged each other I said yes, I was well. 'How are you?'

'I am quite well.'

She didn't look it. I remembered her plump and pretty, now she was thin and her face drawn. Tactfully I did not confess that if she had not spoken first I might have walked straight past her.

'Shall we have tea together, Rose? I was on my way to the tearoom.' She sighed. 'I have such a lot to tell you.'

As I followed her upstairs, memory flashed a signal. I knew where I had heard and seen the words 'Saville Grange' before.

The murder house was next door to Alice's old home, Peel House. Piers Elliott had been an old admirer, whom she rejected for Matthew Bolton who lived with his family in a less pretentious house nearby.

Piers had subsequently married his cousin Freda who was not one of my favourite people. But despite her irritating know-all bossy manner, Alice did not share my dislike and frequently included her in our picnics and parties.

As we took a seat in the restaurant, I little guessed what momentous events were to stem from that chance meeting. Or that there are no coincidences in this life and I was already poised on the threshold of what was going to be my very first criminal investigation.

Chapter Five

Waiting to be served in the tearoom, Alice and I studied each other covertly, our smiles and pleasantries those of two old friends delighted to meet again but conscious that the passing years have brought changes each would be happier to conceal. I don't know how I looked, but sadly, gazelle-eyed Alice had become Alice the scared rabbit.

Questioned, I said that I had returned from America alone and that I was a widow. I did not labour the subject since I did not yet feel strong enough not to break down in public when confiding all the details to an old friend.

To my surprise, it was she who seized my hand across the table and burst into tears. 'I'm so sorry, dear, dear Rose,' she gulped, sobbing into a handkerchief.

I was slightly embarrassed and thought this a little excessive, since she had met Danny only once when we were walking in Princes Street Gardens. I had introduced him and they had not exchanged words, Danny hovering on the perimeter of our conversation, polite and smiling in the diffident, long-suffering manner of men forced to listen to idle female chatter which excluded them.

But Alice's present behaviour was extraordinary in the circumstances. We had not been all that close for years, yet her reaction was that of receiving dire news of a close relative and out of all proportion for a friend's bereavement that was not even very recent since I was not in mourning weeds. Studying her closely, I suspected that it was more, much more than my news that had caused her such distress. Changed in more than physical appearance, she was deeply troubled, in a highly emotional state and hardly recognisable as the easygoing placid girl I remembered.

I watched her narrowly, her hands trembling so much I gallantly took over the teapot, saying: 'Allow me, it is rather heavy.'

She wiped her eyes, drew a deep breath and took a sip of tea. It seemed to calm her a little as she whispered: 'It is so good to see you, Rose. I am so glad that we met.'

I said I was too. Poor, distressed Alice, obviously in great need of an understanding shoulder to cry on. 'How is Matthew?' I enquired.

'Well—why do you ask?' she demanded rather shrilly, a strange response to the natural question that politeness and convention demanded of an old friend regarding her husband. A piece of cambric, a stifled sob and the floodgates opened.

Allowing her a moment to recover, I paid some attention to the scone on my plate, took a couple of bites.

She gained control and said: 'You must excuse me, dearest Rose. I have rather a lot to bear just at present.' Another sob. 'I am most severely put upon—most severely. You see, I have discovered that he no longer cares for me.'

My eyebrows rose at this extraordinary statement regarding Matthew Bolton, with whom I had been perhaps better acquainted than she with Danny. Matthew had seemed the most devoted of suitors, a solicitor in his family's long-established firm with an excellent future, but what Vince called 'rather a dull dog'. I had been in their company during their courtship and later as guest at their wedding.

Now I prepared myself to listen to some tale of marital infidelity. Recalling those first impressions of Matthew, I said: 'You believe he has found someone else?'

'I do indeed. I am sure of it,' she added vehemently.

'Have you talked to him about this?'

'No.' She laughed bitterly. 'But I am well aware of what is going on.' A fierce nod. 'Oh, indeed I am.'

'Alice, if you haven't heard it from his own lips, you might well be misjudging him. There are many things that might be mistaken for such behaviour . . .' I hoped she wouldn't ask me to quote her chapter and verse upon this speculation, since I couldn't think of a single instance at that moment.

She stared at me; hope flickered briefly in her eyes and died again.

I resolved to be practical. Alice, come now. What evidence have you?'

She regarded me blankly for a moment. I

patted her hand, feeling that I had scored a point at last. 'Why not begin at the beginning?' I said gently.

'It started when we moved from Peel House—that was a year ago when our old house was sold.'

Peel House was Alice's family home, one of the few remaining old mansions set in imposing gardens once isolated in country fields alongside Saville Grange. Such grandeur of isolation was before the property developers moved in.

'Matthew found a new buyer,' Alice continued. 'It took some time since I refused the offer of a builder who wished to tear it down and cover the entire area with more modern villas.

'His suggestion that we might occupy one of them appalled me. We could do a lot worse, he said, that with both boys now at prep school and eventually public school and university, it was pointless paying for an army of servants to look after the pair of us.

'Such presumption. But Matthew agreed. As you know, the house is two hundred years old and in constant need of repairs, which cost a fortune.'

I felt that this argument and domestic upset was little reason for a devoted husband to go philandering. I wondered when she would get back to the point of her story. I didn't have long to wait.

'At last we made a private sale to a man who was in trade in the city. An elderly draper with a pretty young wife—his second marriage. Unfortunately he never lived to enjoy the comfort of Peel House,' Alice added with a certain amount of righteous satisfaction.

'Mr Harding died soon after they took possession. His widow, Lily, moved into the lodge and since she had no head for business, a bit of a flibbertigibbet, Matthew said, and he being so wise and thoughtful, he offered to help her set things in order.'

'What happened to the house?'

Alice sighed. 'She sold it to the property developers to tear down.' She paused. 'It is since then that Matthew's behaviour has been very strange.'

'In what way strange?'

She shrugged. 'He has been most secretive, I suspect that he visits her almost every day—instead of going to his office.'

'What about his business? Surely he cannot be spared every day?'

'Indeed no. But there it is. I feel his thoughts and his concern are mainly with this woman and he is neglecting anything else in her favour, delegating work to juniors. He has taken a craze for fitness too—men can be so vain at a certain age. Now that we live nearer the city and there is a perfectly adequate tramway system—which he urges me to use—'

Alice's expressive shudder indicated that she considered this demeaning and didn't care for any ideas of public transport. 'There is a coachhouse at our present house in the Grange but Matthew sold our carriage when we moved in, insisting that we have no need for it and that such things are quite outmoded these days.'

She paused for a moment, biting her lip before adding: 'He said the exercise would be good for me.'

I was expected to make some protest but, for the life of me, I couldn't quarrel with Matthew's reasoning so far.

'However,' Alice continued, 'the coachhouse isn't empty. It's at the far end of the garden and there's a perfectly disgusting man living in it.'

'Surely not!'

'Yes, there is. I saw him one morning after Matthew had gone to work. He looked like a common workman. I got quite a shock. So did he. When I asked what he was doing there he turned his back and, refusing to answer me, darted inside and bolted the door. I banged on it, said I'd call the police if he didn't come out immediately. He just shouted at me: "Leave me alone, missus. Mr Bolton says I'm to stay here as long as I like."

'Naturally I was furious and could hardly wait to tackle Matthew about it. But when I said I objected to having a coarse, low fellow like that on the premises, Matthew got into such a rage and told me I was to keep out of it, that the man was a particular friend of his. A particular friend,' she repeated. 'Can you by any stretch of imagination think of such a creature—a down-and-out tramp—even being a casual acquaintance of Matthew's?'

I shook my head. Frankly, I was baffled too. I could not picture the pompous Matthew, whom even my conventional stepbrother Vince dismissed as 'a frightful snob', admitting to rubbing shoulders with, let alone having friends among, the Edinburgh poor.

'He said this was a man to whom he owed a debt of gratitude,' Alice continued. 'A man who had done him a great service in the past but had now fallen on hard times.'

Again she paused, tearfully this time. 'Can you imagine what the neighbours will think of us harbouring such a creature?'

I shook my head and, disappointed that she was not getting any help from me, Alice sighed. 'That's all there is to tell, really. I just have this awful feeling that Matthew has changed, that he is no longer the man I married, the man I still love with all my heart.' And out came the cambric handkerchief.

I allowed her a small interlude of tears, before saying firmly: 'Alice, none of this makes any sense. Think about it. What on earth has this character Matthew befriended got to do with him taking up with some other woman?'

Now Alice shook her head and looked bewildered, as if the thought had never occurred to her. 'I don't know, Rose, it's just part of the feeling that I'm being deceived, right, left and centre—and that he doesn't want me any longer. Oh, Rose, all this is destroying me. Don't you see, I must find out the truth.'

She studied me intently, helplessly. I was at a complete loss to know what consolation, let alone advice, I could offer, when she went on: 'I must find out what is going on, Rose. I cannot go on like this. I will go mad,' she said and looked wild enough at that moment for me to believe her. 'But Matthew would never forgive me if he found me prying into his affairs.' Leaning across the table, she grasped my hand again. 'What shall I do, Rose? Whom can I turn to?'

I had no answer to that one.

'Don't you see what I'm leading up to?'

I shook my head.

'You can help me, Rose. I beg of you—please say you will.'

I stared at her. 'I don't see how—'

'Oh yes, you do. You were always so clever at, well, sorting things out, finding answers, reasons for everything for other girls—'

I didn't know what she was on about, only vaguely remembering that because Pappa had brought me up to think along his own lines of observation and deduction I was occasionally able to apply them and provide logical solutions to the rather innocent and often fatuous problems of my classmates and friends. When I told Pappa, he would laugh and say they could have worked it out for themselves, as it was more a matter of common sense than detection.

'That was a long time ago, Alice.' I didn't add that I had not been spectacularly successful at sorting out the problems of my own life. In particular, at solving the mystery of a husband who rode out of my life one day, never to return.

'Surely you can advise me, then, just as you used to?' she said desperately. 'I can hardly go to anyone else with such a request.'

I thought for a moment. 'There are probably detective agencies in Edinburgh for just this purpose. You could advertise—'

'No!' Alice shuddered. 'Have Matthew spied upon, his indiscretions made public—a laughing stock to all his friends! The scandal would kill him, ruin him. I am not wanting that kind of vengeance—only my own peace of mind. I shall always love him—always—and forgive him, whatever he has done. Yes, unfaithful or not, it makes no difference to me. I just want him back. But I cannot live with this uncertainty. I must know!'

She banged the table, emphasising the words, shaking the teacups and causing a fluster among the nearby genteel ladies, their feathered hats shivering like alarmed pigeons.

'Rose, are you listening to me? Do you understand what I'm trying to say?'

'Of course I do, Alice.' But none of it was very logical. I could see all the obvious flaws in her argument. In an effort to calm her, I said: 'You are naturally overwrought—I do sympathise, believe me—but the best advice I can give you is not to precipitate a crisis and the best thing—indeed, the only thing in the circumstances as I see it—would be to, well, sit back for a while, wait and see. Given time, the situation might change, he might tire of her—' But I knew I had said the wrong thing.

'No, I will not wait! That I will not do at all! I cannot eat or sleep, I feel as if I am slowly dying, my life draining away.' She stopped and looked across the table, her eyes full of unshed tears. 'Let me tell you something, Rose, something which may make you change your mind. Until today I have prayed and prayed, and still nothing happened. Then the moment I met you again I knew you had been sent to help me.'

She paused for a moment to see the effect of her words and then said slowly: 'It was no coincidence that we met as you were leaving the shop, I knew my prayers had been answered—at last. As if an angel had been sent to deliver me!' she ended triumphantly.

An angel was not quite the role in which I saw myself at that moment as she added humbly: 'I am in your hands, dear Rose. You are the only one who can help me. Don't you see, you can go to Peel Lodge, where this woman—Lily—lives and discover what is going on there. And you can find out about this sinister friend of Matthew's who is living in our coachhouse. Please, please, dearest Rose, do this for me, for the sake of our long friendship.'

It sounded like a mad proposition, maybe Alice had already gone beyond the borders of sanity, but my heart went out to her.

She was a simple soul who had scarcely ever been out of Scotland, her whole existence bound by the conventions of the day. By love and a fortunate marriage to a man she loved, she had fulfilled all that her role in society demanded of a middle-class woman. The thought of losing her husband to another woman terrified her, not only for the personal pain but the disgrace and humiliation, the loss of face that would follow in the eyes of her friends.

And I knew then I would do as she asked. I would try and help her. Perhaps this was exactly what I needed to keep my mind off my own particular nightmare, fears for my own future. 'Very well, Alice, you've talked me into it. I'm not promising anything, but I'll do my best.'

'Oh, thank you, thank you—'

'All right, Alice. Don't upset yourself,' I

begged. 'Please don't start crying again. If I'm to help, I need some practical information from you.' And so saying I took out my 'journal'. 'Just give me some details, dates and so forth, the address of Matthew's business—'

Ten minutes later, the bill paid by Alice at her insistence, we made our way to the front door. About to depart, she eyed my parcels and the worn basket I carried, and propriety got the better of her. 'Just one tactful word, Rose, dear,' she whispered. 'Ladies in Jenners never carry shopping baskets over their arms. It is considered, well, rather vulgar, a duty they leave to their maids.' Observing my expression, she put a hand on my arm. 'I do hope I haven't offended you by mentioning it.'

I wasn't offended, merely trying to keep a straight face as I stifled the desire to laugh out loud. 'Not at all, Alice,' I said soberly. 'But since I don't possess a maid, are my parcels quite correct?' When she nodded I went on: 'A good thing I elected to wear my new coat, rather than carry it back home to Solomon's Tower.'

'Solomon's Tower?' Her eyes widened. 'You're living there—not alone, I hope?'

When I explained briefly that I had inherited the property from my stepbrother she looked mildly surprised. 'I remember when we were children you once took me there. It was full of smelly cats and a mad old man shouted at us.'

'The mad old man was Sir Hedley Marsh and Vince's benefactor. It is no longer full of cats, as you will see when you come to visit me.'

She didn't smile. 'We always thought it was haunted,' she said anxiously.

'I think I can promise you there are no ghosts either. Perhaps, like the cats, they fled long ago.'

'But it is so isolated. You are so far away from the city.'

'Less than two miles, Alice. I realise that can be inconvenient, so I am about to take up bicycling.'

Alice's eyes widened at that. I hoped I wasn't in for another lecture on the impropriety of ladies bicycling, but she merely asked: 'Have you a machine, then?'

'No. I was about to make enquiries as to where I might purchase one when we met—'

'No need for that, Rose.' And for the first time she laughed. 'I told you it was providence that we met. You see, I have a bicycle, a very good one, an 1888 Westminster Ladies Special Light Roadster,' she added proudly. Then sad again, a sigh. 'Matthew bought it for me just before we left Peel House. He has always been a great enthusiast for exercise out of doors. As you'll remember, he was quite an accomplished mountaineer.'

I vaguely recalled an expedition he had organised to the Swiss Alps. He had tried to interest Vince until Olivia put her foot down very firmly.

'I was putting on rather a lot of weight,' Alice continued, 'after the boys, you know. And Matthew who has always been so lean—I do envy him—decided I should get more exercise and that a little discreet bicycling would be good for me. Not in Princes Street, of course,' she added hastily, 'but on our more secluded roads where it would not cause comment. But alas, I never had confidence to persevere, to learn to ride. I'm such a mouse, not like you, Rose.' She took my arm and said earnestly: 'It's yours if you want it. I'd love you to have it. Look, why not come home with me now and collect it?'

I could see no good reason to decline such a handsome offer and we took the tramcar along Princes Street across Waverley Bridge and on into Newington.

Matthew had been right about that. It was a pleasant way to travel and, although I little guessed it at that moment, this innocent meeting with his wife was my first step into a dangerous and terrifying future.

Chapter Six

Outside Alice's Newington home in Portland Crescent a group of ladies were stepping down from two carriages outside her front door.

'Oh dear,' she said. 'Meeting you again put everything else out of my mind, Rose. I had completely forgotten this is the afternoon for our literary group,' she added in a hasty whisper as we approached them.

Polite smiles and introductions were exchanged with the waiting ladies and, ushering them into the hall where the maid waited to take their cloaks, Alice excused herself and whispered: 'The bicycle's in the washhouse—I'll get the maid to bring it round for you. I had a skirt specially made and never worn.' Studying me intently, she frowned. 'I'm afraid it will be too large for you, perhaps you can have it altered to fit—'

When Alice reappeared with the skirt over her arm, the ladies peered out of the drawing-room. Certain that I was a servant 'in need', they smiled benignly and watched wide-eyed as the maid propped the bicycle up against the garden railings.

Alice waved to them brightly, as if she donated bicycles to charity every day of the week. 'Are you sure you'll be all right, Rose?'

she asked anxiously. 'You won't fall off and hurt yourself, will you?'

'Of course not. I'll soon get the hang of it,' I stated confidently. 'Thanks again, Alice. I'm so grateful—you've been very kind.'

'We must talk soon—come on Thursday for tea. I have no engagements that day,' she said.

I gave her a farewell wave and, aware of the literary ladies at the window unable to restrain their curiosity, I set off cheerfully and, with only a couple of false starts, made a wobbling progress down the street.

I'd never manage hills and I'd have to push the machine most of the way to Solomon's Tower. Once into Queen's Park and almost home, I remounted and only fell off twice, unobserved by any onlookers and without damaging anything but my pride.

It wasn't bad for a beginner, I thought, and, putting the machine proudly into the stable, I went indoors deciding that possession of a bicycle might be an invaluable asset in my new role as a discreet investigator of ladies' matrimonial upsets.

Intrigued by Alice's problem, I looked at the brief details I had written down and inserted some queries of my own regarding Matthew's odd behaviour. Such as, who was the sinister working-man living in the coachhouse and why was Matthew Bolton in his debt?

And what of Alice herself?

A curious thought struck me, something rather odd that might be significant. Whereas everyone I had encountered so far since my arrival in Edinburgh had been eager to tell me about the servant girl's murder, especially when they knew where I lived, Alice Bolton had never mentioned it.

The fact that her late home, Peel House, was next door would make one naturally assume that such a dreadful deed would have been, in spite of her own problems, worthy of a mention.

I noted that omission but hadn't the least idea where to begin investigating Alice's husband.

This was the sort of problem Pappa would have relished and I could imagine his quick, incisive mind picking up clues that Alice and I had overlooked. Suddenly I realised how dreadfully I missed him, how I had been longing for some sort of message from his self-imposed exile with the Irish patriot, deemed 'terrorist' with a price on her head, Imogen Crowe.

I wondered if he had persuaded that ardent feminist writer to marry him, or even if that was their mutual wish. I was assuming all was well with Pappa and such was the telepathic bond between us that I would know if anything worse had befallen him than communications and even family letters from southern Ireland being censored. Perhaps they were regarded as containing subversive or treasonable material written by an ex-detective from Edinburgh City Police formerly in Her Majesty's personal service.

I looked out on Arthur's Seat. This was the twilight hour, Scotland's 'gloaming' when the cloudless sky glowed and the first faint star appeared in it. It had been Pappa's favourite hour, the setting sun with crimson clouds a breathtaking reminder of the many occasions we had walked here together.

Not all memories were happy: I remembered dear, wise Pappa—although I hadn't thought so at the time—urging me strongly against marrying Danny McQuinn. Originally I had thought it was because he didn't think a policeman good enough for his daughter, but perhaps I had misjudged him and he was more aware of the perils and hardships that faced a pioneering wife.

After many arguments, finally I had left with a father's blessing. But had some instinct—the second sight inherited from his web-toed seal-woman grandmother in Orkney—warned him that it would end in tragedy? Home again, awaiting those scars to fade a little—alas, I could not believe they would ever disappear and some undreamed-of joy replace them for ever—I wondered what my life would have been like had I listened to Pappa and remained as a Glasgow schoolteacher, patiently enduring until some worthy man came along and made me forget—no, I could never forget Danny—and persuaded me to accept a compromise marriage.

Surely I was better off with the memories of a man I had truly loved since I was ten years old than a dull existence as a suburban wife and mother, I thought, examining the glass-fronted bookcase which had once graced Pappa's study in Sheridan Place. Transported by Vince and Olivia to marshal and tame Sir Hedley's hoard of books which had lain scattered around the house, obviously Vince hadn't wanted any of them, although some were very old and might be greeted with delight by a collector.

Scanning the shelves, I picked up a leather-bound Legends of Arthur's Seat, recalling curious illustrations and how, as a small child, Pappa often read to me from its pock-marked yellow pages when we visited the Tower.

I held it close, as if it were still warm from his hands. The picture that had so fascinated me was of a shepherd lad, staring into a bright crystal cavern. There before him sat King Arthur, wearing his crown and armour, a hunting horn at his side and with him his knights, their swords on the round table, heads bent, all waited. Even deerhounds, with muzzles resting on their paws, ready for the summons to awake and gallop out with knights, their visors down, swords flashing, to save Britain at its time of greatest peril.

'It's not just a fairy story, is it, Pappa?' I had asked, hoping he would tell me once again that there was always someone who said it was true, whose grandfather had heard it from the very lips of the shepherd boy.

'There he was, minding his sheep as he did every night, up near Hunter's Bog. It was springtime, a moonlit night and he heard one of his tiny lambs bleating. He searched for it everywhere and had almost given up hope when he noticed a deep crevasse in a rock nearby. Being small and thin, he slipped inside and walked a few steps down a steep, dark path towards a light shining at the other end.

'Drawing closer, he heard merry voices, laughter and although he was very scared he crept nearer and saw the King, wearing his crown, with his knights around a great table, their hounds at their feet. Knowing that his story wouldn't be believed without proof, he decided to creep forward on his hands and knees, and steal something from the round table. At the King's side was a great cup of gold, shining with jewels.

'That would do! The men were too busy drinking to notice him and, being so small, no one marked his approach. But as he stretched out his hand to seize the cup, one of the deerhounds saw him and barked a warning. Someone cried out, pointed, and the boy panicked, took to his heels. Running blindly back along the dark tunnel towards the moonlight, he thought his end had come when he saw one of the massive hounds guarding the entrance and feared it would tear him to pieces.

'But it didn't touch him, so he ran and ran, and never stopped until he was back in Chessel Close off the High Street.

'There he told the whole story so vividly that a band of men armed with cudgels, sticks and the like set out to find the dog standing by a secret entrance that would hopefully lead them into this magic crystal cavern with its jewelled cup on the table. One and all they licked their lips, thinking of vast fortunes, theirs for the taking.

'But although the lad was eager to go with them and show them the way, he seemed after a while to be leading them round in circles and they never did find the magic cavern. There was no crevasse, no dog, no knights. They shook their heads, shouting about wasted time as they trudged back down the hill, threatening the shepherd lad as they greedily remembered the golden cup with its jewels.

'But the less bold among them gave inward sighs of relief, remembering that inside the hill were caverns known as Goblin Halls, where fairy folk danced and from where, on cold winters' nights, the sounds of music and revelry could be heard. Shivering, they swallowed their disappointment, saying they were God-fearing pillars of the Church who would not have known quite how to face the enraged imperial majesty of King Arthur, to say nothing of his armed knights.'

Arthur's Seat had an intriguing name, conducive to legendary associations in the minds of the imaginative, whereas in actual fact, Pappa told me, it was probably a corruption of the Gaelic 'Ard-na-Saighead'— Height of the Arrows—and the valley known as Hunter's Bog would once have been an ideal place for archery practice.

Evidence of defensive ramparts on the summit dated from Iron and Bronze Ages, and weapons found in Duddingston Loch in the last century suggested settlements on the slopes of the hill. A primeval forest cleared in 1564, it had been greatly favoured by Mary Queen of Scots, with an open-air banquet for a young couple from the court at Holyrood.

'But you prefer a puzzle, don't you, Rose?'

'Yes, Pappa, and had you been alive then, you would have solved the shepherd boy's story,' I said confidently and he had smiled at me, shaking his head.

'Don't be too downhearted, Rose. Rest assured, magic exists in this weary old world of ours if we are prepared to accept it. But there are puzzles beyond us, ones that we aren't meant to solve.'

I put down the book.

Like Danny McQuinn. How would you have tackled that one, Pappa, where would you have started looking for the clues that so obligingly waited to be discovered in your murder cases?

The hill was ablaze with pure golden light from the dying sunset, so bright outside that the Tower seemed gloomier, more menacing than during daylight. Closed in on itself, it became a house of ancient mysteries and puzzles that no one had ever found explanations for, not even my clever father.

The glowing light was so tempting that I decided to take a walk, before I lit the lamp and settled down to read. The fresh air would ensure that I slept soundly in that vast, curtained four-poster.

Truth was that I wanted to escape, not from the remote past of history but from my own more recent past with all its agonies that had blistered my soul, and was ever present, each and every day, like a persistently dull toothache.

Chapter Seven

I set off up the hill, wondering if I could still find the secret path Pappa and I had taken towards the summit past the small cave where he, as a child in 1836, was one of a group of schoolboys who had discovered two rows of tiny wooden coffins elaborately decorated with pieces of tin and each containing a little wooden figure, carefully carved and dressed in funeral clothes.

With no idea of the value or mystery of their find, a lot of horseplay followed and, according to Pappa who was a little frightened by it all, some of the coffins disintegrated. The remaining eight were taken to the schoolteacher, reported in the newspaper and finally donated to a local museum.

Speculation was rife, the most popular belief among superstitious citizens being that they were part of the black-magic rituals. But subsequent history remained silent regarding the origins of the coffins.

Not even my clever father's logical mind could produce a satisfactory explanation but, telling the story, he often shook his head and wondered if this first case of mysterious miniature coffins had not set his feet firmly upon the path of crime detection.

There would be still an hour of fading light and as I walked I remembered less romantic stories about this area. How in the mid-seventeenth century plague-stricken citizens were forcibly ejected from the city to an encampment on Arthur's Seat. Many died and were hastily buried in pits on the hill.

Trying not to think of those unhappy old ghosts in the sudden cool wind from the summit, I was delighted to see that the boulders marking my secret path with Pappa were still in existence. As I climbed, I stopped occasionally to admire this bird's-eye view over the new Edinburgh skyline with its terraces and villas that had sprouted in my absence. The Palace of Holyroodhouse lay grand but dark in gardens, which had once been a debtors' sanctuary and had sheltered an exiled French king.

Suddenly I was aware of being watched. Shading my eyes against the sky, I saw by the crag a tall grey shadow that moved.

Heart thumping, I blinked, blinked again. It was a dog, a grey deerhound; the largest dog I'd ever seen, the size of a pony, and it looked exactly like the one that legendary shepherd boy might have met, as if it had stepped out of Legends of Arthur's Seat.

Enough to make any sane person take to their heels, but I am not easily unnerved: a dog is a dog and, after a band of blood-thirsty Sioux Indians, small fry. Especially this dog, who didn't look fierce at all. In fact, he looked very benign, yawning deeply. As befitted a creature who might be having his first breath of fresh air after several centuries inside a crystal cavern, I thought, still not certain that he was a real dog and prepared on this hill of legends for anything to happen—like his sudden disappearance.

But no, he was watching me, wagging that

enormous tail as if we were old friends and looking not at all unkindly, but gravely from under heavy grey eyebrows, for all the world like an old magistrate on the bench confronted by a tricky case.

As he bounded towards me, however, I must confess I lost my nerve but determined to stand firm, according to dimly remembered advice I had read somewhere—that one should always outstare savage beasts. Not that this one looked savage.

I held out tentatively a slightly trembling hand and said, 'Hello, and where did you come from?'

I didn't really expect an answer but he sniffed my hand, decided its smell was friendly and didn't offend him. I was to be trusted. He lifted his head, glanced back over his shoulder towards the summit of the hill, paused for a moment, apparently listening for something. Then he shook himself as if to shake off whatever or whomever he had left behind.

I stroked his head. I'm not very tall and it reached my shoulder. I guessed he weighed more than I did and his coat was in excellent condition, silky and clean.

A very well-cared-for real dog, no part of any legend and doubtless the proud possession of some frantic owner who might be out at this very moment searching for him.

'Are you lost?' I enquired. He stared at me and if a dog could look puzzled that was his expression. The word 'lost' wasn't in his particular vocabulary.

I tried again. 'Aren't you a handsome fellow?' And the astonishing creature grinned, yes, I'd swear he grinned at me. Showing his teeth, I was to tell disbelieving friends later, when I was to have as much trouble with this real-life dog as the shepherd boy had with his ghostly knights of the round table.

I wasn't sure what to do next. 'Are you hungry, then?' I asked, trying to think what I had in the house besides some as yet uncooked bacon which might appeal to a hungry dog.

He inclined his head, a gesture which in a human might have been interpreted as polite refusal.

'All right. It's been very nice meeting you. Now off you go—home to your master. He'll be looking for you.'

The deerhound stood still, looked quite hurt and then moved a step closer to my side.

'Good dog, yes, you are. But you must go home.'

He yawned again. Then a sound, something beyond my hearing range, alerted him.

Danger, danger, he trembled, staring down towards the park. Then I heard the noise: some wild beast, a very faint roar, from the direction of the circus far below us.

Of course, that was the answer. What an idiot I was. This extraordinary dog was one of the Great Performing Animals from the poster I had seen in the Pleasance. I touched his head, stroked his shoulders. The long, soft grey hair confirmed my discovery.

He had escaped from the circus and might be valuable enough to be stolen, so I must get him back there without delay.

But how? What to lead him with? In the absence of a stout rope, I took the buckskin belt off my skirt and put it collarlike around his neck. It was too large and I spoke soothingly, hoping he wouldn't resist and take a bite out of my hand. I was greatly relieved when he merely regarded this action with mild curiosity.

His behaviour confirmed my suspicions. Remembering how I watched unbroken horses fight against saddles and bridles on the prairies, I guessed that he was used to wearing a collar.

'Come along, now. I'll take you home,' I said. Holding on to my belt, we began to trot briskly down the hill. I hoped he wouldn't try to dash ahead and throw me flat on my face. But no, this amazing, mild and well-mannered creature, who could outcourse a greyhound in the hunting field or bring down a stag, walked obediently at my side, setting his pace to mine and pausing when I faltered.

I was glad of this chance, curious to inspect the circus on the common ground in Queen's Park. It covered a vast area and had spread itself like a small village, firmly entrenched with its caravans and tents, its tepees: an exotic scene with the first lamps and torches lit against the approach of evening and the next performance.

Smells of wood fires, cooking, crushed grass and boiled sweets competed with the more menacing jungle odours of caged animals. The sound of a barrel organ on the carousel, the cries of vendors, still brought a glow of excitement, touching as it did a chord of happy childhood.

The circus was an event much anticipated in Sheridan Place and talked over wistfully with Gran in Orkney, anxious that it would coincide with our summer visit to Edinburgh.

Emily and I spent school holidays with Pappa and looked forward to being with him every day, sure that he would have planned all sorts of treats. Alas, all too often, since criminals did not cease their activities to suit two small girls, Pappa was in the midst of some murder inquiry and our outings were deputised by Vince.

Rather scornfully declaring he was past childish amusements, Vince was eager to pass us on to Mrs Brook. Sometimes he came to the circus, though, and was soon throwing dignity to the winds, the first to shriek with mirth at the clowns' antics or to hush little Emily's fears as the lion's tamer thrust his head into its jaws. 'Nothing to get alarmed about, girls, he's done it hundred of times,' Vince would murmur. 'The beast's been yawning for ages—he's so old and tired they could hardly get him through the wire trap into the big cage. He's probably just had a good meal—or been drugged, or both. That sharp stick he's being poked with, that's the only way they could get a roar out of him.'

The clowns and the acrobats, the trapeze artists and fire-eaters were even then our favourites and I never gave a thought to the other side of seals barking, performing elephants and wild animals, never considered the cruelty involved in their training.

That awareness only came with a wider sense of the adult world.

The deerhound was conscious of the animals, too, and that they were strange and hostile. The hair on his neck bristled.

I didn't want to encounter any cages and, beyond the gate and a small ticket office very busily employed, was a wooden fence to hold the curious at bay. I made a mental note of performance times and resolved to buy a ticket for some appropriate matinée.

There were abundant posters and I found myself staring at 'Chief Wolf Rider of the Sioux'. Complete with war bonnet and warpaint, it was a lifelike poster, and one which set my heart beating faster and turned my blood to water again.

The smell of horses, their whinnying, the

sound of hoofbeats approaching, removed me from Edinburgh straight back to the American West. I felt a sudden pang, the prick of tears. Dear God, I missed Danny so and I found myself shivering as I remembered those renegade Sioux who had broken out of the reservation.

At my side, the deerhound needed no second bidding to steer clear of the horses and wild animals.

As I made my way to where a group of caravans hinted at more domesticated lives, I told my fast-beating heart to be calm, that this was no mirage: I was home and safe.

Nothing could hurt me any more. The future was up to me, but if I were to survive the present, then I must learn always to put the past behind me, those nightmare months of waiting for Danny to return. The long trek back east, the tiny grave of our child, which I would never be able to find again, lost for ever: Danny's son and mine.

As we crossed the enclosure there were voices, a sudden stir of activity in the huge tent as the crowds began to gather, to scramble for the best seats on the wooden tiers.

Outside torches were lit, illuminating other enticing posters: 'Chief Wolf Rider's Wild West Show', 'See the Sioux Ghost Dancers and Custer's Last Stand'.

I shuddered, for the depictions, crude as

they were, touched that chord of memory. Would I ever be able to summon up enough courage to watch a performance, see it as a tame and innocent entertainment? I told myself that the Indians were most likely fakes, white men painted like half-naked savages, remote as the moon from reality . . .

Suddenly a small group on horseback came riding into the enclosure. They looked better fed than I remembered and better clad in buckskins suitable for a British climate.

There was nothing particularly savage about the young riders. They were laughing and looked as if they were enjoying themselves. Without blazes of warpaint and feathered bonnets, the impressive and vivid costumes used in their acts, these tame Indians were a far cry from the savage killers I had encountered. They even saluted me gravely, Christian manners too, and off-stage their leader wore a cross about his neck.

My mouth went dry.

Their shouts to each other in their own tongue, the drum of hoofbeats, now conjured up terrible scenes of lances with scalps, their mirth the screams of the dying.

As they rode past I trembled, wanted to run. Run!

A wave of sickness swept over me. The leader was quite close, near enough for me to see that cross. A crucifix identical to the one Danny always wore.

The deerhound felt my terror. Edging closer, he growled, rumbling deep in his throat, a soft but dangerous sound.

A warning to enemies that he was on my side.

Chapter Eight

The Indians rode out of sight. At my side the deerhound relaxed, danger averted.

But soon darkness would be complete.

With an effort I remembered the purpose of my visit. 'I wonder where your master is,' I said. 'Show me where to find him.'

He looked at me, head on side, clearly bewildered by the request, as if I should be providing the answer.

'Come along, then, he must be here somewhere. And you're big enough to be recognised by folks who know you both.'

We walked through the dusty ground towards a group of caravans. One of them had a look of importance, larger and more ornate than the rest.

'Is this where your master lives?' I asked. But the dog just stared ahead. He made no resistance, however, when I walked across the clearing towards the caravan.

Before I could walk up the steps the door was flung open. A woman, no longer young but gaudily costumed in tights and spangles, appeared. She was in a fine old rage, yelling back over her shoulder to someone inside: 'And you go to hell and take your paramour with you. May you rot in hell, the both of you.'

There was a murmur, indistinguishable but unpleasant, from the unseen occupant which further incited the woman.

'Rot in hell, I said. You can tell her that. And I'll not divorce you. Never. All you want is her money so tell her I want that necklace back you tried to impress her with, tell her that you stole it from me. It was my mother's and there's her curse on it.'

She paused for breath, stamping her feet, dancing with rage. 'Are you listening? Go on, rot in hell. Do you hear what I'm saying?'

It was difficult for the whole circus not to hear her and I stood there, mightily embarrassed at being a witness to this extraordinary domestic quarrel. Obviously here was a woman with no qualms about washing her dirty linen in public.

Suddenly she turned, saw me. 'And what do you think you want?'

Smiling confidently and trying to look as if I hadn't been listening to her tirade, I pointed to the dog. 'I brought him back. I assume he belongs here.'

It was too much to expect this to calm her down, that she would respond to a joyous reunion with a lost dog. She stared at him angrily and I realised she probably didn't even know he had taken off. And seeing her temper I wasn't surprised.

I found it very unnerving at close quarters and suspected that Master Deerhound was a sensitive creature, especially when it came to humans with violent manners who made a lot of noise.

Ignoring him completely, she sauntered over and stopped. Hands on hips, she pointed to the caravan she had just left. 'What do you want with that bastard? Answer me. It's him you want, isn't it—the dog is just an excuse.'

I was speechless but before I could think of a suitably chastening reply, full of righteous indignation that I was a married woman and so forth, she took my silence for guilt and screamed: 'You can take that dog away—right now. Do you hear me?'

'Isn't he yours?' A lame question in the circumstances.

'He is not. And the smell of him will upset our animal acts, spoil their performance.'

Summoning up all the dignity I had left, I asked coldly: 'May I speak to whoever is in charge of the circus?'

She jabbed a finger at the caravan she had just left. 'That rotten bastard in there. He is in charge.' And with a mirthless laugh she came close and stared into my face. 'Another whore, eh? Edinburgh is full of them.'

I was furious at this unwarranted attack on

my character, but made allowance for the smell of drink on her. That, as well as the Sioux braves, took me back a long way to many a bar room of the true wild and lawless West where this lady's demeanour would have gone down exceedingly well for keeping unruly cowhands in good order.

Taking my silence for guilt, she became even more infuriated. She seized my arm in a painful grip. 'Answer me. Another of his whores, is that who you are?' And, staring at the region of my stomach: 'Has he got you with a bairn too?'

The deerhound didn't like her manners either or the way she swayed towards me. Again that warning growl, rumbling deep in his throat.

She was totally unaware of the danger as he strained forward. I hung on to his collar but, fortunately for everyone concerned, at that moment the caravan door opened. 'Daisy. Come inside at once and sober up. Stop making an exhibition of yourself.'

She threw back her head and laughed so heartily that she staggered and almost fell. 'I thought a pretty whore would have you jumping up and down again.'

A tall man was silhouetted against the lamplight from inside the caravan. He came down the steps and hurried towards us. 'What's all this about? I'm Cyril Howe, I'm in charge here,' he added in a voice of authority.

And to my astonishment I found myself staring into the face of the man who had boarded the train at Dunbar in the furtive company of a woman who was definitely not, after the tirade I had just overheard, his legal wife, this loud-mouthed harridan who flounced back into the caravan.

'And what can I do for you, young lady?' he asked, smiling, piling on the charm.

He hadn't recognised me as a fellow traveller from Dunbar to Edinburgh. Not that I was unduly surprised, considering the distraught manners of Mr Howe and his companion on the train that day. I was pleased to see that I hadn't been too far wrong with my assumptions regarding his taste in dress. It was perfectly appropriate for a ringmaster at the circus.

'Don't take any notice of my lady wife,' he said. 'She has a jealous disposition. I'm afraid she is at a rather delicate age.' His accompanying sigh indicated a long-suffering husband with quite a lot to put up with and sorely in need of comfort and understanding.

And all this to me, a stranger. I did not care for his ingratiating smile either. My sympathies were with his shrewish wife who doubtless had plenty of reasons for being thoroughly unpleasant to strange young women who flocked to her door with tearful claims of having been made pregnant by her husband.

Howe pointed to the deerhound. 'You can't bring him in here, y'know, miss. Strange dogs upset the animals.'

'I apologise. I thought he might be yours.'

'What made you think that, miss?' he enquired thoughtfully, taking a better look. 'We only have small dogs in our acts, poodles and the like. They're easy to train—and feed. These big fellows are difficult to handle and eat as much as the ponies.'

I looked at the deerhound who looked back at me with an expression that in a human could only have been interpreted as 'I told you so.'

'Where did you find him?' Howe asked.

'He was wandering about on Arthur's Seat. I assumed he was lost, and with the circus being near at hand . . .'

Howe nodded, somewhat eagerly, came forward and eyed the dog up pretty shrewdly, in the way of one who knows quite a lot about animals. 'Well, now, he seems in good condition for a stray. If he's biddable, I might well find a place for him in one of our acts.'

I could see the way his mind was working. After his statement that big dogs were difficult to train as circus performers, I doubted whether this one would ever do his bidding, unless it was attached to a pony carriage to trot his tiny poodles round the ring, dressed up as little people in frills and flounces.

Howe's expression said he was having

second thoughts. He had decided that this was a valuable animal for breeding and that some dealer would give him a good price, no questions asked.

But the deerhound was sharp. He got the message too.

As Howe advanced and put out his hand, he backed away, showing all his teeth. No benign grin this time. No longer gentle, he growled threateningly. Suddenly ferocious, he barked, twisted out of my belt around his neck and loped away out of the enclosure like an arrow from a bow.

Howe gulped, regained his composure. 'Well, if he troubles you again, remember what I said. I'll be glad to take him off your hands.'

There was nothing more to be said and, bidding him goodnight, I began rolling up the belt I had been left holding and thrust it into my coat pocket.

Howe was watching me. 'That's an Indian belt, isn't it,' he said.

'It is. A present.' I began to walk away.

Howe sidled up to me, put a delaying hand on my arm. 'A moment, miss. If you're looking for work, I might be able to accommodate you.'

Did I look that shabby and poor, I thought, as I said: 'Thank you for the offer but I am not seeking employment. And it's Mrs, not miss. I happen to be married.' I added and, hoping

86

he'd get the message, I looked pointedly at his hand.

He smiled as if that information wasn't important and, quite undeterred, came closer, rubbing shoulders with me. 'Live nearby, do you?'

'Yes.'

He smiled slowly. I didn't like his closeness and he knew it, but refusing to be put off he said: 'Please yourself—missus. But remember, we can always use pretty young women like yourself in our acts—missus.'

He chortled, his emphasis on the word saying that he wasn't fooled and I was making it up, taking refuge in respectability. 'Just remember if you have any . . . problems. We pay good money too—for good services. If you know what I mean.' The accompanying leer left no doubts about that. I turned on my heel with as much dignity as I could summon and made for the exit.

As I was leaving, I noticed Constable Macmerry with another uniformed policeman. They were strolling round the tent but didn't look as if this was a social occasion and they were looking for tickets for the next performance, all prepared to enjoy themselves at an entertainment. Their manner was preoccupied and purposeful. It suggested that they were after something. Or someone.

I hurried across the rough ground, a short cut above the road, still keeping a lookout for the deerhound. There was no sign of him and I realised that he was probably on his way back to his rightful owner after his little adventure and I'd never see him again. Just as well he escaped from Cyril Howe, I thought, or I might have had some explaining to do to a distraught and angry owner about giving away his valued pet.

I put my hand in my pocket. The belt wasn't there.

I realised I must have dropped it. I stopped in my tracks, wondering whether I should go back for it. I had taken the short cut through bracken and across rough ground. It was now almost dark, but for the gleam of a full moon rising above Arthur's Seat that would light my way home.

Realising I had more chance of breaking an ankle than finding the belt, discretion said no and, as if to confirm this, the rain began, a steady drizzle, hiding the moon.

There was nothing for it but to get up early next morning and retrace my steps as far as the circus.

I guessed even then the futility of such a search. I'd never see it again or that blessed dog. Sad and angry, I was ready to blame him. If I hadn't been so concerned for his welfare I wouldn't have lost my precious buckskin belt.

Treasured as one of my last links with America, it had been a symbol given to me by the old Sioux woman who nursed me back to life after my baby died.

Chapter Nine

I had a bad nightmare involving Alice, Matthew and the mysterious widow. It refused to be shaken off and the feeling of imminent disaster remained with an urgency that demanded immediate action.

A search for my treasured belt must wait. I would bicycle to Newington past Alice's old home at Peel House, a nostalgic visit to see it once more before the property developers moved in and razed it to the ground.

My main motive, however, was to inspect the tenant of Peel Lodge. If I were to be of any help to Alice then I had best get the lie of her rival's land, so to speak. A visit on some pretext might reveal information regarding Matthew Bolton's secret life, although I hoped Alice's suspicions were wrong and that he was not having an affair with Mrs Harding. As well as natural compassion for my old friend's distress, I thought of the scandal revelation of such a liaison would cause among their friends, the disillusion and misery their two young sons at prep school would suffer at this break-up of their family life.

Once out on the road again, I was fast mastering the art of the bicycle and could do straight lines pretty well with only a wobble or two when I needed to go round corners or manage the brakes at crossroads. By the time I had reached Peel House, without having fallen off once, I was feeling rather pleased with myself.

The houses were scarcely visible, apart from a glimpse of rooftop or chimney pots beyond discreet high walls and gardens close knit with trees and iron gates to ward off the curious.

Even the birds seemed conscious of their place in this wellbred society and only twittered gently rather than burst into vulgar song or raucous cries.

Today the scene was different. I had not visited the area for many years and wondered if I had taken the wrong turning as further along the tree-lined road a small group of spectators gathered outside my destination. Mostly women, they stared through the gates and along the drive.

What on earth had happened? What new disaster? Then I saw to my relief that they were using this as a vantage point for a good look at that house next door: Saville Grange, destined for a very long time to be known locally as the 'Murder House'.

As I dismounted one woman, imagining my motive was also morbid curiosity, whispered with a shudder: 'Isn't it awful?' She pointed along the drive. 'That's where the poor lass was done in. Strangled she was. I knew her well, a chum of my Peggy.'

It was indeed awful, with Alice's old home just across the garden wall. But it gave me an idea.

Without need for further explanation, but aware that my bicycle might not produce a favourable impression, I parked it by the gate and walked boldly up the drive of Peel House.

The house was not at all as I remembered it, now awaiting its fate, sad and abandoned, with blind, boarded-up windows, its once neat gardens and drive lost under a tangle of weeds.

At first glance the lodge didn't look much better, but a wisp of smoke from one of the chimneys signalled habitation.

I rang the bell, expecting a maid to appear since Alice had inferred that the Hardings had struck a great bargain by selling the house to property developers.

As I waited I listened to considerable activity inside the house. Bolts were being withdrawn on the door. I sympathised with the nervous occupant. I would have taken the same precautions since the spot where I stood was in isolated grounds close to the relevant scene of a brutal murder, behind an ivy-covered garden wall sixty feet away.

There was no maid. The woman who came to the door was in mourning, which enhanced dark-auburn hair, a fashionably—and enviably—alabaster complexion. She was perhaps thirty but looked younger and held a babe in arms.

'I saw you from the window,' she said in tones of relief. 'You've come about the post of nanny. Do come in.'

I was taken aback, already prepared with a plausible tale that I hoped would gain me access.

I followed her into the tiny parlour, heavily overburdened with large furniture and antiques. The relics of the move from grander surroundings looked all out of place, ill at ease at finding themselves moved so far down in the world and in such close proximity to one another.

Taking the seat she offered and flourishing my 'journal', which served so many purposes, I said: 'I'm afraid you are mistaken, Mrs Harding. I am writing a feature for a charitable society on bereaved Edinburgh gentlewomen who might require financial assistance—' I had decided this should be safe enough ground, seeing that she was a woman of means and added: 'Your name was given to me and I wondered if you had any opinions to put forward.'

This bold request made her very nervous indeed. 'I have nothing to say about gentlewomen—nothing at all which would be of any help.' She shook her head and with a disappointed sigh said bleakly: 'I thought you were the new nanny.' She regarded me sadly for a moment as if I might have some advice to offer on the subject of nannies. 'I suppose I needn't hope for many answers to my advertisement. Young women cannot be blamed for being cautious in this . . . area . . .'

She paused. 'I expect you are aware of what happened over there—next door.' When I nodded she continued: 'The newspapers talk of nothing else. I'm sorry for the girl but heartily sick of it all. I don't know how anyone will ever sell a house here again.'

'People soon forget,' I said consolingly and prepared to leave, aware that I had been wrong and there was little to be gained from this interview. With a final look around that stuffy room, more like an antique auctioneer's paradise than a comfortable home, I hadn't the least idea what I was supposed to observe and deduce except the obvious: that the present owner had fallen on hard times.

'I hope you're right about people forgetting,' said Lily Harding as she steered me though the furniture in the crowded passage and opened the front door.

In her arms, the baby stirred and cooed. 'Such a pretty baby. How old is she?'

'He,' she corrected, 'is just a year old. A bit of a handful at present.'

'Then I hope you find a nanny soon.'

Over my shoulder she peered anxiously down the drive as if expecting someone. Then, with another sigh and a murmured good-day, the door closed rather sharply, the heavy armoury shot home once more.

I walked down the drive and there was Constable Macmerry who seemed destined to materialise wherever I ventured these days.

At this moment he was chewing his lower lip, notebook in hand, and solemnly regarding my parked bicycle. His stern and thoughtful expression suggested that he would like to put a lot of questions to it regarding trespass on private property. Hearing footsteps on the gravel, he turned and saw me. I gave him an encouraging smile. 'Is this vehicle yours, Mrs McQuinn?' he asked in tones of surprise.

I said it was and he nodded slowly and pocketed the notebook. 'Visiting friends, are you?' he asked casually, the accompanying glance summing me up as, well, maybe, a possible suspect in a somewhat volatile area of the city. I might look innocent but a policeman on duty can never be too sure.

'I used to visit Peel House. One of my school friends lived there long ago. A sentimental journey.'

He nodded. 'Just in time, Mrs McQuinn. It's due to be pulled down any day now—'

'Is this your area, Constable?' I decided it was my turn to ask some of the questions.

He shook his head. 'No. I'm just helping out. Constable who does this beat is down with influenza. We're very short-staffed with everyone on the search for clues to the poor lass's killer, so I'm keeping an eye on the murder house—'

'You mean Saville Grange?'

'The same.' Pausing, he glanced disapprovingly towards the dwindling group of female spectators. 'Just keeping order,' he added sternly. 'We're very nervous about suffragettes these days.'

'The lady in the lodge I've been visiting will be glad of your protection, Constable. She seemed very scared.'

He laughed. 'You can't blame her when there's a killer on the loose and so close by, too.'

'Oh, do you think he might come back and murder someone else?'

He knew I was laughing at him and said sternly: 'You never know.'

'You have reason, then, to believe that there is some sort of a maniac at large who might strike again.'

He wasn't prepared to theorise on that possibility but, perhaps impressed by my illustrious detective father, he decided to be confidential. 'The signs indicate someone familiar with the district. Despite the fact that the gardener reported suspicious and savage-looking characters lurking about the premises.' He sighed. 'We've drawn a blank with our investigations at the circus so far. Problem is that the Indians—who might well be described as savage-looking characters—

have no English. Apart from their Chief, that is. He seems like an educated man.'

Walking down the road with me, as I pushed my bicycle, he added: 'How are you settling in at the Tower?'

'Very well, thank you.'

'Everything all right?' I said it was and he went on: 'No strangers around?'

'Only a deerhound on Arthur's Seat. No one who could be reported as a suspect, I'm afraid.'

'A deerhound?' he repeated.

'Yes. You don't happen to know if anyone has lost one in the area?'

He frowned. 'No. Can't say I've ever seen a dog like that around here. They're big fellows. Most of the ones I encounter are spaniels or Highland terriers, bad-tempered little brutes. Have a snap at your ankles, sharp as a flash.'

We had reached a crossroads.

'I'll keep a lookout, now that you've mentioned it,' he said. 'Probably escaped from the circus.'

'That was my first idea, so I took him along. He wasn't theirs—I noticed you and one of your colleagues around the big tent, just before the performance.'

But he wasn't going to be drawn any further on that and we went our separate ways.

* * *

As I rode towards the Tower my mind was less preoccupied with the deerhound than with that baby I had just met. His mother said he was a year old. Alice had told me she had been a widow for two years. Then the deceased husband could not have fathered it.

I pictured the little sweet face again and failed to see any suspicious resemblance to Matthew. I wondered how much to tell Alice when I visited her on Thursday. Or if I should mention the baby at all. If what I suspected was true, such knowledge would be disastrous for her present tortured state of mind.

Better for her to remain in ignorance of this even more powerful reason for Matthew's visit to Lily of the Lodge, especially since Alice had a wife's instinct that there was something wrong. Those small incidents of tenderness in a marriage suddenly discontinued can swiftly invite despair—and suspicion that love has died.

Having allowed myself to think ill of Matthew and condemn him without trial, already I was bitterly regretting having agreed to investigate his odd behaviour.

I realised for the first time that I was perhaps out of my depth, that there was a more monstrous explanation creeping into my mind as I remembered the constable's words that the suspected killer was: 'Someone familiar with the district.' A man who knew the area well and who better than Matthew

Bolton? I considered Alice's tale of his weird choice of friends. He would not be the first middle-aged man who after years of contentment had a sudden rebellion against convention.

Supposing Molly the servant girl next door was a bit unscrupulous and a nosy girl and had observed too much of the goings-on in the lodge? What if she were blackmailing him, threatening to tell his wife all? And what if Matthew had taken the matter into his own hands, rushed over to reason with her and, failing to persuade her, had resorted to violence and in a brainstorm killed her?

It was a horrifying thought, this wild, unbounded leap of imagination. We all like to pretend that murders happen to other people and it is unbelievable even to consider that we might number a murderer among our friends or acquaintances.

But I knew better from Pappas cases: that murder, alas, was not just something that we read about in the newspapers after all. Murder could and did happen in one's own parlours, bedrooms—kitchens—committed by loved members of one's own family circle. And everyone who had known them since birth would swear they had not enough malice in them to kill a mouse.

Lily's behaviour regarding bolts and keys suggested that she was scared and had no knowledge of the murderer's identity. If she and Matthew Bolton were lovers, as Alice suspected, she might be ready to protect him, but why then lock doors? Who else did she fear?

As for the role in this investigation Alice had forced upon me, I realised that Matthew was no fool: an intelligent, observant man and, as Alice told me how little I had changed, he would recognise me instantly as his wife's old friend.

A not insoluble problem, however, I decided cheerfully. I could follow him at a discreet distance and, what was more, I had a ready disguise at hand, one none would question or even approach. I was a widow and widow's weeds, the black veil, would be the perfect screen for my activities.

There was one snag. This effective disguise meant that I would have to revert to going on foot or in hired carriages. My invaluable means of swift transport must remain at home. A widow on a bicycle, weeds flying behind her, would be an object of marked interest and, indeed, shocked amusement.

I began to make my plans . . .

Chapter Ten

I had become so unused to regular meals, not to say any meals at all for long periods while travelling across America back to Scotland, that it took the sniff of a pie shop as I rode through Newington to remind me I was hungry.

Scotch mutton pies straight from the baker's oven are mouthwatering. I could hardly contain myself and had I been adept with bicycling and able to eat as I rode, I would have demolished both pies on the spot, instead of waiting impatiently with the tempting smell drifting to my nostrils until I reached the Tower.

As I approached the garden I rather hoped the deerhound would be waiting for me. Instead, a strange man was on his knees studying the forlorn rose bushes Olivia had hurriedly planted before they left.

My unexpected arrival startled him. He leaped to his feet, staring at me open-mouthed, so put out that for a moment I thought he was about to enquire my business here. Then he recovered and, raising his bonnet from a thin mesh of dark curls, greeted me cheerfully. 'Foley, ma'am. Dr Laurie's gardener. I take it that you're Mrs McQuinn.'

He could have been any age between thirty and fifty, a lean, strong-looking fellow with that rather bland 'honest sonsy face' conjured up by Robert Burns's address to the haggis. The kind of face that, when one got used to it, became nice-looking more by habit and repute than actual fact.

Tactfully, I admired his present efforts and added that I had fond memories of the garden at Sheridan Place when my father lived there.

He was pleased. 'That would be in my father's time. Green fingers he had right enough and the keeping of quite a few gardens in that area. I'm glad to say that he passed them on to me.'

'With all the new houses they're building, I dare say you will be getting a few more,' I said.

He grinned delightedly at that. 'Hope you're right, ma'am.' And touching the rose bushes with his foot: 'I expect these were Mrs Laurie's idea, ma'am. She was very fond of her ornamental flowers. But I reckon you'd have problems with such as these. Better invest in some good, nourishing vegetables for the table. There's too much exposure to the weather here. You'll catch every wind and storm that blows across the Forth.'

'I realise that, Mr Foley. A kitchen garden, vegetables and a few herbs are what I had in mind.'

'Very well, ma'am. I'll see to it right away.' And with another salute he picked up his spade.

'You haven't by any chance seen a deerhound around, have you?' I asked.

He looked up at me. 'No, ma'am. Have you lost one?'

'Not really. But there was one here yesterday. I thought it might be a stray.'

He frowned. 'I shouldn't encourage big dogs, if I were you, ma'am. They can make a right mess of gardens—untidy beasts they are and destructive, too. Take my advice and chase him off next time you see him.'

He paused. 'A deerhound, you said. Unusual for city folks. More for country estates, they are. Probably just snooping about. On the scrounge from that circus down the road.'

I didn't want to go into all that again so without further comment I went inside. Despite his warning, I felt somewhat let down that the deerhound wasn't waiting to greet me. And all on the flimsiest acquaintance.

It was such nonsense. He had no doubt by now found his way back to his own fireside and, intelligent beast that he was, decided he would give that woman who tried to sell him to a ringmaster a very wide berth in future.

I could only manage one of the two pies after all and, when I went over to the window to see how Foley was getting along, I noticed a film of dust on the bookcase. In the absence of a maid to do the housework, I had better get to work with a duster and broom.

I didn't find the idea appealing in all truth and, in no hurry to set about the task, I began idly to study the contents of the shelves instead. The Talisman by Sir Walter Scott. I picked it up triumphantly, remembering Pappa reading to me about Roswal. The devoted hound belonging to the Scottish crusader, Sir Kenneth, was the cause of friction between him and his commander, King Richard I. Spinning through the pages, there was a description of Roswal: 'Eager to acknowledge his gratitude and joy for his master's return, he flew off at full speed, galloping in full career and with outstretched tail, here and there, about and around crossways and endlong.' I turned a few pages: 'A most perfect creature of heaven, of the noblest northern breed, deep in the chest, strong in the stern, black colour and brindled on the breast and legs just shaded into grey, strength to pull down a bull, swiftness to cote an antelope.'

The story went on that the King was not best pleased with the deerhound's exuberant activities, since all deer belonged to the crown, and Sir Kenneth and Roswal were guilty of poaching, a treasonable offence with dire penalties. Later, however, King and Knight were reconciled and reached a gentleman's agreement based largely on their mutual respect for the hound Roswal.

*   *   *

A tap on the kitchen door jolted me back to the present.

I had forgotten the gardener.

'I'm done for the day, ma'am, I'll look in later on with some nice cabbage and carrot plants for you. A few onions too, whatever I can gather together.'

About to close the door, I called: 'Wait a moment.' And searching for my purse: 'I must pay you.'

'No need, ma'am. I receive my wages from Mr Blackadder's office.' He looked round the kitchen and said: 'Is there anything else you would like, while I'm here?' And, pointing to the cold kitchen range: 'I could start the peat going for you, ma'am.'

'That's very obliging of you.'

He nodded eagerly. 'Comes in handy for cooking and even in summer the nights get chilly up here. Great things are peat fires,' he added enthusiastically. 'Much less bother and mess than coal fires that are so popular in Edinburgh houses. You can keep peat on embers for as long as you like, if you remember to stoke it every night and not let it go out.'

I laughed. 'I was brought up with peat fires when I lived with my grandmother in Orkney.'

He smiled. 'Then you'll know not to let it

die.'

Gratefully I watched him. What a treasure the man was. Considering how long my fumbling attempts to get a blaze going would have taken, so many burnt fingers, so much frustration, especially since Gran would never trust Emily and me to touch her preciously guarded fire.

Foley was an expert and the warmth and comfort of a peat fire was next best to having a friend in the house.

On his way out he tried the latch on the back door several times. 'If you don't mind me mentioning it, ma'am, a bolt or two is what you need.' He shook his head. 'A young lady living in such a quiet place with no neighbours should have more secure doors.'

'I'd never given it much thought,' I said.

'Possibly not. But things have changed in Edinburgh since the old gentleman lived here. And not for the better. I blame the trains and that railway bridge. Makes us an easy target for all sorts of awful folk who wouldn't have had a mind to crossing ferries and the like. Mark my words, ma'am, Edinburgh was a safer place before that bridge was built.'

He was watching me earnestly, hoping I would agree, twisting his bonnet in his hands. 'There's some rough folk hereabouts these days and a body can never be sure what might happen next. The world's not what it was when I was a lad, ma'am,' he added with a sad shake of the head.

I didn't like to disillusion him that, even lacking such amenities as a bridge and with fewer buildings than there were now, crime had still been, and always would be, rife in a big, sprawling city.

Another pause, another twist of the bonnet. 'Take that poor lass down the Grange,' he said, his voice suddenly hoarse and strained. 'It was me as found her, lying there dead on the kitchen floor.' As he closed his eyes, moving his head to and fro as if to shake off that terrible image, I remembered the account of the gardener's grim discovery. 'I'll never forget that scene, that I won't. It'll never leave me, it'll haunt me till my dying day. Her just lying there, cold and dead. Awful—awful.'

His eyes were tear-filled and I said: 'How dreadful—I'm so sorry. Did you know her well?'

He shook his head. 'Just in the passing. She'd give me bread and cheese, with such a nice smile. Bonny curly hair,' he added and looked at me for a moment as if he were going to add some significant comment. Then he changed his mind, shrugged and said: An orphan from the workhouse, but a good, kind lass.'

He was so overcome that a long pause followed while he dabbed at his eyes with the back of his hand and, embarrassed by this show of emotion, I tried to think of something

106

appropriate to say. 'I hope they get the man who killed her.'

He nodded eagerly. 'All these enquiries that are getting them nowhere. They'd better look sharp or they'll be too late.'

This was becoming interesting. 'Have you some ideas about the man's identity?'

He laughed harshly. 'I have that. And you haven't far to search either.' He looked at me, waiting for my question. When I shook my head, he jabbed a finger in the direction of the circus, 'Down there, ma'am, sure as the nose on your face. One of them savages I saw hanging about the drive when I was doing the garden.'

'Did you tell the police?' The remark was unnecessary since I knew this from Constable Macmerry.

'I did that. But they take their time. I said arrest him straight away or he'll be gone scot-free to murder some other poor lass, but no, they have to wait—until their investigation is complete—that's what they told me. Until it's too late,' he added bitterly.

Poor Foley, I thought, what a terrible experience. I guessed that he had never seen anyone dead by an act of violence. I had—many and often—during my latter years in America. I tried to push it out of my mind but I could sympathise with Foley. The first time is the worst, sudden death swift and unbelievable.

Watching him stride off down the road, I returned to the bookcase and, replacing The Talisman on the shelf, I noticed a yellowed paper folded into the back cover, obviously placed there by some enthusiastic earlier reader. The print was faint and difficult to decipher. It was entitled 'Notes on the Deerhound'.

Can do a steady fast trot for nine miles at a time, overhauling a deer going uphill or on the flat, but if coursing large mountain hares it can also twist and turn as nimbly as any ferret.

From earliest times accompanying the hunting party, in the Dark Ages deerhounds and wolfhounds were once one breed, used by the Celts on all types of large game. Considering themselves and their hounds as one race, not until the human groups separated into Highland Scots and Irish did the wolfhound become a symbol of quality and breeding for its impressive size by the Irish, while the deerhound continued working for its living, combining strength, speed and agility.

Before the introduction of rifles the work of the deerhound was to kill for the table. In the old Gaelic ceremonial, the 'tainchal', hounds and handlers would go up to the deer forest, stalk a suitable group and drive them down into a narrow glen where hunters waited with bows and knives. On more practical domestic occasions the hunter would stalk a solitary deer and slip his hound or hounds to course and kill it. The best hounds felled the deer by overhauling, hitting hard in the shoulder, then killing it with a neck bite as it dropped to the ground. Since less good animals merely haunched the beast, pulling it down by the hindquarters and worrying it, which spoiled the eating, hounds that made clean kills were highly prized.

On the inside back cover, in spidery writing brown with age, someone had written: 'Deerhounds symbolise everything Scottish, huge, granite-grey beasts with coats as rough and battered as Arthur's Seat itself, fierce and impressive, they are gentle and affectionate in character.'

Mention of deerhound and Arthur's Seat together sent a thrill of excitement though me. It suggested that whoever wrote those words was no stranger to a deerhound in this area.

Could it be that Sir Hedley Marsh himself, never known to have visitors, had entertained an acquaintance with the one I had seen? Common sense told me this was impossible, considering the tribe of cats who would be a dog's natural enemies. Besides, as the writing looked very old indeed and the lifespan of large dogs rarely exceeds twelve years, this passage could not possible have related to the same creature I had so briefly encountered.

My discovery that I might be tangling with magic and legendary beasts, as well as brutal murder, made me feel very uneasy indeed.

Chapter Eleven

Foley's words had scared me. I wished people would stop reminding me, as if I needed reminding, that I was all alone in the Tower. I went into the garden and, shading my eyes against the sun, looked at the summit of the hill.

The sheep moved in small groups, cropping grass, indistinguishable as small boulders amid the bright blaze of gorse. Far up in the sky the large black shape of a bird hovered, hardly moving, watching its prey far below.

But in my little garden no bird sang, not a living creature moved, apart from a solitary blackbird digging for worms in the soil Foley had disturbed. All was silent, too, as if a pall had fallen across my new home. I felt very small against the extinct volcano that was Arthur's Seat. Small and vulnerable, as if it might roar into life at any moment and shake me off its side like some irritating insect.

The hours, days, weeks and months stretching ahead suddenly seemed intolerable. Many I knew would follow this exact pattern and I would spend them alone here, longing not for society as such, but just for someone or some creature to talk to, a few garden birds or a pet like a deerhound who had seemed intelligent enough to understand every word I said.

But he had deserted me. He would never come back, he had found his old home again and I should stop hoping and thinking nonsense. So I went inside, closed the door and found to my delight that Foley's peat fire had encouraged the kettle on the hob to boil. I decided to shake off my gloomy thoughts by making a pot of tea, and being useful and domestic.

Before embarking upon anything as ambitious as a clothes washing, I'd tackle my skirt hem, muddied in the bicycling. Afternoon slipped into evening and, going upstairs, I put on my old shoes. Olivia's, although more elegant, were beginning to pinch my broader feet.

As I did so, I thought again about that lost buckskin belt. Whatever my fears of Indians, their crafts were exquisite. Again I felt angry at abandoning all hope of recovering such a treasure. Sand-coloured, I pictured it blending with the bracken, unobserved.

111

Daylight was fading and as I climbed the steep hill it was to an appropriate accompaniment of Indian drumbeats, wisps of smoke rising from the tepees far below in the circus enclosure.

Surveying the distant prospect, my thoughts drifted back to Three Moons, the old Sioux woman who had been my friend. With no language between us, she had every reason to hate a woman of the white eyes who had massacred most of her family and clan, every reason to rejoice and let the fever take me. But Three Moons was what we call a white witch, the Indian equivalent was medicine man or shaman, and she had taken me into her tepee, kept me alive when rightly I should have died. But all her magic couldn't save my baby.

Without understanding a word I said she comforted me, held me in her arms when I recovered enough to cry for him and for Danny—when I pleaded with her to let me follow them into the darkness of death.

Weeping when at last we parted, she wrapped her long grey plaits around my wrists and, placing her hands on my head, I needed no words to know she prayed to the Great Spirit to protect me. And I felt that blessing echoing right down to the soles of my feet.

As if I might, to this day, turn and see her

watching me and while I looked for the track I had taken back from the circus after the deerhound had escaped and I had walked away from Cyril Howe, I knew that language was not always necessary for perfect companionship.

Sometimes Pappa and I could walk together for hours without saying a word and no two people were ever closer—he called it 'companionable silence'. What I would have given for some of that magic time now, for having him at my side—for some consoling words that would give me faith in a future.

Pappa would have found the path instantly with his built-in sense of direction and although I had set off with such high hopes, I was in danger of getting lost. This was the track I had followed before and, since it was too rough to be popular, I might still be fortunate enough to find the belt whose colour would blend with winter bracken, rendering it invisible to a casual observer.

It might even be lying somewhere close at hand. I could picture it beside a boulder, my joy at finding it again.

I soon realised I must give up, for I had covered a great deal of ground in my wearisome search. Slowly, carefully, I walked with my eyes down, examining each side of the track.

All in vain. There was no sign of the belt.

Far below, lights flickered round the circus

113

where they were preparing for the night's performance. The faint roaring of the wild animals sounded eerie, sinister, a little frightening and, although they were safely in cages, they might suddenly appear before me.

Darkness was coming quickly tonight and I must make the most of what little light was left, to make my way cautiously downhill, a more hazardous procedure than climbing upwards.

Suddenly I heard footsteps behind me. Turning, I noticed for the first time two rough-looking men, staggering along the track a short distance away. Broad-brimmed hats, untidy, ragged clothes distinguished them as tinkers. I remembered Foley's words about circuses attracting undesirables. Into that bracket respectable Edinburgh citizens would add thieves, pickpockets and the dregs of humanity.

When I heard them snigger I knew they were drunk and, with the panic of growing certainty, that they were following me. I was their quarry. Heart sinking, I guessed they had probably spotted me from the higher ridge and had been watching, waiting while I searched, in case it was some valuable I had lost.

With a feeling of sickness and terror at the pit of my stomach, I knew my suspicions were correct. For when I stopped, they too stopped, laughing and pushing each other in a very unpleasant manner.

I had to keep a cool head but I quickened my pace, moving downwards as fast as I could.

'Here, you, miss. Wait for us—'

That was the last thing I intended to do. What they had in mind I had no doubt, and I took to my heels and ran through the bracken.

I could see Solomon's Tower in the distance. If only I could reach it, get inside and lock the door behind me and seize that pistol—if they dared follow.

But safety still lay a very long way off and, although I could outrun two drunken tinkers on the flat ground, once I ran into heavy bracken I would be in serious trouble.

I thought I was well ahead, but they were gaining on me. I turned to look round and that was my undoing. My foot tangled in roots and I shot forward on to my face in the bracken.

There was a cheer behind me and the next moment the two men were at me. One of them was holding me down. I could smell the stink of sweat and whisky on him. He was tearing at my skirts, splaying my legs apart, dragging at my underclothes.

I tried to claw at him, to scream. His cohort held my arms and put a filthy hand over my mouth. Laughing, he yelled at his companion to get busy, it was his turn next.

Suddenly the air exploded into a roar, the roar of an enraged animal. A huge grey shape launched itself against the man on top of me, snarling, dragging him off.

I heard a scream of pain as he rolled away, staggered to his feet. His comrade did not wait, both took to their heels, pursued through the dusk, yelling with terror, hunters turned hunted.

I sat up, shaking, adjusted my skirts and wept tears of fright and anger. After all I had lived through in the American West, here I was, about to be raped two hundred yards from my home in respectable Edinburgh!

And as I stumbled to my feet I saw movement in the dim light, a shape. Panic seized my throat—were they coming back?

Dear God, no!

The moving shape grew nearer, became unmistakably a deerhound. Swift and loping he came, sat on guard at my side. Even sitting, his head reached my shoulder and he turned, sniffed at my face with all the concern of a human in that magisterial gaze.

I sobbed. 'Bless you—you wonderful darling creature,' I said, putting my arms around his neck.

As he licked my face, I noticed blood on his muzzle. I shuddered, remembering that I had been reading how deerhounds killed with one neck bite. At that moment I felt no pity and that in the case of the would-be rapists it was richly deserved.

The deerhound raised a paw, stared at me,

barked gently. 'Woof!' Was he asking if I was unhurt, telling me that I needn't be scared any longer because he was here to protect me?

My sigh of relief brought forth a triumphant 'Woof' this time.

I got to my feet and, together, with my hand on his shoulder, he led the way safely back through the bracken and down to Solomon's Tower.

Chapter Twelve

My rescuer followed me into the Tower. I realised he had never been in this, or possibly any, house before from his careful inspection of the kitchen and parlour. He devoted some time head down, sniffing each corner and unseen cranny, staring at the ceiling, registering everything from under those thick, grey, stern eyebrows. At last satisfied, he flopped down at my side.

In the kitchen the kettle was on the hob, but what does one offer a deerhound whom might be a magical beast? I remembered that mutton pie. 'Would you like this?'

He sniffed at it delicately, wagged his tail, opened his mouth and it vanished in one gulp. I patted his head. He tried licking my face by way of thanks.

I started to shiver again, realising this was

delayed reaction. Even after suffering so greatly before my return to Scotland I was still capable of being scared witless. I sat down and began to cry.

'Woof,' said my deerhound and put a paw on my knee. I was amazed at the gesture, my scalp tingled, it was so like the reassuring hand of a human.

'Woof,' he said again, gently. I am here to look after you.

I patted his head and, seeing that I was composed again, he stretched out once more in front of the peat fire and yawned.

He looked very much at home and I asked: 'Would you like to stay here?' The tail wagged and I patted his shoulder. 'If we are to be friends, you must have a name.' I thought for a moment.

Then I had it. The title of the minor noble who acted as official of the king under the old feudal system. I thought of Macbeth's title. Thane of Cawdor, Thane of Glamis. And how appropriate for this magical deerhound visiting me from the court of King Arthur . . . 'Thane—that's what I'll call you. How do you like that?'

He looked at me and I could have sworn he grinned in acknowledgement.

'Welcome, Thane.'

I was suddenly very tired, exhausted by my terrifying ordeal but safe home at last. I longed to sleep. And I knew I could go off to bed and leave my new friend to guard the Tower and me.

Out of courtesy, as he might be nervous about being locked indoors, I left the latch off the back door. I reckoned he was quite capable of using his nose to open it.

Aware of protection, I slept fearlessly, undisturbed, for the night silence on Arthur's Seat is profound. I awoke with sun streaming through the window, to sheep bleating, and close at hand a lark's song soared heavenwards, rapturous in the clear air.

For a moment I wondered if I'd dreamed the whole sequence of last night's events, especially as when I sped down the spiral staircase Thane was gone, the kitchen empty.

Standing with my hands on the table in front of me, I felt strangely empty too, and sad. Opening the door, I looked out past the garden to the summit of the hill and, shading my eyes, called 'Thane!' several times.

Only the sheep continued their grazing and I went back indoors, blew on the peat. With a steady blaze going and a kettle boiling, I made myself a comforting pot of tea, feeling very clever at having conquered the first access of the kitchen range. Some day, if I stayed long enough, I resolved to put that oven to good use.

And so I sat down and wrote to Emily and Vince, telling them only that I had arrived home alone and that I would relate the whole sad story when we met again. As I had only two envelopes I'd write to Pappa later via Mr Blackadder for forwarding to Ireland.

The milk laddie from Bess's farm came past and I asked him to post my letters.

'I will that, missus. I'm always willing to take letters and wee messages from remote houses like yours and deliver them into the city for you.'

He said his name was Billy as he looked up at the bulk of the Tower behind us, dark against Samson's Ribs. 'Seen anything yet, missus? I mean, now that you're living in the house on your own.'

I smiled. 'What sort of thing had you in mind?'

'Well, ghosts and suchlike.'

'I'm afraid not.'

'Folks swear that they often saw the Mad Bart wandering about, long after he had a Christian burial in the kirkyard,' said Billy eagerly. 'They saw him staring out of the window, shaking his fist at them as they walked past.'

I knew that the Mad Bart, alias Sir Hedley, had a strong sense of property and if his ghost haunted Solomon's Tower that was certainly the way he would behave. But I didn't feel his presence. And he didn't resent mine, of that I was certain. 'I don't think there are any ghosts here, Billy.'

Disappointed that I had no gory story to

relate, he sighed and then added encouragingly: 'Aye, but there's time yet.'

Billy knew the area well and went rabbiting, he told me. 'I can bring you one, if you'd like. There's good eating and your maid will ken fine how to cook it.'

When I said I hadn't a maid as yet, but I knew how to skin and cook a rabbit, he seemed mightily surprised by such an admission and even a little embarrassed to discover that Mrs McQuinn wasn't turning out to be such a lady as he had thought her at first.

I made amends by offering him a cup of tea with some bread and cheese. He responded with alacrity and, as he ate, I asked casually if he had seen a deerhound on the hill lately when he was rabbiting.

His mouth was full and I had to wait a moment for his reply. He shook his head. 'Never, missus. A deerhound you say. What do they look like?' An obvious question for a city lad.

I said: 'Big—the size of a pony. Shaggy grey coat.'

'Folk hereabout favour wee dogs. Spaniels, terriers and the rest.' He thought for a moment and laughed. 'Now that you mention it, I heard tell of something like the beast you're on about long ago, in my great-grandpa's day.'

Pausing to drain his teacup, he went on:

'But you won't find any here, not nowadays. They're hunting dogs and you'd have to go to the Highlands to some laird's estate for the sight of one now.'

I gave him a refill and asked: 'Have you encountered any tinkers on the hill?'

He grinned and then looked serious. 'Give them a wide berth, missus. Don't be inviting them in for a cup of tea and a bite of cheese or you'll never be rid of them. They're like flies around a midden.'

And as if this weren't warning enough, he added: 'Be sure to lock your door and keep an eye on your washing line. The men are rogues and their women too. They'll steal anything that isn't nailed down.'

After he left I had that awful flat feeling again. I was suddenly lonely, the house too silent for comfort. Billy was a jolly lad and it was good to have someone to talk to.

The Tower had taken on one of its gloomy moods, shrouded by mist drifting down from the hill. I could no longer see the top of Arthur's Seat, but the bleating of lambs sounded louder, nearer and more distressed. I was miserable, too, conscious of my isolation and vulnerability.

At that moment I would have given anything to hear from Emily. And when she replied to my letter and insisted, as I knew she must do, that I should go immediately and stay with them in Orkney, I knew I'd say yes—

yes, please. I wanted the warmth of kin around me. Gran and Emily, and her husband, too, although he was a stranger to me whom I had met only a couple of times.

The possibility was that I was more scared than I cared to admit about those drunken rapists. Last night came back with sudden force. This rural area of Edinburgh used to be a safe place. Now, people like Bess and Foley who had lived here longer were right to have their misgivings.

Progress had its price and these new streets of houses attracted predators. Or should I blame the circus, which also drew the broken men of society, the bitter dregs of humanity in search of pickings?

Everything around me in the Tower seemed useless then, comfortable but inanimate. I desperately needed living creatures to talk to. At this rate, if Thane failed to return, I'd be reduced to talking to squirrels and wild birds. Even the sheep with their lambs, if I could ever get close enough to them.

*   *   *

I was delighted to hear footsteps outside the kitchen door and to see Constable Macmerry's smiling face. 'Just passing by, Mrs McQuinn.'

I decided I had better report my attack on the hill last night.

Macmerry was very concerned and out came the notebook. 'What did they look like?'

I shook my head. 'Youngish, black hair, dirty faces, filthy clothes, whisky-sodden tinkers.'

'Tinkers? Are you sure, Mrs McQuinn, that they were tinkers? They might have been, well, strangers, Indians from the circus down the road.'

'Not in those white men's clothes stinking of drink. I know the smell of Indians, Constable, and I know the smell. of tinkers.'

He looked at me curiously. I could see him wondering where I got such knowledge but I wasn't prepared to enlighten him.

He shrugged, disappointed. Clearly this wasn't enough to go on. 'I need something more definite to make an arrest,' he said.

'Like my body, bleeding and broken,' I answered angrily. At his shocked face I relented. 'Look, it was dark—I was terrified, too busy fighting them off to make a careful note of what they looked like. I can tell you only what they smelt like . . . a midden. Foul.'

He put the notebook back in his pocket. 'You'd say they were definitely not foreign, though?'

'Foreign—no. I've seen enough tinkers in my life.' I looked at him. 'Had you someone in mind?'

He frowned. 'Well, we're still looking for one of those Indians from the circus, seen lurking about Saville Grange before the Dunn murder.'

I shook my head. 'Sorry to disappoint you, Constable, but I do know the difference. I recognise broad Scots when I hear it, not something your Indians could manage. And I don't think it was murder the tinkers had in mind, just something of a few minutes' entertainment, too trivial to remember,' I added bitterly.

He shrugged. 'Pity, it might have been a useful lead.'

'Getting me raped, you mean?' I said indignantly. 'Very useful!'

'I didn't mean that, Mrs McQuinn.' He looked hurt.

'Tell me something. Was the girl raped before she was strangled?'

Although this was doubtless a routine question regarding female murder victims, he looked uncomfortable and embarrassed.

'I'm a married woman, Constable,' I reminded him.

Consoled, he nodded. 'Well, let's say by the disarray of her underclothing an attempt at, er, intimacy had been made. But the evidence points to only one man being involved.'

'No tinkers, eh.' I shook my head. 'Poor girl.'

There was a short silence when he seemed lost for words, then, eager to change the subject, he said: 'If you should see these tinkers again, or any strangers lurking about, let me know, Mrs McQuinn. You were lucky to be able to fight them off and escape.'

'I was indeed. But then I had a rescuer. A dog—a deerhound I found on the hill. He scared them off.'

He looked at me as if I'd taken leave of my senses. 'A deerhound, did you say?'

'Yes. Do you know of anyone who has lost one?'

He shook his head. 'Probably from the circus.'

'No, I tried them.'

He looked puzzled. 'They're valuable dogs. There are certainly none that I know of in this district. Size of ponies, too big to keep in your average garden or house. Cost a fortune to feed, too. We'd certainly have heard if some owner had lost a dog like that. I'll make a note of it.'

He paused and looked at me. 'And you say this dog chased off the tinkers. Savage was he, too?'

'He wasn't exactly gentle in his dealings with them. They didn't hang around I can tell you. But he saved me.'

Macmerry shook his head. 'I've never heard of a strange dog saving a human before.'

'You're hearing it now and some day, I promise you, I'll prove it to you by showing him to you.'

But even as I said the words I was

126

beginning to guess I had little hope of keeping that promise. Unless I was going mad, I was sure Thane was real. The fact that others hadn't seen him—drunken tinkers apart, who would ken him well enough—was a mere coincidence.

The constable went on his way, and the day stretched long and empty until my meeting with Alice Bolton, and I no longer cared to stay indoors nursing a severe bout of melancholy. So, taking advantage of a windless warm day, I would put my riding to the test by bicycling into the city and exploring the High Street.

Changing into my outdoor clothes, I was about to collect the bicycle from the stable when I heard a scratching sound from outside the kitchen door.

I rushed to open it. Thane had returned!

The newcomer wasn't Thane. The cat who squinted up at me and hissed so menacingly was an extraordinary sight. She looked as if she might have been dug out of Pharaoh's tomb, or was a sole survivor from the Ark when Noah put to sea; not for elegance or dignity, but from antiquity. Mummified with age, a travesty of a cat, a rickle of bones on four unsteady sticks of legs, gnarled and furless.

Her coat, tortoiseshell in colour, looked as if it had suffered from a severe case of moth. At one end of her anatomy was a hairless bent tail, at the other a head with the remnants of one ear, a half-closed eye and a considerable lack of teeth. Where on earth had she come from? Then the truth dawned upon me. I realised that she must have been one of Sir Hedley's feline tribe who had lived with him in the Tower and occupied the fourposter bed, treated by the eccentric old man like animal aristocrats. She must be ancient indeed. How long do cats live? And then I remembered Alice Bolton née Peel proudly presented to us at a party a cat who had celebrated her twenty-first birthday. A cat, I might add, in much better condition than the one who confronted me so savagely just a few feet away.

I did a quick calculation of this lone survivor of a bygone age. The others of Sir Hedley's feline tribe had disappeared, gone feral, mixed their blood with the wildcats that still roamed in the deeper reaches of Arthur's Seat.

There was no cause for concern about their fates or feeding. Although they lived by courtesy in Sir Hedley's home, his half-starved erratic lifestyle could never have supported them. But there was abundance of mice, rats and small vermin, enough indoors and out to keep any cat with a taste for the hunt in health and strength.

According to history that rodent population of Arthur's Seat had been called upon to provide for less fortunate mercenaries during bygone ages as they marched across the hill to do battle in the city far below.

The forlorn creature at my feet miaowed soundlessly, but with a hint of warning. For some unknown reason she had abandoned those secret caves and hollows on the hill and had chosen to return to the Tower. Observing that it was occupied again had suggested to her, with no knowledge of human frailty and mortality, that her kind old benefactor might have returned. And so had she, ever hopeful.

Now the poor beast looked more hunted than hunter and my heart was filled with pity—although I did not care for a closer encounter. The flotilla of fleas I fancied were infesting her shaky body at every movement would have deterred the most determined cat lover from any attempts at further intimacy.

She looked up and gave a strange, shrill scream. I turned and found that a large, soundless grey shadow had appeared at my side. The next moment was quite extraordinary, beyond anything in my experience.

I have been present at many a scene of the vapours among the females of my acquaintance but never of the feline variety. I watched fascinated. This promised to be interesting. Cat leaped into the air, showing amazing agility with all feet off the ground at the same precise instant. Then she keeled over and lay panting, a paw raised to her chest in exact imitation of a female swoon. Extraordinary! Feeling heartless, I could not suppress my mirth.

At my side Thane regarded this eventuality with solemn interest. 'Woof!' he said. It continued to amaze me how much expression and feeling he could put into one bark. It sounded like a gentle reprimand and a note of reassurance at the same time. 'Woof' again. Don't be afraid, was that it?

Cat opened her eyes, rose unsteadily to her feet, shook herself and, instead of taking off in the opposite direction, she staggered towards Thane and, proceeding to rub herself against his front legs (to the consternation and disruption of her resident flea colony), she began to purr like a steam kettle coming to the boil.

' 'Ware fleas, Thane,' I hissed all too late.

Thane regarded her from under those majesterial bushy brows, seemed to smile and, bending down from his lofty height, deigned to lick the back of her neck. She purred in ecstasy and the bond of friendship was sealed.

Thane gave me one of his intense stares that spoke volumes, even without the accompanying woofs. It commanded me to do something about Cat.

I sighed deeply. I had not the heart to turn the poor wretch away and, with a sigh, I realised it looked as if I had yet another occupant for Solomon's Tower. This one would stay outside in the old stable for the summer months. There was straw enough to keep her warm and comfortable at least until I had won her confidence and had the measure of dealing with the insect army that infested her.

She looked half starved. I decided to offer a bowl of milk. She had no objections and accepted a second and a third. Thane, meanwhile, watched approvingly.

When I opened the stable door for her, she had no objections to that either and walked in as daintily and with as much dignity as those old, shaky legs would permit. She even sank into the straw gracefully with an old lady's sigh of content.

It appeared Thane too had decided to take up residence. He settled in a corner some distance away from her. I was overjoyed.

An hour ago I had been quite alone. I now had two creatures to share the Tower with me. There's nothing like a little modest success to build one's confidence in the future, I thought, as I wheeled out my bicycle and set off towards the city.

Chapter Thirteen

Before visiting Alice I had in mind another purpose: to put into effect my role as 'lady investigator' by calling into the office of Bolton and Bolton in the Canongate. Some pretext would do nicely, such as having lost my way.

At this stage I was still certain of a perfectly innocent explanation for Matthew's behaviour. I could not believe I would find him involved in an adulterous relationship with Lily of the Lodge.

I had no wish to encounter him, hopeful only that some of his clerks—helped by a little tactful probing—might provide valuable information, a starting point to my investigation.

Alice was prone to exaggeration, but I remembered that Pappa was a great believer in idle chat spewing out some very interesting clues. If only I knew what I was supposed to be listening for.

As I approached the Old Town lying in the shade of the Castle, I had forgotten the squalor of the High Street, the smells from the closes, the ragged children and beggars.

At least in the so-called Wild West, among the emigrants being poor was a condition of everyone's life. Things were shared and there was good fresh air to breathe and fresh water to drink. People appeared healthier, the children stronger physically, than they did in this piece of the civilised world. I need look no further than the overcrowded 'lands', with whole families living in one room or in stinking closes, to realise the extent of my good fortune.

It had a sobering effect on my self-pity and provided a moral lecture on counting one's blessings, when I guessed at the conditions of other widows and young women who had fallen on adverse times. It did not need a discerning eye to observe the fate of prostitutes who looked old at thirty, desperately plying their trade in daylight hours.

My life, my position in society, by comparison with such women as well as the more respectable folk who watched me pushing my bicycle up the steep winding High Street, was that of a lady of privilege.

In the offices of Bolton and Bolton, Solicitors (the original and long deceased senior members of Matthew's family), one solitary elderly clerk, the sole staff it appeared, looked up from his ledger as the doorbell clanged.

His attitude as he asked my business was clearly hopeful. He looked at once depressed and quite dejected when I explained that I was searching for directions to a bookshop which I knew quite well—or at least it had been there some time ago—on the South Bridge.

As he told me the road I should take I noticed that the office shared his depression and appeared to be seriously in need of upgrading. Spiders' webs were visible in corners and the paintwork was faded and flaking, but a firm and regular onslaught with broom, mop and duster might have worked wonders.

It was hardly a setting to inspire confidence in new clients and, when I decided to take matters a little further by explaining that having recently returned from abroad I had some financial business to transact, I was not altogether surprised that such news heartened the old man considerably.

His manner changed immediately, shoulders straightened, there was even a faint smile and a bow. A slightly gleeful rubbing together of hands was further indication that on the whole, business was far from brisk. 'Mr Bolton is not available at present—'

A fact fairly obvious, otherwise I should not have broached the subject and risked an encounter. Observing my change of expression, which he had taken for disappointment, he said hastily: 'Mr Bolton carries on a considerable amount of his midweek business from his home. However, if you would care to leave your address, I could get him to call on you, madam.' When he added, 'Mr Bolton sees clients in their own homes if that is more convenient,' I wondered if for clients I should read Lily of the Lodge.

The old clerk's face fell when I said I was travelling north to the Orkneys but that I would get in touch when I returned to Edinburgh more permanently.

As I left the office I knew two things for certain. The old clerk's manner had told me without any words that the business was in a poor way and clients few. The depressed and neglected state of the office confirmed my suspicions.

Alice's story about Matthew selling their carriage and walking or riding on tramcars to work for health's sake might be true. In the light of what I had just seen, it took on a new significance as I made my way to Portland Crescent, Newington, where a well-starched maid demanded my business and indicated that appearances were kept up inside the Bolton home. 'Is Madam expecting you?' the maid insisted doubtfully, examining my appearance from top to toe and taking in that bicycle parked by the railings.

I could read her mind: here was that charity woman back again looking for another handout.

She sniffed. 'You'll need to come back later. Madam isn't at home.'

I refused to be dismissed. 'Kindly inform her that Rose McQuinn is here.'

'You'll need to tell her yourself—she is out and won't be home until half past four.' With that, the door slammed in my face.

I stood on the step, wondering what to do next. I didn't want to return to the Tower but I might fill in a little time at a teashop.

As I rode towards South Bridge my front wheel got entangled in the tramway line and I fell off. Onlookers rushed towards me, hands raised me from my undignified position in the ground.

Was I hurt? No, just my pride.

The bicycle? I tested it gingerly. Undamaged. Dusting myself down I left them, heartily wishing I wasn't morally obligated to Alice by accepting her gift of a bicycle, one that I could well afford to buy.

I devoted some further thoughts to Matthew. Considering the shabby state of his office, there might be some good reason to link his odd behaviour not only with Lily Harding but also with some crisis in his professional career, such as embezzlement or blackmail.

Whatever this crisis might be, it had to be quite beyond the normal run of financial matters, since he could not confide its nature even to his wife. And if I was to help Alice and her marriage, that was what I had to discover.

I was completely inexperienced in such matters and, as I rode towards the Pleasance, I never fooled myself for an instant that it would be an easy task.

The wind was blowing from the east, bringing with it sounds of music from a distant brass band. There was even a whiff of smoke and that gamey circus smell blowing from the area of Queen's Park.

All thoughts of teashops disappeared as I watched family groups making their way briskly in that direction.

I soon discovered the reason. Outside the enclosure, clowns on stilts were shouting: 'Ladies and gentlemen—for your free entertainment. We are inviting you to come inside and inspect our performers. Come and see the animals and the clowns.'

Such publicity was an obvious draw. Young children with parents were much in evidence, a Punch and Judy show and clowns who were expert jugglers. The trapeze artists were also clever acrobats.

And there was Cyril Howe himself.

I wheeled my bicycle over to the edge of a group of spellbound children to whom he was demonstrating sleight of hand. As a very clever magician drawing rabbits out of a hat, Howe was an outstanding performer, making doves disappear and reappear, drawing multiple scarves out of his sleeves. Not only the children were spellbound that day.

A master of his craft, he was thoroughly enjoying himself. This Cyril Howe had charisma and, as ably demonstrated from the applause and cries of delight greeting every new trick, his audience was falling into his hands. Soon they would be imploring their parents to take them inside the big tent.

'Where are the Indians, mister?' shouted a small boy.

'They are out exercising their horses, young sir.'

'That's a shame, mister. I came specially to see them.'

'Well, you'll have to come back again this evening. Bring your parents and come to a regular performance.'

'But that'll cost us money,' shouted the small boy's elders, a remark that raised a laugh and a cheer.

'And worth every penny, sir, I assure you. You'll not be disappointed. Take my word for it.'

Personally I wouldn't have taken Cyril Howe's word for buying a penny bun, but admittedly he was a man of many talents. From this distance he looked handsome and strong. No doubt his wife was right and that charisma extended to extramarital activities.

Ever hopeful, too, I thought, remembering his none too subtle approach to me. A very different version from the frightened train passenger at Dunbar, so furtive and preoccupied with his female companion that he failed to recognise me, on our second encounter, as the other occupant of the compartment.

I left, wondering how many other sides there were to Cyril Howe after the caravan door closed and his shrill, unhappy wife removed her spangles.

I didn't envy her. That thought brought a gloomy reminder of my forthcoming visit to Alice Bolton whose matrimonial problems I had cheerfully promised to investigate.

The undeniable fact that I had not the least idea or experience in such matters, or any certainty of where to begin, was now weighing heavily upon my conscience.

Chapter Fourteen

Alice greeted me warmly and upset my plans by saying that Matthew would be joining us shortly. 'When I told him about our meeting and that you were coming, he was delighted and said that although he was very busy just now he would make a special effort to be here. He knew that you were my particular friend and remembered that you were very clever—and pretty,' she added. That pleased her. Her gentle smile was without any malice.

I was furious. Matthew's good opinion or favourable memory was the last thing I wanted. I could hardly conceal my annoyance.

'What is it? I thought you would be

pleased.'

'Please, Alice. Don't you realise that if I'm to . . . follow him, try to find out what is going on with this other woman, it is essential that I don't meet him face to face?'

She had winced when I said 'this other woman'. Now she looked very prim and said: 'I can't understand in the least why you are so distressed about Matthew wanting to meet you—'

I listened despairingly. Obviously she hadn't thought any further than the day or given the consequences of such a meeting any consideration regarding the difficulties it would bring. 'Don't you see that if I meet him', I said, interrupting her protestations, 'he will think it very odd if he discovers that I am trailing him secretly. If he confronts me how on earth can I explain what I'm up to? Alice, please, think about it, use your imagination. He might misinterpret my actions, believe I'm infatuated with him—how embarrassing that would be, for all of us!'

She gave me an odd look and then said: 'Oh, Rose, I'm sorry. He was so . . . nice . . . this morning. He remembered that it was my birthday at the weekend and has promised to buy me a bracelet—' Then she added: 'Since he completely overlooked our wedding anniversary last month, such a sweet gesture.'

A gesture which, I thought, for those not so innocently minded could be interpreted as an admission of guilt by a defaulting husband.

Alice sighed deeply. 'Oh, Rose, perhaps I was mistaken to confide my troubles in you.'

'I beg your pardon, Alice, am I hearing correctly? Confiding troubles are what friends are for,' I added gently and she began to cry.

Out came the piece of cambric. I watched as she dabbed her eyes. I hoped she didn't do this too often in front of Matthew. Tears are a considerable advantage to some women and make them look soft and appealing. Alas, Alice was not one of them; she merely looked red-eyed and red-nosed, snuffly and remarkably plain.

'When he was so nice about my birthday—and about meeting you—I thought perhaps I had been too hasty and had misjudged him. He does work very hard, you know. He is so conscientious about his family firm.'

I listened and said nothing. I wondered how long it was since Alice had seen her husband's office. Being hard-working and conscientious about his clients was not the impression I got from my visit. Or from the old clerk's excuse that his master preferred to meet his clients at home. A fact Matthew had apparently forgotten to mention to his wife.

'Poor Alice. There, there, do stop crying. Is this a complete change of heart you're having? Are you telling me you might have been imagining Matthew's strange behaviour?' I asked sternly.

Alice looked up at me, sniffed and shook her head. 'I wish I could say yes to that. I wish I could say I was wrong, but during the past month he has been like a stranger. So distant and refusing to send that dreadful friend of his away. It's too awful—what our neighbours must think, lowering the tone of the street with tramps living on our premises—'

The tears threatened again and I said: 'Look, do you want me to go on with this? Incidentally I would be the happiest person in Edinburgh if you said, "No, Alice. I have been mistaken."'

'I can't. Things have been so . . . awful, I can't begin to explain. Oh, Rose, what shall we do?'

'I know what I shall do, Alice. I shall go home.'

'Home! But you can't go home—'

'I must. Don't you see it would ruin my plans to meet him at the moment?'

'But what can I tell him?'

'Say I'm disposed—he won't ask questions about that, he's a married man after all—' and, cutting short her protests: 'You'll think up something convincing.'

I left her hurriedly, feeling awful that she was so unhappy and upset. I was sorry about causing her any further distress, seeing that her nerves were already considerably overwrought regarding her wretched husband's mysterious behaviour. And I couldn't honestly believe that any woman with just a mite of intuition could get into such a state without cause.

I made my escape by the front door waved off tearfully by Alice, with a promise to return soon, some afternoon when she might be alone.

I wheeled my bicycle along the road and, once out of sight of the front door, I had an idea. The visit need not be entirely wasted, I thought, as I crept stealthily along the narrow back lane to where, over the garden wall, the back premises of the Bolton house were visible.

I tried the gate, found it unlocked. I was in luck and let myself in, hoping that the shrubbery which hid the coachhouse from the kitchen would also conceal me in the unlikely event of Alice looking out of the window.

From the outside the coachhouse appeared neglected and dilapidated, all signs of paint on the one window and the door had vanished long ago. I couldn't imagine anyone living in such a hovel, even in its better days. An experimental glance through the one grimy window confirmed my worst fears of a gloomy interior, which appeared to be empty.

Taking a deep breath, I tapped on the door. I did not expect any reply, so lifted the latch and let myself in. The one room smelt of damp and was intensely cold. Even on a summer's day the sun must never have penetrated beyond the high garden wall.

I spared a thought for the poor underpaid coachman with his horses who had once lived in this vile place, for when my eyes adjusted to the gloom I saw only bare boards, dust and cobwebs. The squalid scene was completed by a stall long since deserted, the only evidence of an occupant a few wisps of dirty wet straw and a broken harness. On one wall was a tiny grate, which could not possibly have heated more than a kitchen cupboard and obviously had not seen anything as healthy as a fire for many a day.

I looked around, considering. The premises, if such squalor could be dignified by the word, seemed surprisingly deserted to have a resident tenant. One would have expected a shelf of dishes, tins of food, eating utensils and a bed with blankets.

The sole furniture was a rickety old kitchen chair and a large battered wooden box that might contain garden implements. At the moment it served as a table for a stump of candle and some empty bottles, one containing liquid. On the floor, a filthy towel covered a basin and jug.

I decided at least there must be water somewhere and, glad to open the door and fill my lungs with fresh air, I found a tap outside, presumably used for coachhouse and garden.

Inside again I decided to investigate the wooden box. It was firmly locked, a recent innovation since the padlock looked new and shiny.

I was completely baffled. What I was witnessing suggested that Matthew's vaunted hospitality and indebtedness to his great friend did not include the most rudimentary of home comforts.

What did it all mean? I looked around for some clue, wondering what, if anything, I had missed in that cold, unfriendly place. And I reached one positive conclusion. Whatever the reason Matthew had given to his wife, he was not speaking the truth.

There was a much deeper more sinister purpose for his friend's presence. And the word 'blackmail' forced itself in front of my mind.

I was wrestling with the thought, trying to make sense of it, when the door opened and a man appeared.

Even against the light he was a very rough-looking labourer in dusty, stained clothes, wearing a scarf about his neck and a cap pulled down well over his eyes.

That he didn't expect a visitor was obvious. My appearance startled him. Taken aback, his hand flew to his cap, not to raise it politely for sure, and I didn't know which one of us was most scared. 'What d'ye want?' he yelled at me.

I began to apologise and he shouted: 'What are ye doing here, poking about? I'll tell the maister—he'll get the polis to ye.' And, as if to make sure I understood, he seized an empty bottle and raised it in a threatening gesture.

I waited no longer, stuttered out some wild excuse, seized my bicycle and fled, terrified to waste time looking back in case he was following.

But when I turned round at the end of the lane the garden door was firmly closed and, riding fast homeward, I found myself remembering, because I notice things, that he had nice hands.

Nice hands and no manners. And whatever his background, he was no labourer and never had been, that was for sure.

I was still trying to make some sense of it all when the Tower came into view. An elegant carriage with a coat of arms was parked at the gate.

I had a visitor.

Chapter Fifteen

'Vince!'

I could hardly believe my eyes. But nothing had prepared me for the change—no, indeed, the transformation—in my step-brother who stepped out to greet me.

Gone was the rather shy, indecisive young man lacking in self-confidence. His place had been taken by a rather stout, middle-aged man with blond beard and moustache, a gold watch-chain, silk top hat: the air of opulence, the new gravitas eminently suitable for even a minor physician in the Royal household.

It was his voice first of all that told me this wasn't another of my dreams. 'Rose—Rose.'

With a scream of delight I flung myself into his arms.

I was incapable of coherent speech; such high emotions were bound to lead to tears and it was some time before I could find words, or breath.

'Rose!' Vince was similarly afflicted. He held me close, his chin resting on my head. He smelt of cologne—a good smell, something he had despised in his earlier years as unmanly.

At last he spoke. 'Ten years is such a long time, Rose.'

'Too long,' I sobbed.

'Let me look at you,' he said, holding me at arm's length and surveying me with a critical and, I suspected, a well-trained medical eye. 'You look lovely,' he said with a sigh, 'a little too thin and your hair has been bleached by the sun.'

He let a straggling ringlet wrap around his finger, a gesture I remembered from childhood when I sat on his knee and he read stories to me. He grinned. 'Most of Her Majesty's ladies would give anything for natural curls such as these.'

'And yours,' I said.

He laughed, running a rueful hand through his hair. 'Sadly mine are growing somewhat fewer. I have a lot more face to wash these days. But Livvy assures me that the high Roman noble brow suits me. What do you think?'

'I agree with her.' That was true. The blond curls inherited from dear Mamma that had given us such a strong likeness had darkened in Vince and thinned with age. The boyish air they had lent him in youth had been a constant source of aggravation in the early days of his medical career. Certain, then, that no patient would take him seriously, he need have no such worries now. He looked eminently mature and reliable.

Following me into the kitchen he said: 'This is just a very fleeting visit, I'm afraid. We are en route to Balmoral and I have permission to leave the Royal train while Her Majesty pays a brief call at Holyroodhouse. There are redecorating plans afoot for the Royal apartments and she insists on overseeing them personally. Despite John Brown—and now the Munshi's influence and advice—everything planned and decided by Prince Albert's command is sacrosanct. Even after all these years.'

'You will at least have time for a cup of tea,' I said and, looking at him again: 'Your clothes are lovely. You're so well groomed, such an elegant gentleman.'

He laughed at that too. 'You should see the others at court. I pale into insignificance there, I can assure you. I'm just a provincial, a poor Scots doctor, but I'm learning.'

He paused. 'Blackadder told me about Danny. I'm so very sorry, Rose.' And, looking around: 'Did we do the right thing? Are you happy here all alone?'

I looked at his hands holding mine and closed my eyes, wanting this moment of bliss to go on for ever. 'Happy enough, Vince, dear,' I whispered. 'And I can't begin to thank you for giving me this place—such a generous gift.'

'Not at all. I knew you always loved it and I wanted it to be your home—yours and Danny's.'

'It's more like a home than anything I've had since Orkney days. So much of Sheridan Place's furniture too.'

'No thanks to me.' He laughed. 'You should have seen it before Livvy worked her particular brand of magic on everything.'

I remembered how he had hated Sir Hedley and hardly ever set foot in the Tower while the old man was alive when he added: 'I never wanted it.' Again that searching look as he gripped my hands. 'Tell me about Danny. What happened?'

'I wish I knew. He went out one morning after breakfast, just as he had done a hundred times before, and he never came back. It's a long story, Vince.'

I was reluctant to step back into the past, to open up that page of agony again. It hurt too much to talk about Danny, even to Vince. Seeing him again so unexpectedly, I didn't want this moment of intense joy to be tarnished or spoiled. If I began I knew what would happen, I would want to cry at leisure with his undivided attention—not his occasional surreptitious glances at the clock ticking away the seconds on the wall. He would have to go very soon and I didn't want to be left once again drowning in my pool of tears while he switched on to this other life, rushing off, fearful of being late and displeasing his Royal mistress.

'Well?' he said.

I shook my head. 'He was working for the Pinkerton Detective Agency as well as for the Indian Bureau. Tracking down criminals, bank robbers, fraudsters—and there were plenty of them where the finances of the Indian reservations were concerned. He was good at his job—Pappa would have been proud of him. And as a loyal Irishman his sympathies were with the Indians.'

Vince nodded. 'I gathered from our few talks together that he had a feeling for lost causes.'

'He said that no man or woman from Ireland whose family had been exterminated, or from the Scottish Highlands who had been evicted by their landlords—any race at all who had suffered at the hands of the English government—could fail to identify with the American Indians.'

Vince frowned and looked a little unhappy, as if anxious not to be associated with treasonable talk.

'We had been settled in Dakota for a while when there was renewed trouble between the whites and the Sioux. Broken promises, broken treaties, land stolen from them, the usual thing. This culminated in a massacre at a place called Wounded Knee in 1890, five years ago. Two hundred and fifty women and children died at the hands of white soldiers. Renegade Sioux bent on revenge, then a new religion—Ghost Dancers—held sway and brought belief in a future. After Sitting Bull, acting as mediator in an uneasy peace, was shot by an Indian agency soldier.'

Trying to keep my voice calm, I went on: 'Danny never gave up hope, he worked for both sides, back and forth, having faith in a solution. When he didn't come back . . . I knew he had always considered the possibility of a stray bullet, he had enemies, white as well as Indian, and he made me promise that if for any reason he didn't manage to come home after some mission I was to wait a reasonable time and then come back to Scotland. He had set aside enough dollars to cover the journey.'

Vince looked at me. 'The baby. What about the baby?'

I looked away. Arthur's Seat had been replaced by a stark and ugly prairie, a tiny cross—but where? I knew I would never go back, never find it out there in the wilderness. Never in this life would I kneel down and pray by my baby's little lost grave. 'Danny never saw him. Our first child—I'd miscarried twice before wee Daniel was born. He was just three weeks old when we left. We'd been attacked by renegades and took refuge in a white settlement. There was an outbreak of fever. We both took it. I survived,' I said bleakly.

'What kind of fever, what were the symptoms?' The doctor in Vince was waiting for more details.

'I'm no authority—typhoid perhaps—I don't know. Only that an old Sioux woman nursed me back to life again, but my baby was dead and buried. And I didn't have much desire to live either.'

My voice broke. Vince took me in his arms. I could hardly breathe, trying not to cry. Talking, even thinking about it again, did that to me. As if there was a knife at my heart, chipping away at my soul. I wondered if that deadly sensation would ever go away.

I had to break the silence that followed, aching to return to that ecstatic moment when Vince had arrived at my door, to recapture all that had been normal in my life in Edinburgh ten years ago: practical domestic moments, like a kettle briskly boiling.

Vince kissed my cheek and I said: 'Some tea before you go, Vince. Foley lit the peat fire and told me how to keep it going so that I'd have a constant source of warmth and a hob to cook on.'

'Foley?' said Vince, his thoughts miles away in a strange land. 'Oh, yes, our gardener at Sheridan Place. Decent sort of chap. Very reliable. After all these years, such devotion. Glad you found a use for him.'

As we sat at the kitchen table I said: 'Peat fires always remind me of Orkney. What news of Emily and Gran? And Pappa?'

'All seems well. Nobody in the family is a great letter writer, Stepfather least of all. He and Imogen travel a lot. He always wanted to see Europe.'

Pausing, he gave me a searching look. 'As for Emily, you know, it might be a good idea to go back there. You should think about it very seriously if living here alone starts to get on your nerves.'

'I can't imagine that happening,' I lied, brave now, for just before he arrived I had had the most bitter doubts.

'Wait until you've had a winter, snow and sleet—Arthur's Seat can be grim and isolated.' He grinned. 'Of course, you could come and live with us in London. The climate's better there. And we have several rooms.' Warming to the idea, he took my hands. 'Why not consider it, Rose? I'm absolutely serious. And Livvy would be glad of your company, especially with a new baby—'

I listened, smiling and grateful. But did he not realise what agony babies would be when I had lost my own? And as for the older children, would I be forever looking at them sadly and seeing wee Daniel in them, as he might have been had he lived?

Any decision I might have had was cut short by a discreet tap on the door.

Vince leaped to his feet, buttoned his jacket. 'Oh, Rose, darling, that's the coachman. I'll have to go.'

'You've just arrived,' I protested. 'There's so much I want to ask you—how's Mrs Brook?'

'We keep in touch. She's moved from the Highlands and is living in Fife now. Doesn't travel much, she's fairly crippled with rheumatism. Inverkeithing's just across the new railway bridge. Why don't you visit her— she'd love to see you. Always talking about you—you were her favourite—' he added. 'Number 24 Fife Road, that's her address.'

The rap on the door knocker was louder now.

'Must go, Rose, darling. I didn't know you were in Edinburgh. I wasted half an hour going to Blackadder's office for news,' he said.

'The old man's very worried about you, living here all alone with Edinburgh in the grip of a murder half a mile away.' Buttoning up his coat, he said: 'Seems they are rarer than they were in Pappa's day. He was always on a case as I remember.'

'With you to help him, as I remember. Oh, Vince, come back soon, please. I wanted you to meet Thane—'

I opened the back door as I spoke and called his name several times.

'Who's Thane?' asked Vince.

'A deerhound I found on the hill—a stray. I've adopted him. Thane!' I called again. There was no response. 'He's in the stable. He's a bit shy with strangers, I expect. Do come and see him, Vince, it won't take a moment.'

'Next time, Rose, must go. Royal trains won't wait for any man or woman.' At the door he turned round. 'Make sure your deerhound doesn't suddenly attack you. Strays can be unreliable.'

Following him down the path I said: 'Not this one. He looks exactly like the one in the painting that used to hang in the parlour here.'

Had I imagined that too? But Vince laughed. 'It was just an old print. I think Olivia put it down in the cellar. Didn't think you'd want it.'

A swift hug, a kiss, he jumped into the

155

carriage, leaned out of the window and called: 'I'll be back soon.'

'Promise!' I cried.

'I see there's a circus down the road. Happy days. Us all going together, with dear Mrs Brook. Go and see her. 'Bye, darling—'

The carriage was moving. I watched until it vanished down the road, feeling as if my heart was breaking.

I felt so unloved, so unwanted. Of course Vince loved me, but I was low on the hierarchy of loved ones now. I guessed all his visits would be like this one, a snatched hour while the Royal train rested in Waverley Station.

I would have been stupid not to see how we had both changed and I doubted that the blood bond was strong enough to bridge the gulf that life had opened up between us.

I was glad I had not mentioned Alice. Vince would never have understood. Indeed, he would have been horrified at the idea of his 'little sister' being involved in anything as unladylike as a murder investigation. Especially when he knew Matthew Bolton.

There was a further consideration. How would Her Majesty feel about a member of her household—a physician—numbering a murderer among his friends?

It had been a long day, emotionally exhausting, and I fell into bed and much to my surprise slept soundly and without the tortured dreams of Danny which I feared Vince's visit might have encouraged.

Chapter Sixteen

I looked out of the window hopefully, but of Thane there was no sign at all. Nor was he in the stable where Cat, curled up in the straw, had settled down comfortably. Observing my approach was empty-handed, her resentful glare and half-hearted snarl was more of an old woman's grumble at being disturbed than a threat of any kind.

I decided to go in search of the old painting I had discussed with Vince, down the worn steps into the cellar, the debris of Sir Hedley Marsh's long occupation of the Tower, among the spiders' webs and dust, stacked prints, valueless pictures and broken gilt frames.

Searching through them, there at last was the picture that had intrigued me on childhood visits with Pappa: an old Highland shepherd, wrapped in his plaid. Crook in hand, he leaned against a rock, a deerhound at his feet—in the background the antlers of a slain stag, its corpse decently obscured by the heather.

Blowing off the dust, I carried the painting into the light. Thane could have sat for the deerhound and the hill behind could have been some track on Arthur's Seat.

I sat with it on my knee. Was it possible that I had allowed a childhood memory to influence me, a kind of déjà vu of safer, happier days with Pappa?

Had it not been for Thane's intervention when I was attacked by the tinkers and my miraculous escape from them, I could have been convinced that I had invented my deerhound, as lonely children invent imaginary playmates—playmates as real to them as mine were to me.

I decided then and there that I must get a grip on my emotions. I had suffered too many real hardships in recent times to give in to melancholy. For that way insanity lay.

Although the deerhound was the image of Thane, common sense told me it could not possibly be the same dog. This print with the artist's illegible initials had a date: 1845—and no dog lives for half a century.

I must be sensible. I had a new life here in Edinburgh, given the challenge of this strange Tower as my home, four ancient stone walls in which I was determined to destroy any past alienation by an investment of respect and caring. If ghosts or a sinister atmosphere existed, I was certain they could be conquered and I refused to be scared into taking some safe, dreary lodging in the city.

There was always the ancient chapel at the top of the Tower, somehow remote from the rest of the building, a kind of refuge once blessed by saintly hands, a place of sanctity and serenity.

With so much to be thankful for I must learn not to be ungrateful. But at this precise moment I had to escape from this invasion of the recent past.

Vince's visit had sharpened bitter memories, retelling the story of a lost and deeply loved husband and the tiny baby whom I had scarcely time to hold in my arms. Now more than ever, I knew how much I missed and longed for the security of a devoted family, blood kin of my own around me.

He had offered a bleak escape clause. If all else failed, if perseverance and determination did not succeed I could, as he had offered, rebuild my life by going to Orkney or make a life with him and Olivia in London.

My first choice would still be Emily. I could see myself reading her letter, saying of course you must come immediately, Rose. I could picture myself, assured of the warmth and promise of a sister's love and devotion, packing up and departing from the Tower, perhaps never to return.

As for Vince's invitation to live with them in London, I wasn't even tempted. I loved Olivia but I would have no real place, a relative who would be a convenient nanny living among aristocrats more alien, by their upbringing, than the pioneering stock I had lived with in the American West. At least mutual hardships and dangers—and poverty cheerfully shared—were sufficient to clear the social hurdles.

A short visit to London would be agreeable, but never could I imagine living there. I feared that England might be for me, as it had been for Pappa as well as Danny, an alien land.

Footsteps outside and cheery whistling announced the arrival of Billy the milk lad. 'Like a daily paper, too, missus?' An excellent idea. In my new role as an investigator it was important to keep a sharp eye on local events.

'There's a letter for ye. It's from Orkney. Do you ken folk there?' he asked in amazed tones, as if it might be South America or Alaska.

I laughed. 'My sister and my granny live there.'

'Your granny's still alive?' asked Billy, wide-eyed. 'She must be auld.' Since old Bess was his grandmother, the idea of an elderly lady of thirty (as I seemed to him) also having a granny must have seemed one of the marvels of the age.

'She's eighty-eight.'

'That's nigh a hundred!' gasped Billy, shaking his head as he went off whistling down the road, a young lad fortunate indeed to have as his inheritance Bess's farm in the Pleasance.

I looked out of the kitchen door, hoping that Thane had returned. He was nowhere in sight. At least, when I went to Orkney, I would take that print of a deerhound to remember him by, I thought, tearing open Emily's letter.

In my head I was already replying. After the disturbing events of the last few days, culminating in my recent encounter of the tenant of the Bolton's coachhouse, I had no doubts at all about accepting Emily's proposal that I pack my few possessions and take the boat to Kirkwall immediately.

I did feel some guilt, I must confess, about running away and letting Alice down, with her matrimonial problem unsolved. But Matthew Bolton's weird friend was too much for me. I was quite frankly scared of digging deeper into that particular mystery. I felt that there was something very sinister going on and I had been too impulsive in my promise to Alice. As I had neither the courage nor the expertise, let alone the experience, to cope with such an investigation, discretion seemed advisable as the better part of valour.

Such were my thoughts as I eagerly read Emily's letter. But the words I had expected were missing. There was something wrong—this was a reply to my first letter.

Horror of horrors, what I was reading was that Emily did not want me. This was not the enthusiastic invitation I had expected, quite the reverse:

161

Gran has been poorly lately and we have taken her in to live with us. She is getting rather frail to live alone.

We have a lot of problems of our own just now and could well do without any additional ones. So I do wish you well in your new life in Edinburgh—I am sure you will be happy.

Your loving sister . . .

I flung the letter on to the table. Not even the suggestion of a brief holiday much less a permanent home. Nothing!

I realised that Orkney had presented a loophole, an escape from the future that now seemed to stretch empty and bleak ahead of me. I had been relying on Emily, certain of her reaction since we were sisters and because I was now a widow.

In sudden need of fresh air, I went into the garden. Shading my eyes, I called 'Thane'. But today there was no eager shadow loping down the hill. In that moment I was sure Thane had gone, never to return.

I felt very near to despair, to letting go, but that had never been my way in far worse situations than this. So, drawing a deep breath, I went back indoors and, taking up the newspaper, tried to concentrate on the Edinburgh news. It was sadly difficult as the cold words of Emily's rejection swam between me and the print.

How could she treat me like this? As sisters we had been so close and that hurt most of all.

I had to read twice over the latest on the murder of Molly Dunn:

> In the interests of safety for themselves and their families, the citizens of Edinburgh are alarmed that her brutal killer remains at large, ready to strike down other innocent victims. They are demanding that this monster of depravity be apprehended forthwith.
>
> As a desperate measure the police are calling urgently for any persons who might have been in the vicinity of Saville Grange during the twenty-four hours before the murdered woman was discovered to come forward at once with information—

I thought of that tree-lined road, and how few people went that way apart from the residents and those with legitimate business in the area. The off-chance of meeting anyone who happened to be innocently strolling near the murder house and might come forward seemed very remote.

I turned the pages and found an item reporting the death of two labourers on the new high terraces when the scaffolding platform had collapsed in a gale. The work was exceedingly dangerous, their courage praised. WORTH THEIR WEIGHT IN GOLD was the headline. Few men would tackle the daily hazards involved, for a fall meant certain death and builders were willing to pay high wages, for such men were rare and must have exceptional heads for height, particularly in Edinburgh, notorious for fierce winds.

With some relief I turned to the book reviews: Across the Plains, a new book by Robert Louis Stevenson, the Edinburgh writer who had gone abroad for his health and had died in Samoa last December. Both title and subject intrigued me, as I had read that this was the true story of his journey to California from Scotland to persuade Fanny Osbourne to divorce her husband and marry him.

*   *   *

After an interlude of giving vent to my wounded feelings by composing reproachful letters to Emily, letters which I would be too proud to send, I decided go to Thin's on South Bridge and buy a copy of Stevenson's book.

First of all I fed Cat. She was getting used to me but when I attempted to pat her head she snarled. This was a mere gesture of showing her few remaining teeth but enough to make me keep my distance and not destroy the little progress we were making. Something had happened to destroy her trust in humans and I would have to overcome that hurdle before she was ready once again to be a domestic pet sitting by the fireside.

As I wheeled out my bicycle I shaded my eyes, searching the hill for Thane. It seemed silly to keep calling him.

In Newington I was once more aware that females on bicycles were still enough of a novelty to attract amused looks and shocked whispers from ladies.

My progress was also the target for whistles from men working on the buildings and high scaffolds. The steeple of a new church was being erected. The men roosting on their apparently fragile perches were daring indeed to be so diverted by a mere woman's presence far below. Or was this the male's instinct for bravado, allowing their attention to wander even momentarily. One man braver than the rest seemed intrigued by my appearance far below, but when I looked up he had the decency hastily to avert his gaze.

The wind was growing stronger. On most days at Solomon's Tower I was confronted by a stiff breeze blowing across Arthur's Seat. I had yet to experience a real storm with the kind of gale blowing across the Firth of Forth which ripped chimney pots from roofs and sent them flying, while uprooting great trees as if they were no stronger than matchsticks.

At last in Thin's bookshop, having bought Mr Stevenson's book, I browsed through the shelves. And there was one I recognised: Fingerprints by Francis Galton. I took it down and sighed deeply. Published in 1892 while we were in Dakota, Danny had been obsessed by this revolutionary discovery in the science of crime-solving, forever trying to persuade the Pinkerton Detective Agency of its merits. A copy of the book had been my last gift to him. My eyes filled with sudden tears.

A voice behind me: 'Excuse me—don't I know you?'

Mystified, I turned to confront a woman of about my own age. I hadn't the slightest idea who she might be.

'Rose—I'm Freda Elliott—we were at school together before you went to Orkney. And we used to meet in Edinburgh during the holidays. You had a charming step-brother who has done very well for himself, we hear,' she added coyly, holding out her hand.

I took it, hoping my smile signified recognition.

'I would have known you anywhere, Rose. You still have that glorious fair hair. Just as you had in childhood, it hasn't darkened at all. But you are very thin!'

I was flattered by her first observation at least.

But who was she? At last the pieces fell into

place even without the reference to Vince. This was Freda, the schoolgirl I had never liked. But thin lips, narrow eyes and beanpole figure had greatly improved with age.

'How lovely and so unexpected to meet you like this,' she said. 'I heard that you had gone to America and married.'

I shook my head. 'I am a widow now, alas.'

'How sad!' And then a quick change of subject. 'Did you live in New York?'

When I told her the West, she looked disappointed and her eyes widened in astonishment. Such travel seemed beyond her imagination, much too dangerous to contemplate for a genteel Edinburgh lady.

We were now outside the shop and she pointed to a waiting carriage. 'Can I give you a lift somewhere?'

I indicated the bicycle parked by the shop door.

Freda eyed it and, clearly put out as she tried to think of some reason why a lady would want to have such a machine in her possession, asked, 'Um—do you live far away, then?'

'Near Duddingston,' I said casually. Solomon's Tower was something of a shock to the uninitiated, with its sinister reputation, and I was in no mood for yet another lecture on the perils of isolation.

'You are not very far away from me, then. You will remember Saville Grange from the old days.' I nodded and she continued: 'Do let's meet again—soon. We were such good friends.'

Another nod from me, now feeling miserably guilty for not having liked her long ago.

'Are you engaged for tomorrow morning? No. Then come to lunch. I'll send the carriage for you—'

'No need. It isn't far—'

I knew I had said the wrong thing as she sternly eyed the offending bicycle.

Obviously she did not wish the neighbours, assuming they were on the lookout and interested enough, to think she had eccentric modern female friends who belonged to that dangerous new breed of suffragettes.

Her thoughts were quite transparent and, searching for the right words, she smiled bravely. 'I could not permit that, my dear Rose. It might be raining. Besides, the carriage is always at hand,' she added smoothly. 'Shall we say about noon? Have you a calling card?'

'No, I've just arrived back—'

'Of course, of course. Getting organised takes a little time. What is your address?'

I sighed inwardly. There was no help for it. 'Solomon's Tower on the Duddingston road.'

Her jaw dropped. 'Solomon's Tower, I understood that it was a ruin, that no one had lived there for years.'

'My stepbrother inherited it from Sir Hedley Marsh and it is now a most comfortable house.'

'I see,' she said in the confused manner of one who didn't see in the least. And recovering: 'Very well. Until tomorrow, then.'

It was too late now to refuse her invitation and a sudden idea was giving me pause for thought: that this chance meeting might be a piece of luck, although somewhat disguised at the moment, a gift from providence for a novice crime investigator with interests in the vicinity of Saville Grange. I might well learn something to my advantage, even the possibility of unravelling some of Alice Bolton's problems. A closer scrutiny of Freda's next-door neighbour, Lily of the Lodge, would not come amiss although I felt it highly unlikely that I'd be fortunate enough to see her receiving a furtive visit from Matthew Bolton. And in my heart of hearts I still hoped that Alice was wrong about her husband's adultery.

*   *   *

But perhaps Freda had been right about the weather. There was a stiff wind blowing down from Arthur's Seat, bringing with it the threat of a fine drizzle. And there, waiting for me outside the kitchen door, was Thane.

I hugged him and got my face washed

in return.

'You are real. I didn't just imagine you.'

He wagged his tail in complete agreement and, as he followed me into the house, I decided not to miss this opportunity. Taking up my neglected journal, I decided to do a sketch of him. He seemed to know what was involved as he lay on the floor watching me and keeping much more immobile than many a human model I had tried to draw.

Later he trotted behind me to the stable as I carried my bowl of milk for Cat.

She never appeared to move from her straw bed and merely opened her mouth, more grimace than snarl, as if the latter would be too much effort. 'I don't think she likes me in the least,' I said to Thane. 'But she doesn't let her finer feelings affect her appetite. What do you think?'

Thane opened his mouth in that strange approximation of a human grin and settled down on the kitchen floor as I stirred the peat fire into life.

Soon the kettle on the hob was boiling and with some skilful manoeuvring and much patience I cooked bacon and eggs, and fried bread too, discovering that I was very hungry.

Thane watched this procedure intently. 'Do you want some?' I asked.

He looked at the pan and turned his head away with an almost human sniff of dismissal and disdain. Obviously cooked food wasn't one of his requirements.

How did he live out there on the hill? I guessed that rabbits were his staple diet, eaten au naturel, fur, bones and all. I shuddered at the thought but I wasn't prepared to dwell on that or let his eating habits end a promising friendship.

I must never forget that Thane belonged to the animal kingdom. In that savage world, creatures undomesticated by humans, including the wild song birds I found so pretty and utterly delightful, lived and had their being by preying on lesser ones down the survival chain: creatures smaller and more helpless than themselves which they caught and ate while still alive.

Thane remained at my side while I lit the lamp and read my new book. Occasionally he came over and laid his head on my knee to be patted. It was to be a memorable evening, comfortable, safe and measured in terms of what Pappa called companionable silence.

At last Thane stood up, yawned and in another curiously human way he trotted to the door, almost indicating that it was time he took his leave.

I took out a bowl of milk for Cat and when I opened the stable door he looked up at me eagerly. 'Do you want to stay here?'

Trotting inside, after a sniff at Cat which she pretended not to notice, he lay down on the straw, prudently as far away from her as possible.

Bidding them goodnight I went inside, put out the lamps and, preparing for bed, looked out of the window at the great bulk of Arthur's Seat like a crouching lion against a clear, starlit sky. The feeling of protection remained and despite my bitter disappointment over Emily I felt I could look beyond it, with a curious feeling that I was meant to remain here in Edinburgh; that my life, after floundering down many byways, was moving in a positive direction at last.

The day that had begun sadly had ended happily. Happiness is like that. It isn't a time that lasts in our lives but is only to be measured in retrospect, in a series of isolated moments.

Such were my last thoughts as I laid my head on the pillow.

Dreamless sleep was rare of late but there were no hobgoblins from the past to torment me, no demons crouching in the dark corners of my mind.

*   *   *

I awoke refreshed, but when I went out to feed Cat, Thane had gone once more. I didn't feel too badly, confident that he would return. We were friends, we trusted one another, perhaps even shared a strange telepathy, although I would have found it difficult to convince any other human being of that.

Or even that my deerhound existed at all beyond the confines of my imagination.

Chapter Seventeen

There were no curious onlookers on the tree-lined road as the Elliots' carriage took me to Saville Grange.

At the gates of the drive the coachman leaned down and said: 'Would you mind walking up to the house from here? It's just a step,' he added encouragingly. 'And I have an urgent message to deliver for the mistress.'

I said 'of course' but as he drove off I realised that most guests would be taken right to the front door. I'd observed his careful scrutiny of me and my surroundings as he waited outside the Tower. My unfashionable dress suggested that I wasn't one of his mistress's usual smart, well-off ladies.

He had made the obvious mistake that he needn't put himself out and that I was visiting his mistress in some other capacity than that of an old friend. And who could blame him when my appearance suggested a lass being interviewed for the now vacant position left by Molly Dunn's unfortunate demise?

I was sorry I hadn't had an opportunity to discuss that recent tragedy with him as I went down the drive where Foley was bending over the flower beds. My footsteps alerted him and he looked up. Shading his eyes, he stared at me for a moment.

Obviously he hadn't recognised me out of the context of Solomon's Tower, so to speak. Perhaps he had come to the same conclusion as the coachman: that I was a servant looking for work.

'Good morning, Mr Foley.'

He saluted gravely. 'Good-day to you, ma'am. Visiting the mistress, are you? Fine day for it.'

Freda had seen me coming and ran down the front steps. No formality of maids here as she tucked an arm into mine: 'Why on earth didn't Byrne bring you right to the door? I can't think what's got into him. The very idea—I shall reprimand him severely—'

'No need. I didn't mind the walk—'

'But I do! One of my guests—'

'What a lovely garden you have,' I interrupted the tirade which threatened to become embarrassing.

She smiled delightedly. 'You like gardens, do you? Shall we walk around a little? It's clouding over, so we might as well enjoy the sunshine.'

The gardens were vast. If the Elliotts decided to sell, there was ample room for several villas with neat gardens to replace trees and flowers, and tiny secret arbours with stone seats overlooked by stern Greek statues and an ornamental pond. Greenhouses with vine and fig trees flourished lushly on the south-facing walls of the kitchen garden.

It was all very opulent, an impressive sight of urban Edinburgh's wealth. And, as a hint of how dramatically such circumstances could change, tantalising glimpses of the roof and tall chimneys of the now derelict Peel House.

Sadly I remembered Alice's garden where we used to play as children, never as grand as this and now waiting finally to be demolished when the property developers moved in.

There was a saying among the Sioux Indians:

Everything changes
Only the earth and the hills remain

It could have been written as an epitaph for Alice and Matthew Bolton, dealt poorer hands in the game of destiny than their next-door neighbours, I thought, as we turned on to the side path parallel with Peel Lodge, all that remained of a once grand house and abundant wealth.

At my side Freda prattled on, very knowledgeable about plants and flowers. Fortunately my comments were not needed. All that was required, when she occasionally paused for breath and approval was, 'Really? ... Is that so? ... How nice.'

The tour complete, we entered a small courtyard with several doors, one of which led to the kitchen.

At my side, Freda chatted on, assuming I was madly interested in the diseases that infected fruit trees. She paused and, conscious perhaps of my silence, smiled. 'Do shout if there is anything you would like for your garden and Foley will bring a cutting.

'We'll go in this way, shall we?' And, opening the door: 'If you don't mind going in by the servants' quarters, that is?' she added brightly.

Over the threshold and I was standing on the very spot where Molly Dunn had been murdered. The kitchen was spick and span, the walls smooth, unmarked by violence, the stones silent, unblemished by sudden death.

But I had a tingling sense of dread. A girl had been raped and then strangled, she had taken her last breath on this floor.

Freda was still chatting, obviously no listener but a compulsive talker. How had she reacted to that fearful scene awaiting her return to Edinburgh that dreadful day? Had she grieved at all for the poor girl beyond the horror of having her nice home tarnished and made notorious by a murder? Such were my thoughts as she opened the oven door and a blast of hot roasting meat met our nostrils.

As my thoughts were on a particularly brutal murder, the smell was suddenly offensive and despite having felt hungry a few moments ago I felt sick, no longer looking forward to lunch.

'Everything is going splendidly,' said Freda with considerable satisfaction. 'Lizzie will serve us. This is cook's day off, I had completely forgotten when we met . . . Come along.'

I followed her down a dingy corridor to a baize door leading into a vast hall. A glimpse of a carved oak staircase, marble floor and tall pillars, then we were in the handsome panelled dining-room overlooking the terrace, a long shining table set for luncheon.

Inviting me to be seated, Freda rang the bell and Lizzie appeared with the soup tureen. As she served us, I studied her expressionless face and wondered about her secret reactions to the fate of Molly Dunn, about whose character I knew so little.

Doubtless Vince would dismiss this urgent and morbid desire to interview all those in a house where murder had been committed as a direct inheritance from Pappa.

The maid dismissed, as if interpreting my thoughts, Freda said: 'Lizzie is a day servant temporarily. We don't have anyone living in just at present,' she added smoothly.

I made no comment thinking this hardly surprising, considering what had happened in this kitchen we had just left. Any hopes I nursed that Freda might introduce it as a topic of conversation were soon dashed and realising it was not within the bounds of good taste to ask how she felt personally about the servant girl's murder I concentrated on the soup.

The vegetable broth was excellent and, having overcome the finer feelings that had assailed me on the subject of roast meat, I could find no fault with the main course or the dessert, a particular favourite. It was years since I had tasted sherry trifle, Mrs Brook's speciality, and putting aside all thoughts that it was considered impolite and unladylike, I eagerly accepted a second helping.

If this was lunch, I thought, what then was dinner?

A moment later came the explanation. 'Piers is away on business. You know, of course, that he is an MP.'

I didn't. Freda went on: 'He is in Glasgow all this week and I find the days rather tedious; it is so good to have one's friends to share meals with—'

'Do you see anything of our other friends— Alice Bolton? She used to live next door.'

'Alice?' She shook her head. 'We have rather lost track of one another. Circumstances change, you know,' she added and I guessed I had touched a sensitive chord.

Seizing an unfair opportunity, I struck out boldly. 'What of the new tenant—the young widow?'

Freda's sly downward glance, her slight shake of the head, indicated that she enjoyed a bit of gossip. 'I've seen Matthew Bolton, Alice's husband, at the house visiting her.' Watching to see how I took this piece of information, she added: 'Just occasionally.'

'No doubt he has business relating to the property.'

Freda's sigh indicated disappointment in my charitable reaction. 'I suppose that might be the explanation.'

I guessed she didn't for a moment believe this to be so, but she wasn't getting any other speculation from me.

After a short silence she said: 'We didn't communicate much with the Hardings. Mrs Harding and her late husband were, well, never quite the ticket for our social set—' She leaned across the table confidentially. 'I'm sure you know what I mean, my dear. The unfortunate man was in trade—quite ill bred but he had risen in the world, thanks to money—hardly the right sort of people to mix with our academic and professional friends.'

I smiled inwardly at this glimpse of the old Freda. Here was a return to the girl I had remembered and despised. Such exquisite condescension, I thought, to quote Mr Collins, via Jane Austen's Pride and Prejudice. Freda Elliott was definitely living in the wrong century.

We were interrupted by Lizzie. 'Foley's at

the door, ma'am. He's just leaving. Is there anything you're needing before he goes?'

'Nothing, Lizzie, thank you.' As the door closed she said: 'Foley is such a treasure, so willing. Quite dedicated. Knows all about gardens and loves them. A working man who knows his place and his betters, and never puts a foot out of line.'

'He did the garden at Sheridan Place—'

My comment went unnoticed or unheard. 'Such an excellent fellow. He is so distressed about . . . about what happened here. He found the unfortunate girl, you know.'

Here was something at last!

She shook her head. 'He's never been the same since. She was young enough to be his own daughter—it upset him dreadfully and he gets quite intense about tackling the police at regular intervals. Insists they are not working hard enough in tracking down her killer.'

Constable Macmerry had said the same thing. Poor Foley.

'Incidentally,' Freda continued with a swift change of subject, 'if you need a good gardener, I can thoroughly recommend him.'

I smiled. She obviously hadn't connected me with Sheridan Place. 'I know Foley already. He takes care of the garden at Solomon's Tower. Such as it is. Vince bequeathed him to me when they moved to London.'

'How absolutely splendid for Dr Laurie.

180

Imagine the relative of someone we knew as children actually going into the Royal household. Of course, we realise he's only your stepbrother, but you must be so proud of him.'

I smiled. 'And I was proud of him, Freda, long before he had any honours.'

She frowned, thought about that. 'I expect your father spoke up for him, engineered the appointment.'

'My father has been abroad for some time,' I protested.

'No matter, no matter,' she insisted. 'I understand that he had a nodding acquaintance with Royalty in his police work. Protecting Her Majesty at Holyrood and Balmoral. Such important service would not go unrewarded.'

I felt quite indignant on Vince's behalf. 'I don't think Pappa had any hand in Vince's appointment. In fact, I am quite certain it was entirely on his own merits.'

'You're very modest about your stepbrother's achievements, my dear, but Piers and I know about such things as influence. And I'm sure he would say that you are quite mistaken. Anyway, what is important as far as matters concern yourself is that Dr Laurie will see that you receive invitations to garden parties and suchlike at Holyrood.'

Pausing, she beamed on me. 'Such opportunities for you—and your friends—to meet all the right people.'

I wasn't prepared to argue and suddenly I saw very clearly the reason for this invitation. Freda imagined that because of Vince I might be rubbing shoulders with Royalty, I was therefore worth cultivating. Besides, even if hints about friends fell on stony ground and didn't bring any of those opportunities to meet the right people for her, it was a great conversation piece for afternoon tea parties.

As I prepared to take my leave, she insisted on providing her carriage. While she went to summon Byrne I sat by the window overlooking the garden.

She had not shown the least curiosity about my life in America beyond acknowledging that I was now a widow. Was this just genteel behaviour or was she merely bored? Did she even know, or care, that having lost husband and child was why I had returned to Edinburgh?

The visit had been a mistake. The two friends from the past—Alice and Freda—I wished I'd left them where they belonged among the schoolday memories. All three of us had altered with the passing years, such was to be expected when even my beloved sister had changed. So what could I expect of friends with no blood ties?

It was somewhat mortifying.

Suddenly my attention was drawn to movement beyond the garden wall. The door of Peel Lodge opened, a head poked out, was hastily withdrawn in the rather furtive manner of one who does not wish to be observed. Lily came forward out of the shadows. The man turned, grasped her hand, spoke earnestly and leaning forward kissed the baby she held in her arms.

I sat back in my chair, appalled at the significance of what I had observed, hardly able to recover my composure when Freda returned and I followed her downstairs.

At the door she said: 'I have so enjoyed your visit, Rose. You must come again often. It's just a short distance.'

'I'm not at Sheridan Place now,' I reminded her.

'Oh—do give me your card.'

'I haven't one.'

'Oh, of course. I forgot. You're at Solomon's Tower. Well, once you've moved from that old ruin.' She paused. 'I am assuming it is merely a temporary arrangement, until you find something more suitable.'

Words failed me once again. I shook my head.

She put a hand on my arm, took in my shabby clothes in one sweeping glance. 'I'm sure something good will turn up very soon. Vince will see to that, he'll use his influence, see you settled in some good place. That old Tower must be awful.'

'Not at all,' I said, still smiling through gritted teeth. 'I'm very happy there.'

I had learned nothing to help poor Alice, except to see with my own eyes Matthew visiting Lily Harding. A piece of information, like the baby he had kissed, I would keep to myself.

*   *   *

Back at the Tower, Thane was waiting for me. He sat by my side as I made some notes in my journal on my visit to Freda and described the murder scene as well as I could remember it.

I had hoped that setting foot in the kitchen of Saville Grange might yield some valuable clues. But what was I supposed to be looking for? Clues relating to Matthew's possible guilt were circumstantial and any other evidence had vanished long ago from that well-scrubbed, pristine floor.

I suspected that even Pappa with a lifetime's training in observation and deduction, would have had to confess himself defeated by such a scene.

Chapter Eighteen

I awoke to a peal of bells proclaiming Sunday worship from every church spire in Edinburgh. A delightful sound reviving nostalgic memories of Sheridan Place and breaking a vivid dream about Mrs Brook.

I was back in her kitchen waiting for Pappa, watching the clock anxiously, realising that we were going to be late for wherever he was taking us. Missing trains and being late for outings with Pappa had been a constant source of anxiety in my young life despite Mrs Brook's tireless efforts at consolation by way of tea and Dundee cake.

The dream was so real I awoke to the lingering taste of the cake in my mouth, the smell of hot, fragrant tea in the air.

I went over to the window and, as so often when the air is clear and sharp on Arthur's Seat, sounds were travelling a long distance. The chug-chug of a train steaming into Waverley Station a mile away made me decide to visit Mrs Brook in Inverkeithing.

Take a train across the new Forth Railway Bridge. What an adventure that would be, so different from the old days when travel to Fife involved the train being transferred at Granton to the other side of the Forth.

Mrs Brook would most likely be at home on

a Sunday and, even if not, I would greatly enjoy a change of scene, the first since arriving in Edinburgh a week ago. But fortune smiled on my travels, as I set out, a good omen with a tramcar to Waverley Steps from Newington and, at the ticket office, information from the guard that the train for Dundee left in three minutes. 'Look sharp, miss, it's waiting at the platform.'

Taking my seat, I put aside the newspaper I had bought. The journey across the railway bridge on a windy day promised to be exciting enough, exhilarating and even rather scary.

Buffeted by winds, the carriages swayed and shook, clouds of steam poured past the compartment windows, seeping through and leaving an acrid smell. There were moments on that journey when my heart was in my mouth.

No one who ever travels by train can fail to remember the terrible Tay Bridge disaster in 1879 when the bridge collapsed, and the train was hurled into the river and all seventy-five passengers perished.

I wondered if we were to meet the same fate as I stared at the angry waters far below with white horses riding the waves and seabirds screeching past the windows.

Regardless of the fierce wind, men at work on the high girders were hardly a sight offering consolation to the nervous passenger. The newspapers were full of items about the maintenance work needed although the bridge had been in operation just a few years. Accounts almost always ended with gloomy reminders of the numbers who had been killed in its construction, falling to their deaths in the icy waters of the Forth far below.

Dangerous work indeed. Man pays a heavy price for progress, for every new invention takes human lives in its making, I thought, as the wind turned to squally rain before we reached Inverkeithing.

Leaving the train, blown along the platform, I asked direction and found that the Fife Road was half a mile distant. I dare say it might have been a pleasant enough walk on a good day, but in a high wind an umbrella— even if I had the good sense to bring one— would have been useless. I had to hold on to my bonnet, my skirts whipped round my legs, as I was propelled, breathless, along the road.

At last I found Mrs Brook's house on one side of a long grey street. Its exterior was far from imposing, a mean-looking little door, but Mrs Brook's face when she opened it and saw who was standing in the rain was worth every moment of the walk's discomfort. Indeed, it would have been worth walking every step of the miles from Edinburgh to receive that rapturous welcome.

'Miss Rose—my dear—I can't believe it's really you. What a wonderful surprise. They told me you were in America. How is Mr

McQuinn—is he with you? Are you both well? And I hear you've a wee bairn—' All this on the short passage from front door to kitchen, while she removed my coat and bonnet, and set them to dry before the fire.

At last she stopped for breath, smiling at me. Holding my hands without giving me a chance to reply to her questions, she inspected me at arm's length. Strangely enough, whereas with everyone I had met so far, even Vince, I had been reluctant to talk about the tragic circumstances of my return home, I longed to tell Mrs Brook.

I had been warned she was sadly lamed with rheumatism. She was also rather deaf. Sometimes she cupped her ear with one hand, or shook her head and looked bewildered at my fearful adventures.

I believed I could tell my terrible story without breaking down, but no, once or twice I broke down and she was there with her arms around me, my head cradled against her breast, wiping away the tears, saying: 'There, there, my lambie' and returning me to childhood days. To comforts for falls and cut knees, and tears of disappointment when Pappa was suddenly too busy on a crime case to take Emily and me on some long promised and eagerly awaited treat. The only difference this time was that she could no longer say: 'It'll be all right. It'll get better soon.'

There was no such easy answer to my

tragedy but strangely, in retrospect, I know now that was the day the healing process began. No one but Mrs Brook had known the secret—that holding me in her arms and comforting me touched the chord of resurrection in my broken life.

I gained control, wiped my eyes and demanded to be told all about her life since she had left Sheridan Place after Vince and Olivia departed for London.

She was delighted for them but shook her head. 'The time was long past for me to retire. I was getting very slow at moving around and all those stairs were too much for me. Besides, life was never the same after your dear Pappa went to live in Ireland.' And, with a sigh: 'I get postcards from him. He never forgets me. Wherever he's travelling—some mighty strange places, as you well know, I expect—there's always a postcard and one at Christmas, just a line that he's thinking about me and hoping I am well.'

Mrs Brook didn't know it, but she was privileged indeed. Such attentions were more than most of his family ever got from him.

I looked around the small neat kitchen with a box bed in the wall and a door leading into a room that could be used as bedroom or parlour. Besides an outside water-closet shared by several families, that was all there was to 24 Fife Road.

Mrs Brook saw the look on my face. 'It is all

I need, Rose, dear, quite enough to look after.'

'I didn't realise you were living alone. Vince said you'd moved in with an elderly relative—a cousin.'

She made a face. 'I did, but after a week sharing the same kitchen and the same bedroom, I knew I couldn't stand her—nor she me. I have to be honest, I was far too managing and precise. Nothing I did pleased her and her way of doing things wasn't for me either. I knew I would be happier on my own so I moved down here.'

I took those old worn hands and held them.

'Are you happy so far away from Edinburgh?'

'As happy as I'll ever be without your dear Pappa and Doctor Vince. But those days are gone. They can't come back and I'm no use at running a big house any more. Doctor Vince knew that in the latter years but he was very patient and tolerant about it all, and so was Mrs Vince.'

'You must be lonely here on your own sometimes.'

'Not a bit of it, Rose, dear. That same cousin I told you about, Ida, has a daughter. To be honest, she found her mother a trial too. Well, until last week she was nanny in the doctor's big house down the road. But they are selling up, moving south and the children are school age, so she's not needed any longer.' She smiled. 'Nancy looks in every day to see me when she's out with the wee ones.' And, with a sigh: 'She's a dear, sweet lass, ages with yourself. Never married but still hoping, she's like the bairn I never had, we're that close.'

She shook her head. 'Needs to stretch her wings, though. She would dearly love work in Edinburgh. Best thing for her, I can't deny that, although I'll miss her sorely. Inverkeithing's a small village where you know everyone and everyone knows you. I think Nancy could better herself in a big city. Maybe even find herself a nice man to marry before she's too old to have bairns of her own.'

She looked at me sadly. 'I keep telling her she must go, that there's plenty of nannies needed all the time in Edinburgh. She worries about me but there's no need. She can still come and see me in her free time. They tell me things are better these days and if she's lucky she'll get one afternoon off every month and it's not all that far across the bridge. A wee drop more soup, dearie.'

A second helping took me right back. If I'd closed my eyes, I could have sworn I'd open them again in Sheridan Place, right down to the smell of Mrs Brook's kitchen. Nothing would be changed. Pappa and Vince would be there, time turned backwards with my life in America, an evil nightmare, still to be lived.

She asked if I'd found a nice place to stay.

When I said somewhat hesitantly that I was living in Solomon's Tower I expected shocked surprise and yet another long list of reasons why a young woman should not live in such a place in isolation.

There was none. 'I always thought that something could be made of that old place if anyone had the heart to tackle it, put some caring into it. I used to feel sorry for the old gentleman. It was an unhappy house, but in the right hands it could blossom and flourish.'

'My feelings exactly,' I said in surprise. 'And Olivia and Vince have turned it into the beginnings of a charming home. There's a lot of Sheridan Place and not only in furniture found its way there.'

She laughed at that. 'So you don't feel alone either.'

I had a sudden thought. 'You could come and live with me. Oh, please say you will! You could see your Nancy often then.'

She shook her head sadly. 'You're a kind lass, but how would I manage all those hills away from the town? And what about that spiral stair? No, Rose, dear, I'd be miserable. I'm far better off as I am in a village street, long and straight—and rather dull—but with a shop where I can buy all I need. Which isn't a great deal.'

She patted my hand. 'It's when you're young that you need folks around you. And you shouldn't be alone at your age,' she added sadly. 'Not after all you've been through.' She looked at me thoughtfully. 'Haven't you thought of going to Orkney and living with Emily?'

I didn't want to go into that. It sounded like betrayal. 'Some day, maybe,' I said. 'But honestly, I don't feel lonely in the Tower. I feel as if I'd come home.' Encouraged by her attitude I added: 'I have a strange companion.'

So I told her about Thane, our mysterious meetings and so forth, carefully omitting the incident with the tinkers.

She didn't question the deerhound either. 'I never heard tell of a beast like that in my time, but there were such stories when my grandpa was a lad. I expect like foxes and all manner of wee secretive animals they are always there but make sure that no folks see them. That's because they don't want to be seen but it doesn't mean they don't exist, Rose, dear.'

Dear, wise Mrs Brook, I thought, as she went on: 'Remember when you were a little lass you were sure there were fairies? You believed in them and were very upset when folk—not only older folk but like the lasses at your school—said you were making it up. They said fairies don't exist but they existed for you and it made you feel happy to believe in them. That was all that mattered. It was a comfort to you when you needed it and I didn't want it taken away—'

I knew what she meant. Believing in fairies and magic was my refuge after Mamma died and everything changed. Pappa was promoted to Chief Inspector and busier than ever, Vince went to university and became busy about passing exams to be a doctor. Emily and I were left more and more in the care of Mrs Brook, until a visit from our Orkney grandmother took in the situation and persuaded Pappa that we should go and live with her.

'Do you hear from Emily?' I asked.

'Just a card at Christmas.' She looked at me rather anxiously. 'Sometimes I do wonder whether she is happy. If she did right marrying that widowed man. There are no bairns,' she added darkly, as if the measure of a good marriage was the babies it produced.

But in a curious way, because she had known us both so well, I realised she was voicing my own fears. I had been expecting an invitation to stay. It had never occurred to me that I would not be welcome, that there might be some other reason apart from our ageing gran, some matter in her personal life that she was unwilling to confide in her own sister, why I should not come to Orkney.

Watching Mrs Brook brewing more tea, I asked delicately: 'Have you been a widow long?' Even as I waited for the answer I thought of the absurdity of not knowing, since Mrs Brook had been with us all my remembered life.

She turned and smiled at me, teapot in hand. 'I was about your age when I went to work at Sheridan Place with the old doctor before your father bought the house.' She shook her head. 'There never was a Mr Brook, Rose, dear. There might have been but I had only the one sweetheart and he died at the Crimea. A long while ago.'

She sighed, her eyes held closed for a moment, as if picturing that lost love. Then she brightened again. 'Mrs is a courtesy title for housekeepers whether married or not. Invented by the master, keeps us a step above the rest of the staff, most just called by their surnames. Supposed to get respect and keep flirtatious menservants—if there are any—at a distance.' She laughed. 'I found it useful once, when the coachman from Peel House was paying me some unwelcome attention.'

'I met Alice Peel. We were shopping in Jenners.'

'I remember Alice. You were best friends.' She chortled. 'Little demons you were, the pair of you, sneaking down into my kitchen and stealing my freshly baked buns. And then rearranging them on the tray in the hope that I could not count and find some had gone. She must have missed you a lot, used to come round to the house even after you went to Orkney, always asking when were the school holidays and when would you be back.

'A lonely little lass. When she married the Bolton laddie I was pleased for her. He was a nice bairn—my cousin Jeannie who died six years back was housekeeper at Peel House and I used to visit her for a gossip on my way to the shops.

'The tales she used to tell. Matthew was nice but wild, always running away. Once to sea and then to a circus, if you please. The Boltons were frantic, always dragging him back home. They'd made up their minds he was to be a solicitor like his father and grandpa, carry on the family tradition. He was a right little rebel, wanted to travel, to be an explorer when he grew up.

'They couldn't keep him out of trees, he'd climb anything, get stuck, his mother screaming that he'd fall and break his neck.'

She shook her head. 'The poor lad just hated the idea of settling down. There were great quarrels Jeannie overheard—they never kept their voices down in that family. When he met Alice Peel she had the big dowry and he needed it badly. His father had just died and the firm was in a bad way, so Matthew did the right thing and married her.'

This was a different version from Alice's story. 'Alice always gave the impression that Matthew was madly in love with her.'

Mrs Brook shook her head. 'Necessity— like a rich dowry might turn a desperate man into an ardent sweetheart. I'm amazed he's settled down so well. There are two bairns, I hear. Are they happy now?'

'Alice still dotes on him, but I haven't met Matthew since I got back.'

I said I'd met Freda Elliott too.

Mrs Brook nodded. 'She lives where that poor lass was murdered. What a thing to come home to. I'm amazed they can go on living in that house. Or get anyone to work for them.

'I read in the papers that Foley discovered the girl. Do you remember him, Rose? Such a nice, quiet lad. He and his father, before he retired, did your garden at Sheridan Place. Must have been a terrible shock for the poor man.'

We were interrupted by a knock on the door.

'That'll be Nancy now!'

I could see the affection between Mrs Brook and the tall, slim girl with a calming manner and a pleasant face. Impressed by her appearance, it didn't take much imagination to guess that she would make an excellent nanny, I decided, as Mrs Brook gave me a very flattering introduction.

Nancy smiled. 'I've heard a lot about you, Mrs McQuinn. I envy you Edinburgh, such a fascinating place to live. I've only visited, of course, but the Castle and the lovely shops—'

As she talked so wistfully, I got another of my inspirations that day and said: 'I know of someone who is searching for a nanny. At Peel

Lodge. A little boy a year old—if you're interested, may I give your name and address? I assume you have references?—'

Nancy clapped her hands, thanked me profusely.

I was pleased at my cleverness too. While helping Nancy to a situation, it might prove a move in the right direction to find out more about Lily of the Lodge and her possible connection with Matthew Bolton, and a unique chance of discovering some answers to his strange behaviour.

Chapter Nineteen

The Edinburgh train rattled over the Forth Bridge on the return journey to a more peaceful scene. The wind had died down and there was a splendid sunset ablaze the western sky.

I sat back in my seat, content with what had been a very successful day: not only the joy of being reunited with Mrs Brook, but that chance meeting with Nancy, with the possibilities it offered of discovering the truth of the relationship between Lily of the Lodge and Matthew Bolton. I found myself going over the details of Matthew's early rebellion against authority that Mrs Brook had talked about.

In fact, I was still musing over those details as I left the train and, having decided to walk home via St Mary's Street and the Pleasance, a hiring carriage stopped beside me. 'Rose!'

The Boltons were so entrenched in my mind at that moment that I was startled to see Alice leaning out of the window, a glimpse of Matthew on the seat beside her.

'Rose, I thought it was you. Matthew and I are going to a concert at Loretto School. Jump in and we'll take you home, it's on our way.'

There was no way I could refuse and I took the seat opposite. 'You remember Rose, don't you, Matthew.'

Matthew looked put out by this intrusion, cold-eyed, his handshake less than cordial, I thought.

'Dearest,' said Alice, 'why don't we have Rose come to the concert with us?' And to me: 'Do come. There is a very tolerable group playing Beethoven sonatas and there are sure to be tickets—' Turning again to Matthew, she said: 'She must come with us. Do tell her you command it!'

Matthew had said very little. I had inherited from Pappa the ability to catch on fast to atmospheres between individuals. And, even less reassuring, on entering a room I can feel fairly certain when I have been the subject of discussion.

Matthew avoided eye contact and I would

have been a fool to imagine he shared his wife's enthusiasm for my company. He was displeased, perhaps even angry, that she had made the offer of the concert.

Had they been a young couple in love I would have understood immediately that he wished to have her all to himself.

I looked at him and he said rather coldly: 'Of course you must come.' And, with a quick change of subject that left me in no doubt about his real feelings, he asked politely: 'How is your stepbrother?'

'Very well. I've only seen him once since he came home—very briefly on his way north to Balmoral.'

'Balmoral! How super. Isn't it exciting for him, Matthew, being a Royal physician?' said Alice to her husband whose lack of even a polite response indicated his boredom.

Feeling very uncomfortable at Matthew's strange behaviour, I said quickly: 'I've been to see Mrs Brook today, Alice.'

She at least showed some interest. 'That would be the first time you went across our new bridge. Isn't it exciting?'

I said it was terrifying in a high gale and that I had read about the poor men falling to their deaths.

Matthew momentarily withdrew his attention from the passing scene beyond the windows. I took the opportunity to smile in his direction and said: 'You need to have a great head for heights, I'm told. The men are very brave, it gives me vertigo just to watch them on these high buildings. I expect to witness fatal accidents every time I walk past.'

Alice shuddered. She didn't like such morbid conversation. 'You remember Mrs Brook, don't you, dearest?' she said, trying to include Matthew in the retelling of one of many episodes of our early days, involving escapades in the kitchen at Sheridan Place.

Matthew nodded politely and smiled vaguely, a thousand miles away. I wondered why my presence was so disconcerting. Each time our eyes met he looked away hastily.

All this was very disturbing and did not fit the image Alice had presented of an eager Matthew coming home early specially to meet me again and have a cosy tea together. Considering his rather chilly manner, I was glad I missed that treat and that we would soon be in sight of Solomon's Tower.

Then, quite suddenly, I thought I had the answer as I remembered a long-ago encounter with Matthew: a birthday party at Alice's just prior to their engagement announcement—Matthew had been very flirtatious and had tried to kiss me when we met on the staircase.

Until this moment I had entirely forgotten the incident. But was that what he was remembering, embarrassed and guilty about a stolen kiss more than a decade ago?

As home approached and I firmly declined

Alice's invitation on the grounds that I was rather tired and had letters to write, Matthew's relief at my decision was obvious. He was suddenly quite overcome with animation to the extent of throwing in a few polite and conventional words about meeting again, as well as some quite radiant smiles before we parted.

His behaviour was very odd. I thought of my day with Mrs Brook and there was something important in the back of mind that clicked into place.

For the moment it was swept aside by the discovery of a note from Vince pushed under the front door: 'We are going to the circus tomorrow evening. Do come. Will collect you at five.'

Happy and excited at the prospect of being with Vince again, I hardly noticed that the weather was changing.

Despite the glowing sunset, Arthur's Seat was a law unto itself and that night a cold, think, white haar descended on the hill.

*   *   *

I awoke next morning to find that I was entombed in an icy, damp palace with nothing visible beyond the dripping windowsill.

Downstairs I opened the kitchen door and hastily closed it again against the great white shroud that floated towards me. Beyond the garden I could hear the trees dripping, the invisible sheep lamenting this further trial of their uneventful lives. From the direction of the circus came faint alien animal sounds. Obviously this kind of weather spooked them too.

Far off a dog barked. Was it Thane, I wondered, as I went out across the wet grass with Cat's bowl of milk? Setting it before her, I noticed for the first time remains of fur and bones. A quick glance without any desire for closer inspection suggested a meal of shrews and mice.

I considered Cat, lying there so peacefully. She never seemed to move from the barn and I suspected that those shaky old legs were well past the ability to trap even the most slow-moving shrews or mice. So how did they get there? Such evidence pointed to the fact that she was surviving on more than bowls of milk.

Then I thought I had the answer. She was being fed and it could only be Thane, a swift-moving deerhound, capable of catching small animals. A mouthful to him, he was generously donating them to Cat, his natural enemy.

As I went quickly back into the house I realised here was one mystery I would never solve, since there are questions no deerhound, however clever, is capable of answering.

Thankful to close the door, I stirred the peat fire and had another glance through

Olivia's unwanted wardrobe in the hope there would be something suitable for the circus visit.

I unearthed an elegant dark-blue velvet skirt, wearable but, like the sleeves of the matching jacket, in need of shortening by a good four inches. I applied myself to this task, after washing my hair so thick and heavy it would take all day to dry in this weather. I would be fortunate to have it looking presentable before Vince arrived.

As I sewed, occasional glances out of the window confirmed that the mist had not lifted. Noises travel and twice I heard sounds—a galloping horse neighed far off. But who could be on the hill in such weather, especially riding fast? There were plenty of hazards to be avoided even in bright sunlight—boulders, rabbit holes . . .

I heard stealthier sounds than horses, nearer at hand. One of the sheep, I thought, but a lost lamb creates a great racket and these sounds were followed by heavy silence. They made me nervous without quite knowing why, I felt the presence outside was human— what if it was a benighted traveller lost on the hill? I bravely opened the door a crack and called out: 'Hello—is there someone there?'

Silence.

'Thane?' I listened, shivering, told myself it was only a wandering animal.

There were no further sounds and,

retreating to the kitchen, I tackled the lengthy business of brushing out the heavy tangle of my still damp curls.

*   *   *

At last, dressed in my new outfit and with a hat of Olivia's I remembered borrowing for a wedding before leaving for America, I heard the carriage arrive.

Vince leaped out and hugged me. 'So you got my message?'

'I wasn't expecting to see you so soon again—this is wonderful.'

He took my hands. 'Let me look at you. You look lovely—very elegant indeed. Olivia used to have something very similar. It was one of my favourites, but alas, after the children . . .'

I explained that this was indeed Olivia's.

He bowed. 'Perfect for a command performance.'

'You mean the Queen's coming too?'

'She is indeed. Jump in.'

'I thought she would be in Balmoral by now.'

Vince settled himself and said, 'We never got there. Her Majesty has had endless meetings in Holyrood about the new decorations. We were all set and about to leave when she discovered that there was a circus down the road. She had to see it, every engagement to be cancelled—' And as the carriage swayed and we had to hang on to our seats to avoid another carriage heading for the park, he groaned: 'What weather!'

The road was still almost invisible through the mist and only the noise of horses would have warned us of any approaching carriage. On that narrow, twisting road, passing would be a nightmare without proceeding the mile ahead into Duddingston village where it widened enough to make turning possible.

'Let me tell you about this evening, Rose. The programme for specially invited guests, notably the baillies of the city and the Royal entourage, had to be chosen by her. She approved the clowns and jugglers, of course, and the magician, but what she especially commanded were lions and trapeze artists. And the savage Indians in the Wild West Show!'

Listening to him took me back to the past circuses and Pappa's days with the Edinburgh City Police, when Her Majesty's passion for watching other mortals risk life and limb on high wires or with man-eating animals was well known. She had a wistful partiality for brave lion tamers in leopard skins. This savage and somewhat primitive form of amusement did not go unmarked among her courtiers, hinting at wry comparisons with other less sentimental tender-hearted monarchs, namely the Emperor Nero and the gladiatorial circus, culminating in throwing a few Christians to the lions.

No setting was less like the Colosseum in Rome than the gentle one of the Queen's Park, mist or no. And I was thrilled at the prospect of going to the circus at last when, as guests of Her Majesty the Queen, we were ushered in as very important persons to where the Royal box had been hastily but sturdily constructed.

A clutch of uniformed policemen in anxious watchful attendance recalled Pappa's involvement in elaborate security precautions: the certainty that there was no access to the Royal box from beneath as was the case for the wooden tiers of seats for the general public.

There had been many assassination attempts in her long reign and I suspected these were still a nightmare, as well as a considerable expense to the police, for there was Jack Macmerry disguised in plain clothes. He stood near the entrance to the big tent, looking somewhat preoccupied.

At last Her Majesty appeared and was escorted to her seat, having thoughtfully taken the precaution of travelling incognito by adding a thick grey veil to her bonnet. I guessed from the gasps of astonishment and turning heads of the audience, other than the Edinburgh baillies and officials, that the small rotund figure in black was blissfully ignorant that her disguise fooled no one.

One of Pappa's recurring horrors had been of the Queen, an easy target, majestically alone on a raised dais in a frail tent in a huge arena, surrounded by a dense crowd of onlookers from which a single fatal shot could be fired, the assassin making good his escape amid the stampede of panic-stricken onlookers. He used to sigh and say Her Majesty was either remarkably brave or totally lacking in imagination.

I occupied my time before the performance began by spotting the lurking detectives around us disguised as innocent circus-goers. Sharp-eyed, their hands were never far from pistols in their greatcoat pockets.

The show began with the parade of horses and jugglers. High above on the tight-wire were the clowns. As one of them slipped and—almost—fell, the audience screamed, while Her Majesty applauded politely. All part of the act!

In all truth, I was more fascinated by the surreptitious glances at the Royal guest than the circus acts so far. This was the closest I had ever been to her and I wished I had brought my journal along to make some sketches.

The next act was a virtuoso appearance by the magician, Cyril Howe himself. I was near enough to observe that he was sweating, occasionally muttering through his smiles to his assistant, wife Daisy, her spangles trembling. Doubtless both were nervous in case the rabbit didn't miraculously appear from the hat, or Daisy failed to reappear when the magic cabinet door was reopened.

Then, to my surprise I noticed in the front row of the tiered seats Cyril Howe's other lady, she of the dragon pendant. Sure that her presence must have totally unnerved the magician, since she must have been prominently in his line of vision, I wondered if that was the reason he was in such a panic. And why Daisy's spangles were trembling: not with fear but with rage. Poor Howe, I thought, perhaps he wished he could make both ladies disappear as easily as he dealt with the pair of white doves.

Everything went smoothly and to loud applause as the Howes bowed and left the ring. The brass band played a patriotic number while the safety net for the high-wire act was replaced by a ten-foot-high fence of robust iron bars.

A ripple of excitement went around the audience as into that enclosure, bringing with them the smell of the jungle, the lions in their ornate cage were pulled into the arena by plumed circus horses, nervous and less than happy at this burden of ferocity they were escorting.

I glanced at Her Majesty, animated, clapping her hands, enthusiastic as any of the small children in the audience as the lion tamer entered the ring.

Raj (born Abel White in Liverpool) had a muscular frame attired only partially in a small leopard skin, perhaps as a warning to his current charges that this was the fate in store for them if they misbehaved or disobeyed him. Protected by a long pole to keep any unruly charges at a respectful distance, Raj had his lions leaping up and down on the boxes to his command, obligingly opening their mouths in approximations of fierce roars. The more sluggish performers with a tendency to yawns of boredom were prodded into short-lived shows of ferocity.

I was losing interest, still more intent on keeping a watchful eye on Royalty.

At last came the moment she and the rest of the audience had been waiting for. The lesser lions were persuaded back into their ornate cage by the clowns with long sticks and wheeled away. One solitary beast remained and the ringmaster, a silver-clad Cyril Howe, came forward. 'It is essential for Monsieur Raj's safety that we have absolute silence. Any sudden noise that might frighten this savage beast could be fatal to him.'

A roll of drums. Raj bowed to the Queen and, after stroking the lion's mane and murmuring a few words of reassurance, opened his jaws slowly and thrust his forearm inside. Withdrawing it unscathed to tumultuous applause, he bowed again.

Another louder roll of drums. Silence as Raj now thrust his head inside the lion's open mouth, withdrew it and, with no doubt considerable relief, patted the savage beast as if he had no more harm in him than the pussycat by the fire.

Her Majesty was ecstatic and I was sceptical. Perhaps my eyes were sharper than those of Royalty. Sitting slightly to the left side of Raj and his lion I suspected that the man was never in any real danger. And that his savage beast was toothless, elderly and was probably fated to die in tranquil old age, bequeathing that mangy coat as legacy for good conduct to his trainer.

As everyone cheered and clapped, I was inclined to agree with Pappa's reactions. Now, as a grown-up, I was understanding and sympathising with his ready excuses for not accompanying his two small daughters to the circus. He hated seeing caged animals or birds, this failing greeted with wry amusement by his policeman colleagues since his activities had succeeded in putting so many humans behind bars through the years.

The climax was The Wild West Show, Chief Wolf Rider and the Sioux Ghost Dancers, a very impressive performance of daring rough riding on and off and under horses, of jousting with lances. The clowns reappeared in the guise of stern brave Unites States cavalry, who struggled and fell obligingly dead at the Indians' feet, presumably in a re-enactment of Custer's Last Stand.

The Sioux war cries no doubt chilled the hearts of the audience, except that for me they were a mere parody of real life.

I noticed Her Majesty's deep frown, not quite certain whether she should applaud such savagery. No doubt it evoked thoughts of natives in outposts of her Empire where the British flag flew somewhat unsteadily.

I wondered if she had observed that the Sioux were one short. Eleven riders instead of twelve, which put Chief Wolf Rider into some difficulties in the formation riding sequences. Had the missing Indian succumbed to the thick white haar, the atrocious weather, such conditions not readily encountered in his homeland on the sun-baked plains of the American West? Was I the only one who noticed? It was almost impossible to tell individuals apart at long range with warpainted faces streaked white and red but I did wonder if the missing Indian was the young man I had seen with a crucifix like Danny's.

Chapter Twenty

The final parade around the circus ring over, the audience applauded and stood respectfully to attention as Her Majesty left the tent. She had abandoned her frail incognito disguise and the brass band struck up 'God Save the Queen' to loud cheering.

We followed the Royal party. Vince took my arm and at the entrance to the tent we bumped into Jack Macmerry. He looked very surprised indeed to see me in such illustrious company and I felt rather pleased.

'I'll take you home,' said Vince. 'But first let's eat. I'm famished. Café Royale, I think.'

We left the carriage with Vince's instructions to collect him from Solomon's Tower at ten.

'Is that all right for you, Rose? Not too late?'

I was delighted and looking forward to seeing the inside of Café Royale again. As we were led to a table, Vince was genially hailed by one of a trio of men, rather flash and flushed with wine.

'Thomas Carless,' Vince whispered. 'Edinburgh's most notorious gambler. Sails close to the wind in his business dealings, too.'

We had met before, but where eluded me. I gave up trying to remember, happy to be hearing news of Vince's children: Jamie, who was going to be clever and go to an English public school before Oxford or Cambridge.

'Naturally we would prefer a Scottish university, but having been educated in England . . .' Vince seemed apologetic, before switching to my little nieces and sounding just a little reverential about their Royal playmates: so many offspring of Princes and Princesses that I was absolutely bewildered. Impressed, of course, but lost.

I didn't care in the least what he talked about. I was just happy, joyful beyond words to be with my dear Vince, although this rather corpulent balding Dr Laurie was so far removed from the hero-worshipped stepbrother of my early years.

'Met any old friends yet?' he asked.

When I mentioned Alice he twirled the wineglass in his hand and looked mysterious. 'Dear Alice. She had quite a passion for me, you know,' he said idly.

I didn't know, but I wasn't altogether surprised as it was a further explanation of why, according to Mrs Brook, she came to Sheridan Place so regularly when I was away. And yet, so keen to see me, she never mentioned these visits in her exceedingly rare letters.

Poor Alice. And another missing piece of a jigsaw fell into place as Vince went on hurriedly, 'I never encouraged her, Rose. I thought of her as just a little girl, like you, and a gap of twelve years was not a prospect I could take seriously. It was all rather embarrassing and I was heartily glad when she transferred her affections to Matthew Bolton.' He smiled. 'I introduced them, as a matter of fact. Do you see me as an unlikely Cupid? Even I was surprised at the speed of events thereafter.'

He paused, frowned and I asked: 'How so?'

'Well, quite honestly they had so little in common. The Peels were very wealthy at that time, as you know.' He hesitated: 'I realise it's uncharitable but I often thought Alice's money was the answer. Perhaps Matthew saw it as a way out from following in his family's footsteps. He loathed the idea—'

Vince was repeating much the same version of the tale of Alice and Matthew I had heard from Mrs Brook.

He sighed. 'I met a chap in my London club. We got talking and he knew Matthew. This chap hinted that he had got through his wife's fortune somewhat rapidly. He was a compulsive gambler, even as a lad.'

'I had no idea.'

Vince smiled. 'He would bet on anything, sixpence on two dogs crossing the road, idiotic things no one else would ever think of. And I wondered how Alice reacted to this addiction. She was so prim and proper. Except her pursuit of me,' he added.

215

'I suppose life is like that,' I said, suspecting already that in common with many women of my generation she had hidden depths, passions which must be concealed from the conventions of our Edinburgh society.

Vince shrugged. 'Opposites do attract and many marriages are based on compromise—or money. Or both. I assume they have adjusted like the rest of us and are settled and happy together.' He thought for a moment. 'Gambling is an addiction, hard to get out of the system once it takes a hold. I suppose Matthew restricts himself to a rubber of bridge or the horses at Musselburgh races.'

I said nothing. I couldn't bring myself to go into Matthew's strange behaviour or his weird friend in the coachhouse. Perhaps I should have sought Vince's advice, but it was Alice's confidence, her secret I would be betraying.

At last it was time to return to Solomon's Tower and the doorman summoned a hiring carriage. Princes Street and Waverley Bridge were busy at this hour of the evening. Pedestrians as well as private carriages were making for theatre and concert hall with gentlemen hurrying to their private clubs.

'We're off to Balmoral at the end of the week,' Vince told me. 'I'll try and see you again, if I can be spared.'

'I hope so—surely doctors aren't needed every moment of the day.'

'You'd be surprised,' was the rueful reply,

'with an extensive household on the move, how many sore throats, stomach upsets, cut fingers and imaginary ailments can be produced every day.'

Pausing, he looked out of the window. 'This damned mist! Can't even tell if we're on the right road.'

I assured him that we had turned on to the Queen's Drive. Arthur's Seat was just visible in the gloom of early darkness.

When we stepped out of the carriage, while Vince paid the cabman I shivered. The mist had lifted very slightly but it was bitterly cold and clammy.

'Of course I'm coming in for a while. See what's been happening in the Tower since you took over. Don't suppose you have anything to drink?'

Considering that he had consumed most of a bottle of wine with our hearty supper, I felt the offer of a cup of tea might be more appropriate.

He grinned, reading my thoughts. 'You are quite right, Rose, dear. We do get into very bad habits in Her Majesty's service.' And, patting his rather tight brocade waistcoat with unmistakable satisfaction: 'There are the inevitable results you see before you. Ah, well, there's a price to pay for everything. Would a cigar offend you?'

'Of course it wouldn't.'

Lighting up, he trotted after me, admiring

everything, up the spiral stair and down again. Back in the kitchen he was pleased to see the kettle boiling and pronounced the peat fire a great success. 'A decent cup of tea, at last.' He sighed. 'No one in Holyrood—or in St James's for that matter—seems to have heard of how to make tea. Hot, not boiling water—dreadful. Weak as water. Even Her Majesty complains that no one could make tea like dear John Brown. Apparently he had his own methods of improvement, by doctoring it with whisky—'

As we sat at the table happily gossiping, with me wishing the evening would last for ever, I was telling him about my visit to Mrs Brook when we heard the sound of trotting horses.

A carriage stopped on the road outside.

'That'll be for me. Dammit! Just when I was enjoying myself so much. Dearest Rose, we seem always to have so little time—'

'Before you go. I haven't fed Cat. The last of Sir Hedley's great feline tribe. And quite incredibly old. She's out in the stable—you must see her.'

'Must I?' said Vince grimly, his glum expression reminding me that he had never liked his benefactor, despite the old man's devotion to him. And 'never liked' was putting it mildly.

As he put on his evening cape I poured milk for Cat, longing to keep him here on any excuse until the last possible moment, to extend the glorious evening, knowing how long the hours would be, tonight and tomorrow and the next day, without him. Loneliness, homesickness for my ain folk that got worse.

'I haven't shown you a drawing of my deerhound.'

Vince laughed. 'The hound that never was, you mean.'

I made no comment as I produced the drawing I had made of Thane the day before. Even to my own eyes it was a creditable likeness, although there was still work to do on the shaggy coat, the final touches.

Vince handed it back and smiled. 'You're teasing me, Rose, dear. That's very naughty!'

'What do you mean?'

'I mean this is an exact copy of the old print I told you about.'

'No, it isn't. Look behind him, there's the hearth—the fire.'

But Vince frowned, shook his head.

'I'm telling you. It's him—Thane. He came in and sat where you are standing now, as he often does—and I drew him.'

Watching his expression I felt annoyed and cross with Thane, too, that he never put in an appearance, proving that he was no figment of my imagination and that I was speaking the truth. 'You think I'm making it up,' I said sadly.

He put his arms around me, kissed my

cheek. 'Of course not, silly girl.' He paused and, as if wanting to change the subject, said lightly: 'You know, when you were a little girl you could draw the most convincing fairies.'

I knew what he was getting at. 'And they didn't exist. Is that what you're saying?'

'No. What I'm saying is that you always drew very well. Well enough to have been a very creditable artist, made a career of illustrating books.'

When I laughed, he said: 'I'm serious, Rose. You could have done it easily, if you hadn't—' He shrugged.

Hadn't rushed off to America to marry McQuinn and waste your life were the unspoken words.

I didn't want our lovely evening to end on this sour note because, being me, it was these last few moments together I'd keep on remembering. 'I must go and feed Cat, before it's completely dark.'

'Off you go, then. There's a novel by one of the Brontës that Olivia was given as a present. It came over with the other books from Sheridan Place by mistake. I'll just have a look for it.'

He went over to the bookcase while I took the other lamp and walked across to the stable with Cat's bowl.

As soon as I opened the door I knew something was amiss.

Cat wasn't in her usual place.

Instead, there was a man's arm, brown and bare and unnaturally still, sticking out of the straw.

I took the lamp closer. What was this? Another drunken tinker?

With Vince close by in the house, I went forward bravely, touched the man's arm with my foot. 'Hello there!'

There was no reaction. I leaned down and seized the bare wrist. It felt like ice. Even a drunken tinker would have moved. I expected groans and curses.

Nothing. I carried the lamp upwards for a closer inspection of this mysterious intruder.

Lying face downwards was a motionless form, the head turned into the straw at an unnatural angle.

I waited no longer and rushed back to Vince. 'Come quickly. There's a dead body in the barn. A man—I think he's been murdered.'

*　　　*　　　*

The man was young, very dead and even discounting the buckskin jacket he was Indian. The twelfth man missing from Chief Wolf Rider's troop we had seen performing at the circus four hours ago. And this one I had seen before. He wore a crucifix around his neck.

Vince looked up from his examination. 'Murdered? No, Rose. I suspect he died

221

naturally from a fractured skull. He also has a broken arm. Though what he was doing here in your stable I have no idea.'

'He's from the circus. They exercise their horses on the hill every day.'

'That's the answer, then. Probably took a fall. There's plenty of bruising. Of course, he could have been waylaid, attacked and severely beaten, crawled to the nearest habitation for help.'

'He may have been murdered, then.'

'I can't tell for sure. But I don't think so.' He looked up and smiled grimly. 'How the mind immediately turns to murder in this family, doesn't it, now?'

'How long has he been dead?' I asked.

'Some time. Rigor has set in so I would say six to eight hours—offhand. It's some time now since I worked on corpses and I may be severely out of practice.'

'Then I can tell you exactly when I think it happened.'

Vince stared at me. 'How on earth?'

'This afternoon, about two o'clock, I was sewing and I heard a lot of movement on the hill. You know how sounds carry in the mist.'

'What sort of sounds?'

'A horse galloping—neighing. Other weird sounds—I can't say exactly because I didn't feel like going out to inspect.'

'That was wise of you.' He was studying the crucifix. 'A Christian Indian. Didn't your

Danny wear one like this?'

'Yes. And I noticed this poor lad particularly because of it. A group of them rode past me the other day. I wondered then—'

Vince shook his head. 'No, Rose. If you're wondering whether it belonged to Danny I can only say that would be the coincidence beyond belief. There are millions of these worn by Roman Catholics the world over.'

'But he was from Dakota, where Danny disappeared, chasing renegade Sioux Indians—most likely from his tribe!'

I was glad of Vince's arm around my shoulders. I was shivering.

'You're clutching at straws, Rose, dear,' he said gently. 'But to be practical we must inform the police at once. I'll give a note to Everett. And we'd better let the circus know right away. His friends will want to make arrangements.'

He looked at me. My teeth were chattering although it wasn't from cold. 'Not scared of a dead man, are you?'

'Of course not.'

'Don't worry, I'll be with you until they take him away. If you don't feel like staying here on your own, then I can put you into a hotel in town—'

'No. I'm fine. I'm not scared. I've seen dead Indians before.'

But this was different. An Indian on my

property in Scotland, who might have been murdered.

While Vince was writing notes, a police carriage drove up, nicely blocking the road. We could hear voices, Everett protesting.

I opened the door to Jack Macmerry.

'Sorry to disturb you so late at night.' He paused and looked at me rather intently. 'Especially when you have a visitor.'

'Come in.'

He followed me into the kitchen and was considerably put out to find that my visitor was a man, very presentable, and that I was alone with him at ten o'clock. A moment later he had the situation in hand. 'Evening, sir.' He saluted Vince. 'Sorry to intrude on you.' And, turning to me: 'I just had to know that you were safe, Mrs McQuinn. You see, there's been another murder . . .'

Chapter Twenty-One

'There's been another murder . . .'

I stared at Jack Macmerry, my first thoughts the young Sioux Indian lying dead in the barn. 'How on earth did you know that?'

It was his turn to look bewildered. 'At the circus tonight. Mrs Howe, the magician's wife. Her husband discovered her a couple of hours ago. She was strangled and the killer left his belt around her neck. We're looking for him now.'

He paused and regarded us grimly. 'Mr Howe believes it was one of the Indian riders, Wild Elk. And that he's on the run, since his horse rode in without him. He can't have gone far, doesn't know the district and so forth. We have men out combing the hill.' He looked at me earnestly and said, 'You were my first concern, that you might be in danger. Thank God you're safe and we got here in time.'

Vince's heavenward glance at this dramatic statement, his raised eyebrows, clearly indicated without necessity for words what I already suspected. That I had a new admirer in Jack Macmerry who gazed resentfully at him. It was the look of a potential rival and I decided that an immediate introduction was necessary: 'This is Dr Laurie, my stepbrother.'

Relief changed the scowl into a smile as they shook hands. 'A doctor, sir?'

'I am indeed. And your search is over. You need look no further. We've got your man.'

'You have!'

'Yes, as a matter of fact we were just about to send for you,' I said. 'He's out in the stable.'

'No need to hurry,' said Vince as Jack rushed forward. 'He won't be going anywhere.'

'You have him secure?'

Vince shook his head. 'He's dead.'

'Dead! Did he attack you, then?' said Jack, with an anxious look in my direction.

'Of course not,' I said. 'He was dead when I found him. When I went out to feed the cat about half an hour ago.'

'Had he been dead long?' Jack looked bewildered.

'I examined him and I'd say as rigor was established that he had been dead for at least eight hours,' said Vince.

'Eight hours!' Jack frowned. 'Then he can't have murdered Mrs Howe.'

'I should think it extremely unlikely that he could have strangled anyone within that time period. He has a broken arm in addition to other injuries, including a fractured skull. Injuries which suggest he might have been the victim of an attempted murder himself.'

Jack shook his head. 'Howe was convinced it was this Indian lad, Wild Elk.'

'On what evidence?' asked Vince.

'Well, he was the most likely suspect. According to Mr Howe, he'd been hanging around the caravan. Mrs Howe was strangled with an Indian belt.' He shrugged. 'And when the horse came back riderless, it looked as if he was on the run, trying to get away from Edinburgh.' He sighed. 'It all fitted in so neatly, especially as our only lead in the Dunn case is that a young Indian from the circus was seen in the vicinity of Saville Grange around the time of her murder. Difficult, since there are twelve of these young fellows—and they all look a bit alike, with their long black hair—' Another long-suffering sigh from Jack. 'There's this man—the gardener from next door—swears he saw him. Never off our doorstep. Hardly a day goes by without him plunging in to see if we've made an arrest yet. And if not, why not?' He shook his head. 'I must say when I heard Howe accuse this lad, I thought "Great—that's both murders solved. Peace at last."'

The doorbell clanged noisily to announce the arrival of two uniformed constables and a middle-aged man in plain clothes.

Introduced as Inspector Gray, he grasped Vince's hand. 'Laurie! Great to see you again. Heard you'd gone to London. Miss the golf, do you?'

'Not much time for that now, sir. What about you?'

'Still manage a few rounds here and there. Handicap's still improving—'

I was fascinated by the inspector. Nondescript is the best possible disguise for policeman or criminal. And his name Gray described his appearance and his features to perfection. Five minutes after he left, I'd be hard pressed indeed to describe him. 'Well, what's been happening here, Macmerry?' he asked.

Listening to Jack's very concise statement as Gray seated himself at the kitchen table and spread out his legs in a very relaxed fashion, I decided that crimes in Edinburgh must be on the decrease since Pappa's day when senior inspectors raced to the scene. Not that Pappa was ever tempted by golf. Going after murderers and lesser malefactors would never have left him time for such leisurely activities as chasing a wee white ball round eighteen holes.

Gray stood up. 'I'd be obliged if you'd accompany us to view the dead man, Laurie, and give a statement to Macmerry here.'

'Of course.' And Vince handed him a very elegant card. 'Will this do as my reference?' he asked idly.

Jack's eyes widened, this was an occasion for awe and respect.

Gray, who already knew of Vince's promotion, said: 'As you're a member of the Royal household, sir, that will be enough in the absence of the police doctor to pronounce cause of death for the Procurator Fiscal's report. You don't need to come with us, Mrs McQuinn,' he added, heading towards the kitchen door.

I ignored that. 'I've seen dead bodies before, they're no new experience. And since I discovered this one, there might be questions you want to ask and my statement, too.'

Gray merely nodded, although Jack was clearly impressed as I produced more lamps and we trooped out to the stable.

228

A sad, unhappy scene awaited us and whatever my brave speech, the sight of a dead man chilled me.

Gray knelt down beside him. 'What have we here?' He touched the crucifix. 'A heathen converted, eh?'

'We'd better speak to Chief Wolf Rider, sir,' said Jack. 'He might know something of the fellow's background.'

I thought that was a good idea.

Watching Vince make a further examination of the dead man, details of which he related to Gray and were duly noted by Jack, I wanted to know more about our dead Indian wearing a crucifix identical to Danny's.

Gray rubbed his chin thoughtfully as Jack produced an impressive-looking box and proceeded to take the dead man's fingerprints. 'We'll see what they tell us about Mrs Howe's death.' And, turning to Vince: 'What do you think, Laurie? Does the condition of the body suggest to you that we might have another murder on our hands? Was he killed first and his body planted in the stable here?'

Vince shook his head. 'My first look at the body was fairly hasty but now I am almost convinced that we are not looking at a murder. I'll be very surprised if fingerprints help in this case.'

He stood up. 'I am almost certain his death was the result of a fatal accident. Evidence?

The riderless horse indicates that he was thrown. His injuries suggest such a possibility. And consider the atrocious weather today. There still is a thick mist out there. It was worse earlier in the day so perhaps the beast stumbled into a rabbit hole. Some animal suddenly appeared on their path—like a sheep . . .'

Or Thane, I thought privately.

'The fall broke his arm, there is bruising down his side. He also hit his head and that, the internal haemorrhage, killed him. Although he managed to survive long enough to crawl this far in a desperate bid to seek help.'

Gray sat back on his heels and looked at Vince. 'You'll sign a statement to that effect, will you, Laurie?'

'As it is my firm and considered opinion, sir, I will be glad to do so.'

Jack had departed with the two constables who now returned with a stretcher. Gray followed them as they carried the body across the garden and into the waiting police carriage.

When he returned with Jack he said: 'I'd be obliged if you'd come with us, Laurie, if you please, to talk to our police doctor.'

'Of course,' said Vince, preparing to leave,

Jack turned to me: 'What about you, Mrs McQuinn?'

'Rose, please—' I said. 'This is too grim a

business for polite formality.'

His smile was wholehearted. 'All right, Rose. Do you want to stay here alone after all this?'

'Why not? This is my home,'

'But—there's just been a dead man . . .'

'Who has been removed. He can't hurt me, Jack. Please don't worry about me. I'm not in the least scared.'

He looked at me solemnly. 'I know that. I think you must be one of the bravest women I've ever met.'

I grinned, feeling pleased. 'I've had my moments.'

'In the Wild West, eh?'

'Exactly.'

He still look worried. 'I could get you a night's lodging with one of my colleagues. His wife rents rooms in the High Street.'

'No thank you. I'll be fine, really.'

I felt Vince's hand on my arm. 'And I will be looking after her.' I guessed by the suppressed amusement in his voice that he had been listening to this conversation between us.

'Oh, I see.' I heard the relief in Jack's voice. 'Holyrood, is it?

'Alas, indeed it is not.' Vince laughed. 'I can't imagine Her Majesty being amused at one of her minions bringing home an uninvited guest for the night. So I'll stay here with Rose. I can sleep over there,' he added, pointing to the box bed.

My protests fell on deaf ears. 'I insist, Rose. I'll send Everett back with a message.'

'What if you're needed, a sore throat— something serious, like a heart attack? You must go. Never mind me—'

Vince shook his head. 'Even Her Majesty will be impressed by the priority of my assistance with a fatal accident. I'll return as soon as I can.'

Jack frowned, regarding me in the manner of some fragile flower ready to wither and die without his constant attention. 'I would rather we didn't leave you here alone, not even for a short while.'

There were more tedious arguments in which Inspector Gray took no part, but I had almost to throw the other two well-intentioned men out into the night. Both were determined that they were leaving behind a helpless young woman who would be terrified to stay alone in a gloomy ancient tower. Which had now added to its already bad reputation with a dead body found in the stable. Not to mention a murder at the circus just down the road and a possible killer on the loose.

Finally it was the production of a pistol and the assurance that I could use it that convinced them. I had almost to demonstrate its use to prove to Inspector Gray that this was a weapon I had handled with great effect in South Dakota.

He greeted this statement whimsically by asking how many men I had killed. I had no reply to that. Whether I had killed any of the renegades I had not waited to find out. I preferred not to know or have such matters on my conscience.

At the door Gray poked his head out of the police carriage. 'Perhaps Mrs McQuinn should accompany us to the circus tomorrow morning and tell her story to Cyril Howe.'

'I'm afraid he is going to need some convincing, being so determined that Wild Elk has killed his wife,' said Jack.

'Then you had better prepare a copy of Dr Laurie's statement. That should help convince him. Especially as his prime suspect had already been dead himself for four or five hours before his wife was killed.'

After they left I sat by the fire for a long time with all the lamps lit in the windows.

Where was Thane? My deerhound was never around when he was needed—like now. I would have given much for the comforting reassurance of his presence in my kitchen. Why did he stubbornly remain out of sight when there were other visitors to the Tower? Would I ever work out this puzzle?

But there were other questions needing answers. Questions of considerable urgency.

Someone had killed Daisy Howe but it could not have been Wild Elk. However, if his fatal accident had happened at eight o'clock instead of two, then the police would have been able nicely to round off and file away both murders as neatly solved.

He was the 'savage lurking about' who had killed Molly Dunn and, in the case of Mrs Howe, after strangling her he had rushed from the scene and, in the anxiety to escape, plunging recklessly into the mist the horse had thrown him.

There was only one problem. While Chief Wolf Rider's troop were one short at the performance, Daisy Howe was still very much alive and assisting her husband in his magician's act.

I thought about Inspector Gray's quiet reactions to all the evidence. He was a slow-moving man, who didn't make much fuss but obviously reached the appropriate conclusions.

Even without the new concept of fingerprints, I wondered how Pappa would have reacted to the known facts.

It was a frightening thought that such discrepancies in time also made perfectly clear that there were now two killers on the loose in Edinburgh, two crimes to solve.

Molly Dunn's murder with its circumstantial evidence still worried me most. I awoke during the night and heard Vince moving about in the kitchen.

Startled for a moment, but too weary to investigate, I realised he had interrupted a very strange dream. I was on the verge of apprehending Molly's murderer and Matthew Bolton's eccentric friend was threatening me.

Chapter Twenty-Two

Not only had I a ringside seat at a Royal command performance at the circus one day but on the very next I was to have a ringside seat at a murder enquiry!

I awoke at dawn to the sound of a carriage on the road outside. It was still dark. I thought of Vince asleep downstairs and decided it was someone heading to Duddingston. Too weary to go to the window I fell asleep again.

By the time I opened my eyes fully to greet the morning, eight was striking on the grandfather clock in the parlour.

There was no sound from the kitchen and I dressed hastily, hurried downstairs. But Vince had already gone, the box bed carefully made up. I was disappointed—I had hoped we could have a leisurely breakfast together before he went back to Holyrood—as I read the note he had propped up on the table: 'Sorry, Rose, dear, had to rush. Everett came with an urgent summons. One of the infants has a fever.'

Dreading my visit to the barn, I found that Cat wasn't there either. The events of yesterday must have scared her off. I left the milk and bicycled down to the circus.

Jack was there with Inspector Gray. I could hear Cyril Howe's voice raised in anger even before I reached the caravan.

Seeing me did nothing to put him in a better humour either. I gathered that Gray had produced Vince's statement that, according to his examination of the dead man and because of the time factor involved, Mrs Howe's murderer could not be Wild Elk.

Cyril Howe had made a fuss about having fingerprints taken in the caravan and, refusing to listen to Inspector Gray, he yelled: 'Whatever a damned doctor's been telling you and all this damned new-fangled fancy rubbish'—he glared at Jack—'I know best. I'm her husband and I know what I'm talking about. It was that damned savage killed my Daisy!'

'You are mistaken, sir,' said Gray more respectfully than the man deserved. And to me: 'Would you repeat what you told the police, Mrs McQuinn.'

'I was at the performance last night and Mrs Howe was alive then, helping her husband in the magician's act. By the time I reached home two hours later the Indian Wild Elk had already been lying dead in my barn for several hours.'

Howe's sneer dismissed a mere woman's evidence and he tried constantly to interrupt as Jack corroborated this statement. He got us all annoyed by adding that in his experience all doctors were incompetent crooks who could be, and mostly were, wrong.

'I must remind you, sir, that Dr Laurie is with the Royal household,' said Gray sternly.

Howe looked momentarily subdued. 'How many corpses does he see there every day? Not many, I'll bet, if he knows which side his bread's buttered. So if that savage you're all intent on protecting didn't kill my Daisy, suppose you listen to my facts?

'After the second performance I thought she'd gone back to the caravan to change and had gone to bed. I had things to do, people to see—'

I thought about 'she' of the dragon pendant as he spoke.

'I found her in bed all right. Strangled with an Indian belt. Plain as the nose on your face. What more evidence do you want?'

'Is this the belt?' asked Gray.

'It is indeed. The very same.'

Gray looked at Jack who shook his head. 'The fingerprints don't match the dead man's, sir.'

I was staring at the belt in horror. 'But you'll find mine on it. That's my belt, Inspector.'

Gray frowned. 'And when did you lose it, Mrs McQuinn?'

'Earlier this week. I found a deerhound wandering on the hill behind Solomon's

Tower. I assumed that he was lost and belonged to the circus. I had nothing suitable so I used my belt as a lead.'

Pausing, I looked at Howe. 'You remember, I thought he had escaped from here.'

Howe stared at me. 'I don't know what you're talking about, Mrs McQuinn. A deerhound?' He laughed. 'I don't remember any deerhound.'

'But you must. You offered to take him off my hands.'

Howe laughed. 'Now what would I do with a deerhound? They're hunting animals. You could never train them as circus performers,' he added with a look of appeal in Gray's direction.

'You said you'd find a place for him in one of your acts,' I said indignantly.

Howe shook his head, looked at the three men and said soberly, 'I'm afraid this young woman is having delusions—'

As he said it I realised something odd and rather terrifying. Howe was the one person who had ever seen Thane with me. The only person, apart from his dead wife, who could prove that Thane existed.

Gray frowned. 'This is definitely your belt, Mrs McQuinn?' When I said it was he asked: 'When did you last see it?'

'Thane—the deerhound I brought here—was wearing it as a collar. He ran away when Mr Howe offered to take him off my hands.'

Howe's snort of disbelief indicated that this was a pack of lies.

'Why should the dog do that?' Gray asked gently.

'Because he seemed to understand what was going on, that Mr Howe wanted to buy him,' I said desperately, aware of how daft it sounded.

'So he was still wearing your belt?' said Gray.

'No. He broke loose and left me holding it. I pushed it into my pocket. Or I thought I did but when I got home it wasn't there. Next day I went out and retraced my steps across the hill, back towards the circus here, to search for it.'

As I spoke I looked at Jack, knowing that whatever the others thought, he would believe me.

Howe laughed again. 'That's your answer then, gentlemen. That bloody young savage found the belt on the hill and used it to kill my Daisy.'

Gray looked thoughtful. 'A moment, sir. Was there any reason that you know of why he should kill her?'

Howe shrugged and Gray continued: 'Had you seen them quarrelling, for instance?'

'Not exactly. But these Indians all hang around with nothing to do between performances. My Daisy was good to them, kind—gave them food.'

'They would hardly kill her for that,' said Gray gently. And, looking in my direction: 'What about . . . other favours?'

'If it's sexual favours you mean,' I put in, noticing how the men winced at the word, 'Sioux Indians don't want them from white women.'

'And how does she know so much about it?' sneered Howe.

'Because I've lived with Indians in Dakota. The same tribe as your riders.'

'Mrs McQuinn has just recently returned to Edinburgh,' said Jack.

Gray nodded, that seemed to satisfy him. 'Was there anything missing from your caravan?'

Jack produced his notebook.

'Some trinkets, jewellery and that sort of thing,' said Howe vaguely.

'It would help if you could be a little more specific, sir. Descriptions and so forth,' said Gray.

Howe shook his head. 'That's beyond me. I don't know the contents of my wife's trinket box—'

'The box is still there?'

'Yes. But I don't know exactly what was missing. She was always buying cheap earrings and bracelets to wear with her costume in the ring.'

I remembered the dragon pendant his other woman was wearing at the performance last night and how the first time I came here with Thane, Daisy and Cyril were quarrelling about it, screaming that it was a valuable piece that had belonged to her mother and he had stolen it. 'These Indians wouldn't steal cheap trinkets. They have good jewellery, the very best,' I said. 'The silver and turquoise they wear is real, sometimes with religious significance.'

Howe gave me a murderous look. 'Whose side are you on, lady?' he sneered. 'Not Queen and countrymen, that's for sure.'

Gray didn't like that, neither did Jack. 'If we aren't needing Mrs McQuinn any more, sir?'

'Not at the moment, but we may need you again later. Is that all right?' said Gray.

Jack went out with me. 'I'll walk you home.'

'I have my bicycle.'

He grinned. 'Then I'll run alongside if you promise not to go too fast, seeing it's uphill all the way.'

'We'll both walk, then. I've just remembered there's something I'd like you to see.'

As we fell into step I asked: 'Tell me something, why aren't you in uniform?'

He laughed. 'Because I've been promoted. Came through two days ago. You've brought me luck. I'm now a sergeant, permitted to wear plain clothes.'

Back at the Tower I produced my journal

241

and showed him the drawing of the couple on the train from Dunbar.

'That's jolly good,' he said. 'Wait a minute, that's Howe, isn't it? You've got him exactly—a perfect likeness. But the woman—'

He frowned, studied it again. 'I couldn't be sure but . . .'

'It's not Mrs Howe.' And I told him about the train journey, their furtive manner at Dunbar Station before entering my compartment. And how they had parted company at Waverley, like strangers, as if they did not wish to be seen together.

'She was at the performance last night, sitting right at the front. I'm sure Daisy Howe knew of her existence. She could have reached out and touched her. And most important, even more outrageous when you come to think about it, she was wearing the dragon pendant, which I'm sure was what I overheard them quarrelling about the night I took Thane down—'

'Thane? Oh, yes, the deerhound.' Jack didn't argue, he said: 'You realise that this gives us a new slant.'

'I do and if you want my theory purely on circumstantial evidence, I think Daisy Howe recognised the pendant, tackled Cyril. They quarrelled and he killed her—'

'With your Indian belt. His fingerprints will be on it, but that's acceptable as happening when he was trying to release her.' He paused.

'If it's yours, Rose, how on earth did it get into Howe's possession?'

I thought for a moment. 'That's easy. I have watched his performance as a conjurer and magician. And I'm convinced that he took it out of my pocket that night when we were talking together, after the deerhound ran off. He said if I ever wanted a job I could join one of his circus acts.'

Jack's brow darkened. 'The cheek of the man! What would a lady like yourself want to do with circuses?' He nodded grimly. 'And if that's the way of it, Rose, then this crime must have been carefully planned, waiting for the right place and opportunity.' He whistled. 'The vanishing Indian must have seemed like a gift from heaven. What a villain the man is! I was prepared to give him the benefit of the doubt. An angry man, a jealous harridan of a wife, he seizes the first thing that comes to hand to shut her up and, in a murderous rage, strangles her accidentally.'

'That's the usual way with domestic crimes, isn't it?'

'I'm afraid so, but not this one. Well, we still have to prove it, Rose. But you're a genius!' And leaning forward, he kissed me gently on the cheek.

'Thank you, Jack. That was very nice.'

'And I meant it, too.'

We looked at each other and said a lot of things that didn't need any words at all.

He clasped my hands, held them tightly. 'Will you come to a concert with me in the Princes Street Gardens one evening?'

'I'll be delighted. If you're not too busy solving crimes.'

He grinned. 'I'll be there. And I'd like to take you to meet my parents—'

'Steady on, Jack, first things first. We've just met, for heaven's sake.'

He laughed. 'Oh, I don't mean right away. I was thinking ahead and, besides, they live at Peebles.'

As he was leaving he said: 'We'll be interviewing the circus people, just the usual routine business after a murder. But Chief Wolf Rider has asked to see where Wild Elk died. He's very insistent, seems that it's very important. Is that all right by you? No need to be scared. We'll send someone along with him to see you're all right.'

I laughed. 'Jack, there's absolutely no need. I know enough about the Sioux to understand his motives. He isn't going to harm me. He might want to burn down the barn, of course.'

I shouldn't have said that. Jack took it seriously and I had to persuade him that it was only tepees that were burnt when their owners died.

'All right, but I'd be happier if one of us came too,' he said darkly.

I watched him go, not quite so hopeful now as I was when he first kissed me. I liked Jack although I was by no stretch of the imagination in love and I doubted whether that ecstasy would ever happen with another man.

But having Jack as a friend had interesting possibilities. Especially if Howe was guilty, as all the evidence suggested, and Wild Elk was dead, we were no nearer to proving whether he had killed Molly Dunn. I was convinced that he was innocent of the servant girl's murder long before I met Chief Wolf Rider.

So the question remained. Who was her killer? And more important was the nagging thought that he was still out there somewhere, laughing at all of us, a murderer on the loose perhaps even now stalking a second victim.

Chapter Twenty-Three

Even without his feathered war bonnet Chief Wolf Rider was an impressive sight. One of the handsomest men I had ever seen with features that might have graced a sculpture of an Aztec warrior. In the course of our talk it emerged that his grandmother was a Sioux chief's captive. Offered to return to the white man's world, she refused, having settled down happily with her new family. Perhaps mixed blood makes a stronger race and Wolf Rider was a fine example of the true Westerner.

He declined my invitation into the Tower and suggested we sit on the stone wall by the stable. As we did so, I had an odd sense of déjà vu, that I was reliving some past event. There were moments when I knew before he spoke what his next words would be.

While he related the story of his early years, I recognised the way he took a broken branch and drew lines in the soil at our feet, that smiling, narrow-eyed sideways glance.

With a sense of shock I knew whom he reminded me of.

Danny McQuinn. I had never expected to meet a man of Danny's calibre again and I thought how he would have liked and respected Wolf Rider and how they might have been comrades. Two men born in different cultures, in different worlds, yet hewn from the same rock.

He needed to see where Wild Elk had drawn his last breath. Wolf Rider, it transpired, was a shaman—a medicine man.

'There is a ceremony to be performed on the exact spot where Wild Elk's spirit will linger until his soul is released to soar into that other world—' He took a deep breath.

'Where the Great Spirit waits to receive his faithful disciples.'

Disciples, Wolf Rider had called them. When I looked surprised he said: 'Wild Elk was a Ghost Dancer, a believer in the new religion of the Dakota Sioux with its promise of salvation, that a messiah was to come and save them.'

He paused and smiled bitterly. 'Any new faith was good enough for a desperate people to believe in after the massacre at Wounded Knee. When we do the Ghost Dance in the circus, I wonder how many of the audience realise the significance of a new Sioux religion?'

His glance was a question. I knew the answer. 'They believe that it will restore to them an earth soon to be covered with new soil that would bury all the white men. New grass and trees would grow, streams would run clear and the buffalo herds would return to the plains.'

He laughed. 'You amaze me. How come you are so well informed, lady?'

'They also believed that the shirts they wore were sacred and impervious to bullets.'

'How wrong they were.' He sighed.

And I told him that I had lived in his land and knew at first hand the appalling conditions by which the Dawes Land Allotment Act had robbed the Great Sioux Reservation of a hundred million acres of their land and left a hundred thousand souls landless and in direst poverty literally to starve to death.

Wolf Rider nodded. 'Sitting Bull, our great leader, said that there was only one promise the white man made that he kept. And that was to exterminate the Native American race. The Ghost Dance scared the white people—a pernicious system of religion—which in fact was based on non-violence. When they came to arrest Sitting Bull, it was one of the agency policemen, one of his own tribesmen, who fired the fatal shot, as he had prophesised.'

He went into the stable and I waited on the stone wall outside in the sunshine. Our talk had taken me back again to dangerous days in a harsh world I had only narrowly survived. At that moment I would not have been surprised if the hill had vanished and I was once more in the desolate landscape where I had last seen Danny McQuinn ride out, never to return. Where our little son lay in an unmarked grave.

I heard him chanting but it was all over very quickly and when he came out, he handed me the crucifix that Wild Elk had worn. I held it to my breast and tears welled in my eyes. 'So he wasn't Christian after all.'

Wolf Rider stared straight ahead. 'Only as much as we all worship one God whatever name we call him by. Be it Great Spirit, Jehovah, Allah—'

'Then why did he wear this?'

Shading his eyes, Wolf Rider searched the summit of Arthur's Seat as if it might provide an answer to where Wild Elk had received the injuries that had killed him. Then, turning to me again, he said: 'He wore the Christian cross as a penance, a reminder of a man he had killed in Dakota.'

My heart pounded—I could feel the blood in my temples. 'Was this man—' I croaked. 'Was his name—Danny McQuinn?'

Wolf Rider looked at me sharply. 'Your husband?' And with sudden compassion he shook his head. 'I have no idea, nor, I think, did Wild Elk ever know his name. I knew only that he was white. I had assumed he was one of the pony soldiers.'

'Do you know what happened?' I gasped out.

'No. Wild Elk never told us except that he had not meant to kill this man. They were not enemies. It was a terrible mistake—he had broken the Ghost Dancer's sacred vow.'

There was a long pause. 'But he came from this land, your land—somewhere on this side of the great Atlantic Ocean. But whether England or Scotland I have no idea.'

Again he stopped talking; frowning he stared towards the summit, the look of a searcher. But for what? 'When we arrived here in Edinburgh, Wild Elk went out with the others to exercise their horses on the hill here, but he became distressed, certain that he was being followed.'

'Followed? But he was a stranger. Who would be following him out there?'

I didn't believe in ghosts. Most likely it was a policeman keeping an eye on him. They were taking no chances. Foley had seen an Indian near Saville Grange and they were on the lookout for possible suspects. 'You say he liked going out alone? Did he by any chance extend his riding to other parts of the town?'

Wolf Rider looked at me and with that strange insight into my mind. He said: 'If you mean over there'—he gestured towards Newington—'where this young woman was murdered, the answer is no. Very definitely no, as I have told the policemen who keep asking the same question. They are very eager to believe that someone of his description was seen in the area.'

His smile was sardonic. 'To white men, all Indians look alike. A bunch of red savages. This particular Indian was seen on foot. On foot indeed. As I keep telling them, we are under very strict rules that our troop of riders remain in the Queen's Park area. They are at liberty to exercise their horses singly or in groups but are required by the terms of our contract—as foreigners—to check in and out, in case of any misunderstandings.

'As for Wild Elk, he would never go anywhere without his horse. He had a cautious nature and it was out of character for him to wander off on his own.'

'Can that be proved?' I asked.

He shook his head. 'Alas, no. Wild Elk had problems like many young men, but they would not be solved by killing a defenceless young woman in a remote part of Edinburgh.'

'Have you any theories about Mrs Howe?' I asked, changing the subject to yet another murder.

He looked grim. 'I have plenty. One in particular, but it does not concern Wild Elk. The Howes were always quarrelling. And they did not keep their voices down.' He shrugged. 'Maybe some significance. That is for your policemen to find out. But as far as our riders are concerned, Mrs Howe showed only the usual contempt for anyone who was not white—and rich.'

'Her husband says she was kind to Wild Elk. Gave him food and suchlike.'

Wolf Rider laughed. 'Whatever suchlike means! He is either mistaken or lying. And if he is accusing a dead man of his wife's murder, there is only one logical reason.'

'You mean that he killed her himself?'

Again that mocking sideways glance. 'Exactly. One thing is certain, Wild Elk never believed that one of your policemen was following him.'

He paused thoughtfully before continuing: 'Who or what was stalking him, setting him apart, singling him out from his comrades was not as simple as that.'

My spine tingled with fear as I stared over my shoulder, over and away up the blank and empty slopes and ridges towards the summit of Arthur's Seat.

Wolf Rider could feel my fear, I was certain, although he stared ahead impassively. 'We believe that the spirits of those who die by violence can then enter into animals. In Wild Elk's case he began to believe that the soul of the white man he killed had followed him.'

'Surely not here—in Edinburgh?'

Wolf Rider nodded solemnly. 'In this very place. He believed his victim was hunting him, tracking him down. Seeking vengeance in the body of a giant dog.'

My heart thumped wildly. 'What kind of dog?'

'A huge creature.'

'A deerhound?' I whispered.

'Is that what they are called? Are they hunting dogs?'

'Yes.' I could hardly speak.

'You have seen this creature, then?' he demanded sharply. 'He is real?'

'Yes, very real. He saved me when I was attacked on the hill out there by drunken men.'

Wolf Rider thought about this, said nothing but continued to regard me as if reading my thoughts. Confused and terrible thoughts to which I could give no name. He breathed deeply. 'You are aware how Wild Elk died, what killed him.'

'His horse threw him. That is what they say.'

'I think there is more to it than that.' Again

he took up the branch and began drawing patterns on the soil at our feet. 'I believe that this animal—the spirit of the man he had killed—caught up with him, spooked the horse.' He stopped. 'And so he was avenged.'

I put my hands over my ears. What he was suggesting was outrageous. Everything I had ever learned, even been taught to believe in, refused to touch it, give it logical thought.

As for Danny he would have been horrified too. As a staunch Roman Catholic, it was against all the tenets of his religion to believe that Thane was the embodiment of a human seeking vengeance, protecting me—

It was nonsense, nonsense. I could not— dared not—give the suggestion credence. The crucifix seemed to be burning my hand.

Wolf Rider said it had belonged to the man Wild Elk had killed, a white man but not an American soldier—

I dared not believe that it was the same one Danny had worn.

'Hello there!' It was Jack, at that moment, the worst and yet the best possible moment for an interruption to restore sanity to the madness swirling around in my brain.

He strolled across the garden, looking at us both curiously, perhaps aware of the strange atmosphere he had walked into. 'Got everything you need, did you, sir?'

Wolf stood up, nodded. 'Everything Wild Elk needed for his soul's rest and peace.'

Turning, he took my hand, bowed over it. His smile linked Jack and me, as if he had another vision that he would have liked to talk about. Then he was leaving, going away. He knew so little about me. I wanted to tell him all about Danny, have confirmation for my fears.

God knows what I wanted. But whatever it was, the moment of closeness between us was past, as if it had never been, and had turned us into strangers again, we who could have been so much to each other in some other world.

For ever, now, we would walk our own paths. They would never cross again.

*   *   *

Wild Elk was laid to rest in the local cemetery, as the evidence of wearing a crucifix entitled him to Christian burial. This decision must have relieved Chief Wolf Rider and the members of his troop, since the Sioux manner of laying the dead out on high trestles and allowing the buzzards and wild creatures to consume his remains would not have amused Her Majesty, nor those who enjoyed pleasant Sunday afternoon walks in Queen's Park.

'On the other hand,' Jack reminded me. 'You can never be sure. The days of public executions are over, but they are still within living memory. And we must not forget that they were once highly regarded as a suitable outing the whole family could enjoy. You can never tell anything with human nature. There is a touch of the ghoul in all of us.'

The funeral ceremony made headlines in the local newspaper and produced a rash of letters signed 'Indignant' and 'Disgusted' from city worthies who considered this burial unethical.

'The police were also present,' Jack told me. 'But with Wild Elk in his grave we are no nearer to solving Molly Dunn's murder, further away than ever. In fact, this promises to be another unsolved crime where we'll always have difficulty in persuading folk that it wasn't "that savage Indian".'

'Wolf Rider tells me that once the police have arrested Daisy Howe's killer the circus moves on, down to England. I think they'll be glad to go.' He smiled. 'He is joint owner with Howe and he's been very helpful. A fine man, didn't you think?'

'Very,' was my only comment.

Chapter Twenty-Four

Each morning I expected to see Thane loping down the hill, but it seemed that the Tower had been deserted by my two strange creatures and I wondered sadly whether I'd ever see either of them again. Although I was almost persuaded to have grave doubts about

Thane's existence, Cat had always seemed real enough.

I concluded that animals are very sensitive to deaths and that the recent demise of Wild Elk in the stable had scared them off. I hadn't seen Cat since; although I put out her bowls of milk, they remained untouched and I decided that she had returned to the wild again.

I couldn't blame her. I didn't care to linger in the empty stable either. It would always be associated in my mind with the horrifying discovery of a dead man lying there.

Considering that clearing out the straw might make me feel better about putting the building to some use, armed with broom, matches and a sense of purpose, I opened the back door to find Cat sitting on the step.

At the sight of me she miaowed plaintively. She hadn't an ounce of menace left in her but I suspected she was very hungry.

'Come along—come inside.'

Meekly she followed me into the kitchen for the first time, looking around cautiously, tail arched. When I put down the milk she lapped it up eagerly.

Watching her, I realised I couldn't put her out into the stable again. Nor did I wish to, as I remembered an old straw laundry basket at the back of the cupboard with a shabby, faded velvet cushion no doubt overlooked from Sir Hedley's day. Setting it by the fireside, I said; 'Welcome to your new home, Cat.'

She needed no second invitation. Leaping into the basket, she sniffed at it delicately then, looking up at me, she purred like a steam kettle. Was I hearing right? Such progress! After a minute and careful inspection, she settled down and allowed me to stroke her head. As I did so I noticed that her coat was in better condition too. So I hoped the fleas had abandoned her for a more insalubrious host.

*　　　*　　　*

I was to have tea with Freda once more. She came by carriage especially to see me, she said, hoping that would find me at home and if not then prepared to leave her card.

She was the last person I had any wish to see as I heaped straw on to a fire outside the stable.

Politely ignoring my dishevelled state, she said: 'I'm on my way to the Summer Fête at Duddingston church. Perhaps you would care to accompany me.'

Heaving some remaining straw on to the blaze, I was seized by a fit of coughing which rendered me temporarily speechless.

'You don't need to do that kind of menial work, Rose,' she stated severely. 'That's the gardener's job.'

'I enjoy the exercise, Freda.'

'You don't need any exercise, my dear.

You're far too thin as it is,' she continued with an unmistakable note of envy. And, turning her critical gaze towards the kitchen door: 'The Tower is quite attractive at close quarters and I am sure you have made some remarkable improvements,' she added wistfully as the reason for her impromptu visit became clear. Curiosity had driven her to see how I was living.

I took up the challenge. 'Perhaps you would like to come in for a while, if you aren't in too great a hurry.'

'Oh, yes, indeed. A few minutes. If that doesn't inconvenience you.'

'Not at all,' I said dousing the last of the blaze. 'My work is finished now.'

As she trailed behind me, frowning, her eyes darting everywhere, I refused to apologise for accumulated dust as she ran her hand over the parlour windowsill and withdrew it hastily. 'How are your plans to employ a maid? I am sure I could find you a very reliable person with excellent references among my acquaintances.'

I declined firmly, saying that when I was quite certain of my future plans I would let her know.

'You are considering going to Orkney, to your sister?'

I nodded vaguely with a speedy change of subject, helped by her favourable impression of the parlour, despite lack of polish, as she commented on the handsome furniture from Sheridan Place.

The comfortable stone-flagged kitchen with its whitewashed walls also met with her approval. 'Quite a transformation, I'm sure.' She paused for breath as I led the way up the spiral stairs. 'I believe it was very decrepit when the old gentleman lived here.'

In the bedroom she sighed. 'Such a lovely old four-poster. I know they are no longer fashionable. Piers insisted that we got rid of ours, so unhealthy those curtains, he said. But this does look comfortable, especially in such a draughty old room,' she said, looking in alarm at the old tapestries Olivia had resurrected to add an illusion of comfort and warmth—warmth and life, as they were never completely still, activated by cracks that let in air through the ancient stone walls.

At the door, she asked: 'Well, is there more to see?'

'There's a private chapel, long disused, but if you're interested . . .'

Puffing her way breathlessly up the remainder of the now steep and narrow stairs, interested she was, but not in the way I expected or felt. As I opened the door, the afternoon sunlight was streaming through the old stained-glass window, a narrow-arched slit high in the wall. It cast bright splashes of colour on to the stone floor where the altar had once stood.

I felt again that air of tranquillity and benediction.

'Quite churchlike,' remarked Freda at my side. 'But just a little creepy, don't you think?' And, looking round the rough-hewn walls: 'Perhaps a few pieces of elegant furniture would make all the difference. You could use it as a second bedroom.'

That was sacrilege, I thought, but said nothing.

She had noticed hanging on the wall below the window the crucifix that Wolf Rider had given me and on the raised floor the candle I had lit for Danny. 'Why, Rose, this is a surprise. After all these years and I never knew you were Roman Catholic.' She succeeded in making it sound like a particularly nasty and fatal disease.

'I am not,' I said, 'but my late husband was born in Ireland. He was brought up and educated by the nuns at the Sisters of St Anthony's Convent down the Pleasance.'

'You did not turn, then. That's a relief.' Pausing, she regarded me thoughtfully. 'But were you not afraid? I mean, mixed marriages can be most unfortunate, such a disaster socially too.'

'Ours was not so. We were very happy and we never felt threatened by how we believed. In fact, we could always see some good in both churches.'

Freda suppressed a sniff of disapproval and

260

a tightening of her lips indicated her feelings on the matter as without another word she headed down the stairs and out into the sunny garden. There she breathed what could only be interpreted as an audible sigh of relief at a narrow escape from Popery.

Tapping her foot on the path, frowning at a small group of weeds, she said: 'I really must get you some plants. Foley will bring them over. He has put down a few quick-growing trees and shrubs. They would be a great improvement, just what you need to shelter the back garden. They'll take away that bleak feeling—'

'You are very kind,' I said, following her out to where her carriage was waiting and thinking I really enjoyed my wild garden, likely to outwit the keenest gardener's attempts to tame it.

'Well, my dear, that was very nice. If you are absolutely sure you can't come to Duddingston, perhaps you'd come and have tea with me tomorrow at four. Meanwhile, I'll discuss plants with Foley.'

'Thank you. May I come on my bicycle?'

She frowned a little at that. 'If you wish. But I had thought to send the carriage round for you.'

I felt very happy that evening, with a book to read and Cat curled up in her basket at my feet. With time and patience I was sure she would graduate to sitting on my knee. Leaning back in my comfortable armchair, it was a pretty domestic thought. A glimpse of a world remote as paradise from my nomadic life in a savage land with Danny and its tragic ending.

Next day I cycled to Freda's to find that I was too early. Maggie, the maid, came to the front door looking cross and with a disapproving look at my means of transport, she said: 'The missus isna' back yet. She's awa' to the dressmaker's to have her new gowns fitted. Ye can come in an' wait, if ye like,' she added disagreeably as if that would put her to considerable personal inconvenience.

I declined her suggestion and, as the day was pleasantly warm, the garden was a preferable option. I could see Foley's head and shoulders at the far end emerging from a deep trench he was digging, with shrubs and small trees ready for planting.

I walked towards him. This was an excellent opportunity to discuss not gardens but something of vastly more interest: Molly Dunn. I was curious, for the newspaper's bland account revealed nothing of her character. No doubt Foley could fill in some details . . .

He heard my footsteps on the path. Straightening, he put up his hand to shade his eyes as I came out of the sun. He stepped back, startled for a moment.

'Good afternoon, Mr Foley.'

Maybe he wasn't used to Mrs Elliott's

friends passing the time of day with him. He touched his bonnet politely. 'Afternoon, ma'am.'

'Mrs Elliott says you might have some spare trees and shrubs for my garden.'

'That is so, ma'am. The mistress mentioned it and I'll gladly put some aside for you. We have more than enough. I'll come along and prepare the ground for them.'

'Thank you. I'll be grateful.' Preparing to put my waiting time to good purpose, I took a seat on the low brick wall supporting the cold frame, an excellent vantage point to oversee Peel Lodge. I realised chances of seeing Matthew Bolton emerge once more were remote indeed. Doubtless endless patience was required by those who investigated and solved murders where the hand of coincidence played a very small part indeed.

I just wished that the main suspect was not my friend's husband. However, my surveillance was not to be. Foley appeared from the greenhouse carrying a rather ornate garden chair.

'You'll be more comfortable sitting on this, ma'am,' he said and clambered back into the trench.

Thanking him, I remarked: 'You seem to enjoy your work, Mr Foley. Have you worked long for the Elliotts?'

Pushing back his bonnet, he scratched his forehead. 'Nigh on five year now.'

'Then you must have known poor Molly.'

'Aye, I did that. She came here straight from the workhouse when she was twelve,' he looked balefully in the direction of the house. 'She was right glad of a friendly face, I can tell you.'

His expression was an insight; it told me more than any words about how the Elliotts treated their staff.

Foley sighed. 'Such a bonny lass she was.' He looked at me. 'Right bonny complexion and lovely fair curly hair. Like yours, ma'am. Just a picture.'

Faintly embarrassed at such flattery, I asked hastily: 'Was she happy here, do you think?'

'Happy enough, happy as any of them,' he added darkly.

'She must have had friends among the other servants?'

'Nay. They were all too old for her.'

There was a moment of silence, before I said: 'Can you tell me something that rather worries me?'

'If I can, ma'am.'

'I'm curious to know why they allowed her to stay on alone in the house that weekend.'

He looked at me sadly. 'It's a holiday time for the staff when the master and mistress are away. But the lass had nowhere else to go. No family or friends like the others. No one'—he paused and pulled out a weed at the side of the trench—'but me. I live down Priestfield way but I couldn't take her there. Wouldn't be proper. I live alone since my father died and I'm not a married man.'

How lonely he sounded. Poor Foley. I wondered if anyone had ever loved him. And if when he was young he had loved someone and a shy man, too diffident to declare himself, his affection was not reciprocated. 'When did you last see her . . .' I forbore to add 'alive' but Foley understood.

'A few days afore . . . afore it happened.'

'Tell me, did she have a sweetheart?'

Foley bunched his fists. 'No, she did not. What chance had she in this place to meet young lads? They worked her like . . . like a slave.'

I smiled. 'That doesn't stop most girls, Mr Foley. There are always ways and means. Isn't that why the lower windows of the new villas have bars on them? Not to keep burglars out, I'm told, but to keep the maids in.'

He turned round, his face furious. 'She wasn't like that. She didn't like young men hanging around. She was very prim and proper about things like that.'

No young men, I thought. So that took care of the jealous swain. As for Foley, he sounded exactly like a stern father.

I wondered if he had heard about Wild Elk's death. It had been reported in the newspapers but perhaps Foley hadn't noticed, didn't—or couldn't—read. I certainly didn't

265

intend bringing it to his attention. He would hear eventually. That couldn't be avoided. It would be the talk of the local inns, if he frequented such places in his spare time. I wished he could have been spared such news. He would be dreadfully upset, having set his heart on the 'savage Indian' as her killer, to have to come to terms with the man being innocent.

I imagined the police wouldn't be too pleased either if he began tormenting them again, as Jack had told me, with his daily calls, his insistence that her murderer was still on the loose and why weren't they out looking for him?

He was digging again. And so was I, for information. 'When you found her that day, it must have been a dreadful shock, so awful for you?'

He turned to look at me, his eyes full of tears. With the back of his hand he brushed them away.

I felt terrible, reminding him so brutally of what had probably been the worst experience of his whole life.

He nodded slowly as if seeing it all again, laid aside his spade. 'I tried lifting her up to revive her. At first I thought the poor lass had just fainted. But she was cold. So cold. Like ice. I tried to warm her hands—then I knew she was dead.'

He had tried lifting her up. 'Was she

quite small?'

He stared at me. 'If you mean little, like yourself, ma'am, no. She was more like the mistress in size. In fact, she told me the mistress often handed down clothes she was done with.'

I thought about that. Foley was not more than average height, lean and wiry. I couldn't see him carrying someone the size of Freda Elliott, trying to get help. On the other hand, Matthew Bolton and his labourer friend were tall, strong-looking men.

'Was there evidence of a struggle?'

'A struggle. Of course there wasn't. He . . . he just crept up on her—that devil. She didn't stand a chance.'

'So there was no sign of any disturbance where it happened.'

He stared at me. 'Not a thing out of place. Everything was neat as a pin. Tidy—the way she always kept the kitchen. Proud of it, she was.'

I thought about that. A big strong lass like Molly should have put up a fight. 'Doesn't it strike you as rather strange?'

'What d'ye mean, strange?'

'Because if she didn't put up a struggle, don't you think it might be because this man she let into the kitchen, who then attacked her, was someone she knew?'

'Someone she knew?' He frowned. 'Why should it be someone she knew?'

'Don't you see, if it was a stranger, forcing his way into her kitchen, she would have picked up the nearest object to defend herself. A knife, a rolling pin. Kitchens are full of useful weapons in a tight spot and all near at hand.'

Foley's eyes widened slightly as if that thought had never occurred to him before, then he shook his head firmly. 'Course she didn't know him—it was that Indian done it!'

I couldn't tell him that the evidence proved it wasn't Wild Elk or that my conversation with Wolf Rider had indicated that the rest of Edinburgh beyond Queen's Park was out of bounds to his circus troop.

This talk with Foley left me more confused than ever and did nothing to help my own deductions.

And there it must rest. I could hardly go around interviewing the Elliotts' servants without causing undue comment and consternation.

But what Foley had told me didn't fit. I thought of Molly opening the door to a faceless man she knew, a man who had been a visitor to the house. 'Knowing her place', being polite as he made advances. Until it was too late. And Matthew Bolton's face furtively leaving Peel Lodge intruded. Was he Molly Dunn's murderer? Was he protecting someone else? I thought of that uncouth character lodging in his coachhouse. Was

Matthew being blackmailed into protecting him, shielding a brutal killer?

The law wouldn't see it that way and poor Alice would be even more distressed when her beloved Matthew went to prison as accessory to murder.

Perhaps I should let well alone, allow the murder of Molly Dunn to rest where it belonged: an unsolved case.

For I realised that the solution I had in mind, once it was proved beyond reasonable doubt, must break poor Alice's heart.

Chapter Twenty-Five

'Rose! My dear, I do apologise—'

Foley retreated to his digging again as Freda hurried across the garden.

'That dreadful woman—unspeakable. She actually kept me waiting thirty minutes for my fitting. Then she told me calm as you like that the evening gown wasn't ready. Such excuses, of course. She'd been ill and so had her baby. Four children under five years old, if you please—and an invalid husband with TB. Or so he claims—' As she spoke she led the way towards the house. 'How awful that Maggie left you out here with the gardener. I shall reprimand her severely—'

'No need,' I interrupted. 'It was my choice

and Foley was very helpful.'

'Really. I always find him exceptionally dull. You must bring out the best in him,' she said with a curious look: 'But then you always did, even as a girl. Everyone loved you at school. Especially the teachers. We were all quite envious,' she added with a little trill of laughter, her rather mocking look indicating that I wasn't to take my popularity too seriously.

That was the moment when I decided my childhood instincts about Freda had been right. I hated her snobbery, hated the thought that we were linked by birth into the same social class. We had nothing in common. After a wearisome hour of Freda airing names of all the famous and important people Piers knew and the hectic life of an MP's wife, I took my leave. Earlier than was strictly polite and on my feeblest of excuses, but I was beyond caring. Enough was enough!

However, I felt considerably better, my patience restored, when at the front gate I saw Nancy, Mrs Brook's young friend, pushing a pram in the direction of Peel Lodge. 'Mrs McQuinn,' she greeted me. 'I'm so glad to see you. I got the situation, thanks to you. I'm now nanny to wee George here.'

Pausing, she drew back the covers to let me see his sleeping face. 'Isn't he gorgeous? He's so good, too. I'm so grateful to you, Mrs McQuinn. I came for the interview and Mrs

Harding wanted me the very next day. She loves wee George. Her sister died when he was born, now her man has remarried and wants his bairn back. Such a nice lady, too. Giving me every Sunday off—not many nannies get more than a day off a month. So I'm lucky.'

She looked pretty and animated, wholesome as a breath of mountain air, after my recent visit to the house next door. I suspected her conversation would be vastly more interesting as well.

When I suggested she visit me some afternoon she was delighted. Explaining how to get to the Tower, I added: 'It's rather far for you.'

'Not at all. I'm used to walking and I'll bring wee George, if you don't mind.' I didn't and she smiled. 'I'd love to see your old tower. I like old buildings and churches. History was my best subject at school. I wanted to be a teacher, but it wasn't to be.' She added sadly.

As she was leaving, I said: 'Call me when you're passing—any time, I'm mostly at home—'

I left her, thinking that at least Matthew was cleared of fathering an illegitimate child.

A nearby church clock struck five and on impulse, as I was only ten minutes away from the Boitons' house, I decided to call on Alice. It didn't cause me any anxiety that such informality was frowned upon and leaving calling cards was the polite rule expected in Edinburgh society.

Even as I told myself that Alice and I were old friends, I knew the purpose of my visit was to see Matthew who arrived home each day, according to Alice, at five o'clock prompt. I needed urgently to see him in his domestic surroundings. 'Catch him off his guard,' whispered my alter ego, the investigator. Pappa had told me long ago that there was much to be gained by observation and deduction when people—especially suspects— were least prepared for a visit.

I was in luck. Alice was at home and pleased to see me. I had a story all prepared. There was a summer bazaar in one of the Newington churches (information obtained from a quick look at a poster on my way from Saville Grange). 'I wondered if we might go together.'

'That would be delightful, Rose. Friday would be better as Matthew often stays late in his office on Fridays. He likes to prepare his court cases for the week ahead, you know. It's his busy time just now—'

I listened amazed and thought that business must have improved greatly since my recent visit to the offices of Bolton and Bolton.

'He came home early today. He's in the study,' she whispered, looking across the hall. 'He has a visitor, an old friend.'

At that the study door opened. I heard

272

voices, one of them was faintly familiar. I wondered for a moment if Matthew's uncouth friend from the coachhouse had been elevated into polite society.

But the man who emerged could not, by the greatest stretch of imagination, have been the rough labourer I had briefly encountered in the coachhouse.

Over six feet tall, very thin with an apostle's face and a beard, he was very well dressed. I had seen him before. 'Thomas Carless. You met at our wedding, Rose.'

This was the man Vince had pointed out to me in the Café Royale, known to sail close to the wind in his business dealings. Was Alice ignorant of his reputation?

Matthew was watching me narrowly. When our eyes met he was polite, he smiled a lot, but there was something reserved and evasive in his manner. As if he were greeting a client whom he didn't entirely trust, and who might turn out to be difficult and even dangerous.

He was nervous, sweating slightly. Was I mistaken? Was it his recent interview with this old friend Carless and not myself that had disconcerted him? His countenance cleared a little when the maid announced that 'Mr Carless's carriage has arrived'.

Shortly afterwards Matthew joined us in the drawing-room, his manner noticeably more relaxed, almost normal in the circumstances, in keeping with a husband politely receiving an old friend of his wife's, whom he hardly knew at all. I doubted whether that stolen kiss of long ago lay heavy on his conscience.

'Alice tells me you have recently returned from America. If you are interested in Robert Louis Stevenson, I have a copy of his book, Across the Plains, which might appeal to you.'

When I said I had bought a copy he said: 'It is quite excellent. I have several of his novels, Treasure Island, Kidnapped—'

'Matthew knew him personally,' Alice put in proudly. 'They studied law together.'

'He wasn't a close friend, Alice,' said her husband sternly.

'Of course not, dear. I realise that he was something of a tearaway, quite unconventional despite his upbringing. But then people who write often are strange,' she added, sounding disappointed that they could not claim the now famous author as a close friend.

Glad of this chance to pursue a common interest in books, Matthew said: 'Has Alice shown you our library yet?'

She hadn't and rather proudly he led the way across the panelled hall into a large room with shelves on all four walls, from floor to ceiling. Most of them were packed with books and hardly needed the modest explanation: 'I have a fairly good collection.'

'Fairly good!' exclaimed Alice good-humouredly. 'There are books everywhere. Old, dusty volumes no one ever opens.'

'At least you don't have the dusting of them,' was the sharp retort and to me: 'My wife has no head for heights.'

Alice shuddered. 'Even those library steps make me feel giddy.'

I felt she would have liked to expand upon this unfortunate disability but Matthew, impatient at the interruption, turned his back on her and, with a smile for me, went on: 'I gather you are something of a reader, so do feel free to borrow anything that takes your interest.'

'You are very kind.'

The chiming clock reminded Alice that she was expecting two ladies from the Women's Guild to discuss the autumn programme. 'They are staying to supper, since Matthew has another engagement. Perhaps you would care to join us, Rose.'

I declined the invitation. The prospect of two worthy ladies possibly of Freda's calibre, I thought uncharitably, would be too much in one day even for my strong constitution.

While we were talking, Matthew went into his study and emerged with several letters which he put on the hall table.

'If they are ready for the mail, there is a box at the end of the street,' I said.

'Maggie will take them. It is quite a walk.'

'But I have my bicycle.'

'Very well. And thank you.' As he handed them to me I noticed that his hands were dirty and I wondered if he had been indulging in a little light weeding and had not had time to wash his hands before his visitor arrived.

Alice kissed my cheek and, after some argument about a meeting place, we agreed to meet inside the church hall.

I had my own reasons for insisting. For my plan to succeed it was necessary to include my bicycle.

I was curious enough to read the addresses on the three letters before dropping them into the postbox. None of then meant anything to me or seemed of any significance to the purpose I had in mind and retaining them might prove embarrassing.

But by the time I had made my way back to the Tower, Matthew's grimy fingernails had triggered off the wild course of action I had been considering, lurking at the back of my mind ever since Wild Elk's death.

*   *   *

When I pushed my bicycle along the path towards the now empty stable, Thane was waiting for me.

Delighted to see him again, I hugged him and he was real enough to give my face a good wash. Thrusting firmly aside nonsense about a vengeful spirit who had pursued Wild Elk to his death, I stroked his head.

He looked pleased, that ridiculous almost

276

human grin. He was a dog, only a dog. Not a phantom, not magical nor malevolent. Somehow he had found his way to Arthur's Seat. That silky coat was too well groomed to belong to a stray. Some day an owner would turn up and reclaim him. That I must believe; I mustn't get too attached to him.

The fact that no one else saw him, that he was never around when I had a visitor at the Tower, was because he didn't wish to be seen. Doubtless he had his own canine reasons for being wary of humans.

Thane was a lost dog who had come into my life by chance when I needed him most. And that was coincidence, or providence, or what you will. Every other assumption based on what Chief Wolf Rider had told me was complete and absolute rubbish, I told myself, looking at Thane lying so peacefully by kitchen fire.

I just wished I could believe it.

Chapter Twenty-Six

Next morning, while I was having breakfast, Foley arrived with the carter, unloaded saplings and shrubs plus a large spade.

Freda had been very kind. If her generous contribution took root, survived the battle with the harsh elements and exposure of

Arthur's Seat, then the Tower would be protected by an impressive small wood.

I took Foley out some bread and cheese, which he received gratefully, offering further suggestions about putting down a winter vegetable patch. This discourse was interrupted by the arrival of Jack, in uniform today, striding across the garden. Acknowledging Foley by name and a cheery greeting, he said: 'Shall we go indoors, Rose? I have some important information for you.'

We left Foley staring after us, obviously impressed and naturally curious about what a policeman was doing at the Tower before nine in the morning.

Emptying the teapot for Jack, as he sat at the kitchen table, I said: 'So you know Foley too. Small world, isn't it.'

He grinned. 'We frequent the same public house in Duddingston. I have an occasional game of cards with him and his cronies.' Declining my offer of bread and cheese, he added: 'I'm on my way to the Central Office and I thought you'd be interested to know that you were right. Howe is guilty. He murdered his wife. Wild Elk's fingerprints are nowhere in the vicinity or near where Daisy was strangled.'

Pausing, he regarded me thoughtfully. 'Nor on the belt he allegedly strangled her with. However, there are plenty of Howe's own prints and others, which I assume to be yours.'

'Would you like to check?'

He laughed. 'You're not serious?'

'I am indeed. My last husband was obsessed by the discovery that fingerprints could be used in solving crimes. I saw Galton's book in Thin's. I bought it for him once.'

'Have you read it by any chance?' Jack asked eagerly. When I said no, he went on: 'It's a fascinating work. There was a great deal of scepticism but now it has taken on and is in regular use. It isn't all that new, really. The ancient Chinese used thumb impressions to seal documents and in our own century they were used in India to identify illiterate prisoners. However, it wasn't until 1880 that a Scots physician, Dr Henry Faulds, came up with the theory that each individual's fingerprints were unique and might offer a possible method of personal identification . . .'

Realising that fingerprints had cleared Wild Elk of Daisy Howe's murder I said: 'Did they fingerprint the kitchen at Saville Grange after Molly Dunn's murder?'

Jack nodded. 'They did indeed. There were prints all over—and all pretty useless since they were mainly of servants, none of whom had been present at the time. As well as Foley's, of course, since he had discovered the body. Mrs Elliott objected strongly to having her premises—and her servants—fingerprinted.' He shook his head. 'She made a great fuss about the mess involved, threatened to have her husband bring it up in the House.'

Listening to him gave me an idea. 'Can I ask you a great favour?'

Jack smiled. 'Anything.'

'Don't say that until you know what it is— would you check some fingerprints for me?'

He grinned. 'Some sort of a game, is that it, Rose?'

'Something of the sort.' A grim game, but exactly what I had in mind.

* * *

I met Alice as arranged at the bazaar and bought a crocheted table centre and a pretty shawl for Mrs Brook.

Alice was choosing romances from the bric-a-brac stall. 'I can recommend this author, Rose. Her love stories are so poignant and quite tearful,' she added with a sigh. 'Some for you?'

I declined that pleasure but this discussion gave me another idea. 'I would very much like to take up Matthew's offer. I'm very keen to read some Walter Scott again.'

'Of course! Come home with me and you can help yourself.'

Obligingly I pushed my bicycle along and she didn't seem to mind that this received occasional stares. She was being very brave today about showing that I was her friend and she didn't care a fig for middle-class conventions.

In the library I hoped I had remembered correctly that Scott's leather-bound works were on a high bookshelf. 'Up there, Alice. If I may borrow Old Mortality please.'

She laughed. 'Really? Surely you don't want to read such a dull book.' And, patting her recent acquisition of romances, she said: 'Wouldn't you rather have one of these?'

'Thank you, Alice. I may take up your offer in due course. I take it you don't read Sir Walter.'

'Never! I prefer something lighter to put me to sleep.' She sighed. 'The books you see here are all Matthew's—they are first editions. He's an avid reader. He's read some of them several times. Amazing!'

As she spoke, she wheeled the library steps into position and regarded the top shelf with some hesitation.

'I wonder . . . I hate going up there.' She shuddered. 'Heights make me so light-headed. Would you mind, Rose?'

That suited my purpose excellently. Climbing the steps, I took down the volume very gingerly and popped it into my basket. Shopping baskets for ladies might be frowned upon in elegant shops like Jenners, but they were considered right and proper for ladies at church bazaars without their maids in attendance.

I watched the clock anxiously as Alice chattered happily, unaware of my lack of concentration. I had to be away before there was any chance of meeting Matthew, wending his way homeward. At last I made my escape, with Alice saying that I must come to dinner with them both one evening soon. At the front door she whispered anxiously: 'Have you got any news for me yet?'

I smiled reassuringly. 'Only that I'm fairly certain Matthew isn't having an affair with Lily Harding.'

She clasped her hands together. 'Oh, Rose, you've made me so happy.'

I didn't like to add that her husband might be guilty of something much more terrible, so before she could ask any more questions I mounted my bicycle and rode off.

Sure I was no longer visible from the front door, I quickly turned down the back lane and, praying that the garden door was unlocked as usual, a moment later I was once again outside the coachhouse.

I tapped on the door, hoping that Matthew's sinister friend was not already in residence. If so my plan would be ruined. There was no reply and with a sigh of relief I lifted the latch. The interior was grim and gloomy as ever but I did not intend to linger. I looked around. Ah, an empty bottle. The very thing. A moment later, wrapped in my handkerchief, it was safely stored in the bicycle basket and I made my way home, exceedingly pleased with the day's work. All I had to do was wait patiently for Jack to arrive the next day.

*   *   *

I felt very happy and confident as I took my journal out on the hill, sketched the Tower, to draw it as it looked when I first came to live here. Before all those trees and shrubs rendered it invisible from higher up the hill side.

My other reason was that such concentration was the perfect activity to calm my anxious thoughts about the future.

Thane found me sitting on a boulder. He greeted me with his usual animation and flopped down on the ground beside me.

Comforted by his presence and our usual companionable silence, when it was too dark to continue drawing our ways parted. He declined to return to the Tower and loped away back up the hill. I wondered about his world, what fascinations existed that no human would ever see or understand.

*   *   *

It had rained heavily during the night but the mist had cleared and a thin watery sun was with us once more when Jack arrived that afternoon.

I put the book and the bottle before him. 'Let's see you work one of your miracles of detection,' I said.

He regarded me solemnly. 'This is just a joke, Rose.'

I smiled. 'A harmless game, something to impress one of my friends.'

'Very well,' he said and I watched him as he dusted the book cover and the bottle with very fine black dust and, like magic, the fingerprints became clearly visible. The thumb was strongest, the four fingers tended to blur.

By using a magnifying hand lens, a few minutes later I knew I was right, that thrill of pleasure, the delight in having my suspicions confirmed.

I might have confided in Jack then and there, but fate deemed otherwise.

A ring at the door and I answered it to Nancy, with wee George in the pram. 'I was walking past the circus, I wanted to have a look at it and when I knew I was quite near . . .' she said.

I cut her apologies short. 'Do come in, Nancy. It's lovely to see you.'

Jack was looking out of the parlour window, his back to us.

'Oh, Mrs McQuinn, I'm sorry. You have a visitor.'

Jack turned round. 'Nancy—Nancy Craig—isn't it?'

'Jack Macmerry—'

The next moment the pair were hugging each other, laughing delightedly. Suddenly they remembered me.

Still holding Nancy's hand, Jack said: 'This is wonderful. Nancy and I knew each other long ago. We were next-door neighbours in Duddingston.'

Pausing, he looked at her fondly. 'We were childhood sweethearts, weren't we?' he said shyly.

Nancy regarded him gently, eyes bright, as if she too remembered. Then she shook her head, said sadly: 'We moved away. Things changed and I never expected to see Jack again.'

'Nor I you, Nancy.' Jack seized the opportunity to give her another hug.

'I heard you had gone into the police.'

'I heard you were working in Fife.'

'And now meeting again like this.'

'It's wonderful.'

I looked at them. Wonderful for them, I thought.

The conversation over a cup of tea belonged to things past and I was no part of it.

Listening and observing their closeness, I felt envious. I had been guilty of seeing Jack Macmerry as part of my new life, perhaps even of my future. Once again, I thought sadly, I had been wrong.

Was I witnessing a lovers' meeting destined

for a happy ending, sentimental as any in Alice's romantic novels?

Later, watching them walk away down the road together, if I were to be perfectly honest, I experienced another emotion. Once I had a husband, had been loved. And I knew the lack of that passionate lover. My body cried out for the need of a man to hold me in his arms again.

Whether I wanted him for life or just a passing hour, Jack could have fulfilled that role.

And now I knew I was jealous.

He never looked back. The two were absorbed in each other and I was forgotten.

I went inside and closed the door, doubting whether there would be any more invitations to walk in Princes Street Gardens, or to meet his parents.

At least not for me.

They were well suited, an ideal couple. Jack with his new promotion, ready to marry. And Nancy would be the perfect wife and mother of his children. Of that I had no doubts at all.

But for now, I had other dangerous business on hand. It was time to confront Matthew Bolton.

Chapter Twenty-Seven

It was half past three, and there was still time to tackle Matthew and to get this unpleasant business over with today.

Where was this confrontation to take place? I could go into the High Street to the office of Bolton and Bolton, but Matthew was a devious character and the chances of finding that this was one of his rare days at his desk were not encouraging, despite what Alice had told me at the bazaar while we having tea.

This was her evening of helping in the soup kitchen for the poor of the parish and, as she was never home until eight, poor Matthew would have to make do with a cold collation. 'He is very patient,' she told me.

With Alice out of the way, I could go to the house, say I had an appointment with Mr Bolton. And risk being turned away by the maid. And should she mention it to her mistress, wouldn't Alice think that odd?

So left with the coachhouse as the only alternative to catch Matthew on his way home, I made my decision.

It was a sordid place to have to spend time waiting, my mind full of misgivings, but as the church clock struck the half-hour, my patience was rewarded by the sound of footsteps outside.

The door opened and the rough-looking labourer strode in.

Blinded by the sunlight outside, he didn't see me at first. The interior was dark, my presence concealed by the shadows.

With the tired sigh of an exhausted man, he began to remove the scarf about his chin and his bonnet. Suddenly he knew he was not alone. Turning sharply, his eyes widened and he shouted hoarsely: 'What do you think you're doing, sneaking in here? Get out of here,' he added, his fist raised angrily.

I stepped forward. 'It's no use. The game's up.'

'What are you talking about?' he demanded. 'Get out of here—at once—or I'll tell the master—'

As if he hadn't interrupted, I went on: 'I think not. The game's up, Matthew, for you and your eccentric friend. Except that there isn't any friend, never has been, eccentric or otherwise, living in this vile place.' I shook my head. 'No mysterious friend from the past to whom you owe a debt of honour.'

He groaned as I added: 'It's always been just Matthew Bolton, playing a dramatic role, hasn't it?'

Defeated, he sank down on to the rickety chair. 'And how did you find out?' he gasped.

'By this,' I produced Jack's sheet of paper. 'These fingerprints at the top are from one of your novels, which I took the liberty of borrowing from your library. Underneath are prints from an empty bottle which I found lying on the floor here.'

'So—'

'So, if you look closely you'll observe that the two sets of prints are identical. They indicate without any doubt that there is only one man—yourself.'

He was staring at the prints, ready, I was sure, to protest, to question the accuracy of such evidence.

'Take them to the door, examine them properly in daylight,' I said.

He shook his head, but made no move.

'Well, perhaps you'd like to tell me instead just what is going on, Matthew.'

'Does Alice know about this?' he demanded.

'No one but us.'

He sighed. 'Thank God for that. It's nothing illegal, you know.'

'I believe you.'

He groaned again, put a hand to his head. 'I have no idea what your part is in all this, what it can possibly have to do with you. But all I can tell you is that you are almost too late with your fingerprints.' He looked up at me. 'The charade, the game I have been playing for three months, is almost over. Just two more days, that is all I needed to complete it.'

He paused suddenly, demanded sharply: 'Did he put you on to it?'

'Thomas Carless, you mean? No.'

'But you do know him. Are you working for him?'

'No, Matthew. I'm working, if you might call it that—the term I use is investigating—at your wife's request.'

His eyes widened at that. 'For Alice? I don't believe you. She has no idea. I've been at great pains to keep it from her.'

'At such pains that she believes you are having an affair with another woman. Lily Harding to be precise.'

'Lily Harding!' he exploded. 'I hardly know the woman. I saw her after we moved from Peel House, to help her sort out her finances, and I've paid her several visits lately on legal matters. She wants to adopt her late sister's baby, but since her brother-in-law has recently remarried he now wishes to reclaim his son.'

'Surely you could have told all this to Alice? She would have been interested and sympathetic.'

'Interested I dare say. But sympathetic, no! Mrs Harding has long been a sore point between us. No doubt it relates to our change of fortunes and having to sacrifice Peel House to the Hardings. Even since the poor woman was widowed Alice has been quite irrationally jealous. She's got it into her head that Mrs Harding is some sort of a femme fatale and I've learned, in the interests of a peaceful life, to avoid mentioning her name.'

Especially with wee George, I thought. The baby even I suspected might have been fathered by Matthew.

He frowned. 'Who told you of my visits to Peel Lodge?'

'You were seen recently by your former next-door neighbour, Freda Elliott, who happens to be an old acquaintance of mine—and Alice's.'

'I still don't understand why Alice involved you in this.'

'Because, Matthew, she loves you and she's heartbroken by your current strange behaviour. Certain that you have changed and no longer love her. When we met again recently she was quite desperate. She had to tell someone and, as we were once close friends, she pleaded with me to try to find out what was going on.'

'For pity's sake—spying on me, was that it?' he said indignantly.

'It's called investigating in polite society, Matthew.'

He shook his head. 'I expect I have changed lately. I've been under tremendous pressure, but I've never ceased to love her. It's a long story, Rose. How much of it do you know already?'

'Not a great deal and that only guesswork, I'm afraid. By piecing together information about your past.'

'My past?'

'Your love of adventure, how you wanted to be an explorer and how you rebelled against going into the firm.'

'I still hate it, you know.'

'I also knew from my stepbrother that you were a great climber, here in Scotland and in the Alps. Then one day I saw someone very like your bogus labouring friend on a scaffolding in the Pleasance.'

He grimaced. 'I saw you that day, looking straight up at me when the lads were all whistling. I was fairly sure that you didn't recognise me, though.' And, with a grim smile: 'Well done, Rose. I think it's you who should be in the legal profession, not me,' he added bitterly, 'putting all these odd facts together and coming up with a solution.'

'I haven't quite reached that yet. All these facts, as you call them, were strange enough but the question remains, why did you take on this ridiculous charade in the first place?'

I gave him a moment to reply, before asking gently: 'Do I take it that you are being blackmailed, Matthew?'

He laughed. 'Indeed I am not. You are quite wrong about that. The correct answer is simply money. Steeplejacks are in great demand, since it's highly dangerous work. As you'll realise from the casualties you read about in the newspapers, there is a lot of money to be made by skilled climbers with good heads for heights.' He sighed. 'Truth is,

I've always been a gambler. I can't help it or cure it and we are in desperate need of money. Although Alice hasn't the slightest idea, I might have been faced with bankruptcy and prison, if I hadn't met my old college chum, Thomas Carless, again at my club one night.

'Thomas is a great gambler, always was, so when he heard my story, he bet me a thousand guineas that I couldn't work for three months as a steeplejack and keep it secret from everyone, including my firm, which was the hardest part of all. And my wife.'

His eyes brightened. 'It was a challenge and, dammit, one I enjoyed and was certain I could win. It was going very well, except that I was so tired by the end of the day that I was short-tempered and neglecting poor Alice.'

'Couldn't you have told her? She would have understood—'

'Which shows just how well you know Alice. She would have been appalled. She has a terrible fear of heights—witness those library steps the other day. And she's always hated me going climbing. I had to promise to abandon it when we married. The idea that her husband, a middle-aged man, was doing a dangerous job every day, perched on high scaffolding in all weathers, would have sent her into terminal vapours.'

He smiled wryly. 'There is another reason, too, which probably has not occurred to you.

What would the neighbours think if they found out that Matthew Bolton was working as a common labourer?' Sadly, he shook his head. 'No, Rose. She would never have forgiven me for that, for the scandal and the gossip. We would never have lifted our heads again, a laughing stock, the outcasts of our social circle.'

'So that was why you invented the old friend in the coachhouse, the tramp who had fallen on bad times. A bit tenuous, wasn't it?'

He shrugged. 'It was the only convenient way I could change into my labouring garb each day and back again into more gentlemanly wear when I returned home every evening. Don't you see, I had to have a safe place where I was unlikely to be disturbed—or observed.'

I pointed to the wooden box. 'There lies the real Matthew Bolton.'

He nodded and smiled. 'Correct. I have to hand it to you, Rose, you've been very clever. I expect it's your upbringing, living in a policeman's house.'

'Maybe so. But you scared the life out of me at our first encounter here. You were a very convincing labourer. I almost gave up that day you yelled at me. You should have been an actor—'

He laughed. 'You've guessed it. Another of my unfulfilled ambitions. A pity we have only one life to live.' And then, soberly: 'I was even more scared than you were. I could see the whole charade falling to pieces, my hard-won wages and Carless's thousand guineas vanishing into dust.'

'Even without the fingerprints, your hands were too elegant for a workman, although your nails were dirty when we spoke in the library the other day.'

'That was always a problem. Steeplejacking is dirty work and, although I could wash my face and hands reasonably, I needed hot water and a brush to clean them after some of the dirtier work.'

'What are you going to do now?' I asked.

He straightened his shoulders. 'Tell Alice, confess all and throw myself on her mercy. And then, whatever she says, I must finish the job.' He looked at me. 'Trouble is, Rose, I shall miss it when I'm sitting safely back behind a desk again. It's been a challenge and has renewed my taste for danger. There is something so . . . exhilerating about being way up there above the city, almost like being back in the mountains again,' he added wistfully. Then, taking my hand: 'If you'll forgive the grime, Rose, I hope now we can be friends, that we will laugh—some day, with Alice when the shock has worn off—about this escapade.'

I wasn't too hopeful about that and, leaving him to change back into Matthew Bolton and tell his wife the whole story, I would have given much to be a fly on the wall.

As I returned to the Tower I was glad that I had been wrong about Matthew, all those fears that he had killed Molly Dunn because she was blackmailing him over Lily Harding.

Such flights of fancy. But the frightening fact remained. Even if the police were ready to close the case and mark it 'unsolved', someone had killed her.

And that faceless 'someone' was still at large.

Chapter Twenty-Eight

Thane was in the garden when I reached home. He was investigating Foley's trench and the plants that lay alongside.

It was a beautiful, soft, calm summer evening, an unseen army of insects buzzing in the gorse bushes, a pair of hawks hovering on the summit of Arthur's Seat.

As I sat on the wall with Thane at my feet, my hand on his head, I felt at peace with the world and quite proud of myself. I could hardly wait until tomorrow to see Jack again and tell him of the successful experiment with the fingerprints. My first case!

At that moment I believed I would be ready

to congratulate him even if he told me he was wildly in love with Nancy and that he intended to marry her.

I had survived worse things and, considering what I had lived through during the last two years, another disappointment would hardly seem a major catastrophe.

Thane was oddly restless, though. He wasn't sharing my feeling of peace and kept getting up, loping across the garden, staring up at the hill. On any other face but a dog's his expression could have been described as puzzled and anxious.

I guessed there was something in the wind that night beyond my human ken. Could it be the restless hovering birds of prey reminding him he hadn't eaten for some time?

I patted his head. 'What's wrong? Are you hungry? Is that it? Are they hinting there's food ready for the picking?'

He turned his head on one side, giving me his wise look. And then, with that oddly human grin, he jumped the wall and loped away up the hill.

I stayed outside until the last of the sunset faded over the Pentland Hills, then I went inside and lit the lamps. I fed Cat and, taking up my book, I thought about tomorrow.

Perhaps it was because the mystery of Matthew Bolton was solved that I had no positive plan. Suddenly there seemed no future, as if everything had ceased.

This was my first case. Perhaps it was a normal reaction after the day's excitement and when I had established myself as a professional investigator I would get used to it.

A noise alerted me. Was it Thane returned, his appetite satisfied? Opening the door I met only blackness. The moon would rise later but at the moment nothing separated Arthur's Seat from the horizon. The outline of hill and sky were one.

I decided I was quite tired after all and was on my way up to bed when there was a sharp rap on the kitchen door.

Jack, I thought excitedly. An unexpected visit but very welcome considering my feelings about him at that moment.

I opened the door to Foley—a very different Foley from the gardener in his rough clothes. This Foley had smartened up, wearing a suit and cloth cap, and smelling strongly of ale. That didn't bother me, I was used to men smelling of drink. He worked hard and had doubtless been celebrating his one well-earned evening off.

'Good evening, ma'am,' he said, tipping his cap. 'I wonder if you've had a chance to look at the plants I left—to approve of them, like . . . They're ready to go into the trench.'

'Heavens, Foley, you can't be gardening at this hour of the night.'

'Correct, ma'am. I'm on my way back from

the Sheep's Heid, down the road. I saw the light was still on and thought I'd better warn you.'

'Warn me? What about?'

'I don't want you falling into that trench I've dug.'

He must be drunker than I first imagined, I thought, and said: 'I'm aware of the trench, I was in the garden when you were digging, when Sergeant Macmerry arrived—'

'Oh, aye, the policeman. I ken him fine. We play cards together.' His rather contemptuous laugh hinted that he was a better player than Jack. Suddenly he squinted past into the kitchen, as if he thought Jack might still be around. 'It's a nice old place you have here. I often came past in the old days, that would be when you were a wee lass at Sheridan Place. I used to wonder what it would be like inside,' he added giving me a hard look.

I let that slide. I certainly wasn't taking any broad hints, suspecting already that once inside the house he might be difficult to get out again.

'Shh.' He looked over his shoulder, held up his hand for silence. 'Did you hear something?'

'No.'

'You must have heard it. I did!' And so speaking, he brushed past me and before I could protest he was in the kitchen. He looked around for a moment, then said: 'Mrs

McQuinn—I'm being followed. You see, I know who killed that poor lass at Saville Grange.'

'You do?'

That pleased him. 'I knew you'd be interested, the way you talked to me about her when you were visiting the mistress.'

'Yes,' I said vaguely, wanting to get him to the point. 'And now you've found out who killed her.'

'Oh, aye, I ken him well.' He chortled and, without waiting to be invited, sat down at the table. Looking across, he wagged an unsteady finger at me.

I remained standing. 'Suppose you tell me then,' I said coldly. I didn't like the way he was making himself at home, sprawled across my table. He was very drunk and I was pretty certain he knew nothing about Molly Dunn's killer and was using that to get into the Tower. My patience was growing thin. I just wanted him out, as quickly as possible. 'Why don't you tell me tomorrow?'

He thumped his hands on the table. 'No, I want to tell you now! Don't you want to know? You were curious enough before.'

His suddenly aggressive attitude infuriated me. But perhaps it was better to humour him.

He didn't know what to make of my silence. 'Have a guess!'

I shook my head. 'I haven't the slightest idea.'

That didn't please him. 'They're saying it wasn't that savage bastard after all. The lads in the pub were saying they read in the papers that he didn't do in that circus wife either, Rosie.'

Rosie indeed! I felt angry at this liberty. No one—not even my own family, except Pappa—ever called me that. 'I think it's time you went home, Mr Foley,' I said, emphasising the 'Mr'.

Elbows on the table, he glared at me. There was no longer anything servile about this Foley. 'Why don't you listen to what I'm saying?'

Another thump of his fist that rattled the vase of wild flowers. It rattled the last of my patience too. 'Very well, tell me what you have to. Then will you please go.'

'Ah, that all depends.' Another sly look and something else that I couldn't quite define.

'Depends on what?' I asked shortly.

'On whether you're going to be nice to me—'

'Nice to you!' I was shocked. I could hardly believe my ears. The cheek of the man!

The table was between me and the door. With as much dignity as I could summon, I walked swiftly towards it. But he was there before me, leaning with his back firmly against it.

'I've had enough, Foley. Will you please get out of here. Go—now!' And turning, I tried to raise the latch.

I wasn't prepared for him to grab my arm, his face peering into mine. 'Not before you listen to me. Ah, don't be like this, Rosie,' he pleaded. 'You must ken I always liked you, even at Sheridan Place, when you was a wee lassie. Right bonny you were then, still are.'

He raised a hand to touch my hair and I ducked out of the way. That made him furious. 'You're just like her, aren't you. I thought you'd be different, being married—used to men—and all that.' Another glare. 'This is the way she went on that night. Whenever I wanted her to be nice to me, she'd push me aside—as if I was dirt. Just like you. Well, she did it once too often—'

I stared at him. I was rooted to the spot as suddenly I realised who 'she' was. Sickened, I knew what he had wanted me to listen to, what he was telling me. 'You killed her. It was you, wasn't it? Oh, my God.'

He made another grab at me, seized my head between his hands and tried to kiss me. I struggled but my back was against the door. He was a strong man, his body hard against me. I could smell the sweat on him, the smell of sex.

Oh, dear God. For a moment I panicked, knowing what he intended. Then I remembered the way saloon ladies dealt with this situation. I raised my knee, thrust it hard into his groin.

He gave a yell, clutched himself, doubled

302

up and let me go.

That was all I needed. I opened the door and raced out into the black night.

But where was I to go?

Aware of my terrible peril, I thought of the hill. There I was on good ground. I was used to the paths, sure I could outrun him. And I remembered the drunken tinkers.

But there was no Thane to save me now. Such miracles don't happen twice.

Darkness was my enemy. I got as far as the trench by the garden wall, began to climb but one of the stones was loose and I stumbled.

'Got you now, you bitch. There's your grave all dug ready, Rosie, dear,' he yelled. There was something raised in his hand.

The spade.

I ducked and slipped, screaming, into the deep trench. As I tried to scramble out, he hit me hard.

I fell back, stunned.

There was soil on my face, in my eyes and hair.

'Help me—please,' I sobbed.

He was shovelling in the earth as fast as he could.

I was being buried alive.

I was suffocating, struggling to free my arms, to clamber out, grasp something solid. But there was nothing, nothing but crumbling soil. Falling on me . . .

A faint sound growing louder far above me.

Then silence.

*   *   *

I opened my eyes to a biblical scene of Pharaoh's daughter rescuing baby Moses. His basket was moving gently in the bulrushes. Was this what it was to be dead?

A shadow moved, came between me and the tapestry. I was lying on my bed in the Tower, with Jack bending over me, wiping my face clear of soil with a towel. My jaw ached where Foley had hit me and the grave smell of wet earth was everywhere. In my nose, my mouth. I began to sneeze and choke, unable to breathe properly.

'There, there, Rose. You're safe now,' said Jack.

I tried to sit up and the room whirled round.

'Steady on. You had a nasty shock—'

'Thank God you got there in time,' I whispered. 'Where's Foley? He told me he killed that girl.'

'Did he now? And he meant you to go the same way,' he said grimly. 'We've been watching him for a while now. You know the rules—when it wasn't the Indian lad, there was only one other logical person it could be. There were plenty of clues, especially the way he insisted we find her killer. The old story of returning to the scene of the crime. A touch of insanity—'

I sat up. 'I'd love a cup of tea, Jack.'

He insisted on carrying me down to the kitchen as if I were fragile and might break into tiny pieces. At the table I watched him brew the tea from the kettle already boiled for water to wash the soil off me.

'Have you arrested him?'

'He ran off after that dog attacked him, but he won't get far.'

'What dog?'

He grinned. 'Your deerhound, I suspect.'

'How . . .'

He put the cup between my trembling hands. 'Drink up and I'll tell you. There was no way we could prove Foley killed Molly Dunn, but we knew he drank a lot at weekends. Then one of the lads in plain clothes who lives nearby was having a drink with him and encouraged him to talk, especially as he had been bragging to his cronies that anyone could get away with murder if they were clever enough to fool the police. He'd also said that lasses like Molly Dunn got what was coming to them.' Jack shook his head. 'This didn't fit the grieving Foley who pounded into the Central Office every other day.'

He studied me, frowning. 'When I came into the garden today he was digging that trench. You weren't aware of it, but he was watching you. With a look any man kens fine as lust. I realised that our humble gardener fancied you a lot. When I went to the pub tonight he was drinking heavily so I decided to follow him. Instead of heading home to Priestfield, he set off across the hill. It was dark, I lost him and lost my way into the bargain. My one thought was to get to you. I had this awful feeling that you were in danger. And then, as I stumbled about, a very odd thing happened.'

He looked at me. 'A big dog, your deerhound, appeared. He ran up to me, stopped, ran a few steps ahead, stopped again. Like a dog who wants some fun, wants you to throw sticks for him. But the direction he was heading was downhill, towards the Tower. I ran as fast as I could, but he got there first and by the time I jumped over the wall he had Foley on the ground. I called him off. He just lookcd at me, wagged his tail as if to say: well, I've got your man for you. Then he loped away back up the hill. I was going after Foley when I heard a groan from the trench, saw a shape half covered with soil—' He shuddered. 'Dear God, Rose, I'll never forget that moment. I thought I was too late. That you were dead. That devil was burying you alive. Oh, Rose—' With a stifled sob he took me into his arms and held me. 'I thought I'd lost you.'

His kisses were real enough to convince me, but I said shyly as I came up for breath: 'I

306

thought I'd lost you—to Nancy.'

'Nancy!' He laughed. 'Whatever made you think that? Childhood sweethearts rarely become life partners, didn't you know that? Besides, I'd made my choice, long before Nancy appeared again.'

He paused. 'You know what I'm saying, Rose.'

We kissed again,

'I know, Jack. You can stay, if you like.'

*   *   *

That's almost all there is to tell. Except that they found Foley in his home. Dead. He'd taken arsenic. If he'd lived, he would have hanged. Poor Foley, despite it all I still had a shred of pity in my heart for a lonely man, unloved and unwanted.

I wondered if that was what had twisted his life and turned him into a monster. And if anyone would ever discover that sex is a powerful instinct and obsession a form of sickness.

Howe confessed to his wife's murder. He was in love with a rich woman who wanted to marry him, but he refused to give the police any information regarding her identity. Arrested, he was put in the local jail awaiting trial. And somehow he managed to escape. He just disappeared. It seemed that he wasn't a magician for nothing and this was his

307

greatest performance.

For a week or two it was sensational news, then all was forgotten and, for Alice, forgiven. Her marriage saved, she was happy again with her Matthew, even insisting that he join a climbing club.

As for Thane, he comes to the Tower when he feels inclined and I'm happy to see him. But I don't try to own him. No obligations.

It's the same with Jack. For the moment, anyway, while I prepare for my next case. And until that dream finally fades, the one where I open the door and Danny McQuinn walks back into my life again.